SHADOW
TARGET

SHADOW
TARGET

DAVID RICCIARDI

BERKLEY
New York

BERKLEY
An imprint of Penguin Random House LLC
penguinrandomhouse.com

Copyright © 2021 by David Ricciardi
Penguin Random House supports copyright. Copyright fuels creativity, encourages diverse
voices, promotes free speech, and creates a vibrant culture. Thank you for buying an authorized
edition of this book and for complying with copyright laws by not reproducing, scanning, or
distributing any part of it in any form without permission. You are supporting writers and
allowing Penguin Random House to continue to publish books for every reader.

BERKLEY and the BERKLEY & B colophon are registered trademarks of
Penguin Random House LLC.

Library of Congress Cataloging-in-Publication Data

Names: Ricciardi, David, author.
Title: Shadow target / David Ricciardi.
Description: New York: Berkley, [2021] | Series: A Jake Keller thriller
Identifiers: LCCN 2021000502 (print) | LCCN 2021000503 (ebook) |
ISBN 9781984804693 (hardcover) | ISBN 9781984804716 (ebook)
Subjects: GSAFD: Suspense fiction.
Classification: LCC PS3618.I275 S53 2021 (print) |
LCC PS3618.I275 (ebook) | DDC 813/.6—dc23
LC record available at https://lccn.loc.gov/2021000502
LC ebook record available at https://lccn.loc.gov/2021000503

Printed in the United State of America
FIRST PRINTING

To Chanti and Bubi—Don't take it personally . . .

Life can only be understood backward,
but it must be lived forward.

—Søren Kierkegaard

A man cannot be too careful in the
choice of his enemies.

—Oscar Wilde

SHADOW
TARGET

ONE

THE SCENE WAS still, despite all the violence.

A breeze blew up from the valley. A raven soared over the treetops. A hot piece of metal ticked as it cooled in the freshly fallen snow.

Jake Keller opened his eyes.

Debris was scattered across the mountainside. Wisps of smoke rose into the air. Jake wiped the blood from his face and lifted himself to one knee. Everything hurt.

The air smelled of charred plastic, burnt jet fuel, and death.

Jake rose to his feet and staggered through the wreckage: past twisted metal and torn leather, around bundles of scorched wires, through a graveyard of personal possessions. Off to his left, a piece of the landing gear stuck out of the snow: a smoldering rubber tire attached to a sheared-off metal strut. To his right, at the base of a thick pine tree, was the lifeless body of the man who'd been sitting by the right wing. He'd been launched headfirst from the fuselage when it had broken in two.

Jake stumbled to what had been the nose of the aircraft. The pilots had done a commendable job, guiding the plane down onto a relatively flat section of the Alps, but they'd been given an impossible task. The crash had driven the engine, and what was left of the bent and broken propeller, back through the cockpit and into the passenger compartment. Both pilots had suffered massive trauma, as had the English couple sitting behind them.

Jake was the only survivor.

He looked to the east, across the Three Valleys. The light was fading quickly, but the warm glow of the setting sun reflected off a distant object floating above the horizon. The faint whir of a helicopter echoed through the mountains, growing louder as it flew toward the crash site.

Jake glanced downhill. There was something in the snow— something man-made. Though there were many man-made objects scattered amid the wreckage, Jake knew this one was significant, though he knew not why. He looked at the helicopter, looked at the object, and realized he could not reach it before the helo arrived. He headed uphill instead—by instinct driven into the woods—and used a downed evergreen bough to brush away his footprints. The hasty deception wouldn't survive careful scrutiny, but time was just another item on the list of things Jake Keller needed but did not have. He crawled into a pit at the base of a towering pine tree and hid.

The helicopter arrived. It was a black twin-engine Airbus, large and powerful and very much at home in the French Alps. It orbited the wreckage a hundred feet off the ground, with its lights off and its side doors locked open, generating its own blizzard as the downwash from its rotor simultaneously blew snow down from the trees and up from the ground.

The helicopter slowed to a hover over the crash site and a thick rope fell from its open door. Two men slid down swiftly amid the cloud of blowing snow. They wore cold-weather hiking boots and insulated parkas, and each carried a small backpack with snowshoes, climbing ropes, and an ice axe strapped to the outside.

Serious mountain gear.

Twenty seconds after it had arrived, the helicopter flew away.

The site was still once again. The two men made their way to the forward end of the fuselage and worked their way aft, past the victims. The plane's tail section had settled on its side and one of the men used a flashlight to illuminate the interior—the exact place where Jake had been seated. The man spoke into a radio, but Jake was too far away to hear what was said or even what language had been spoken.

As the sun fell below the distant peaks, the men switched on red-lensed headlamps and began an organized search. Starting at the center of the crash site, they repeatedly walked north, east, south, and west—methodically extending each leg of the pattern by a few paces. They'd been searching for just three minutes when one of them squatted in the snow to examine something he'd found.

Footprints.

Jake's footprints.

The man reached inside his jacket and removed a pistol with a sound suppressor screwed onto the end. His partner pulled a folding rifle from his pack and put it to his shoulder. The men moved uphill cautiously—their heads swiveling in every direction—like predators tracking dangerous prey.

Which of course, they were.

Jake Keller had been with the Central Intelligence Agency for seven years and part of its elite Special Activities Center for the last two. He'd traveled the world, fighting America's enemies wherever he was needed. From warmongering theocrats in Iran and rogue politicians across Asia and the Middle East, to sadistic warlords in Africa, the mission to protect his homeland and its citizens had driven

Jake to some of the most dangerous places on earth. It had never been quick, it had never been easy, but he was tenacious, tough, and a lethal threat to any and all who wished harm to America.

But today's battle was one he could not win.

Routine passenger screening for the short commercial flight had seen to it that he was unarmed, and he was too battered to run. The best he could do was hide.

The searchers were fifty yards distant, sweeping their headlamps across the increasingly dark mountainside, when Jake used his bare hands to burrow into the snow. The cold stung his skin, but frostbite and hypothermia could be treated—certainly more so than the alternative.

The men were twenty yards away when Jake brushed snow on top of himself, hoping that darkness and a miracle might let him see another sunrise.

But the men kept coming, the snow crunching underfoot with each step. Darkness and a healthy fear of the unknown slowed their advance. They'd closed to within ten yards when something froze them in their tracks. It was the muted thrum of another helicopter, resonating through the winding valley. The men doused their lights, looked and listened. Aircraft were common in the area, but not after sunset, when the mountainside Altiport closed for the night.

The second helicopter roared over the nearest peak and began a wide, arcing turn back toward the crash site. The two men bolted, running downhill through the deep snow to stay outside the intense beam of the helicopter's xenon searchlight. In just a few seconds, they'd vanished into the darkness.

Jake watched the helicopter descend amid the trees and settle into a hover a foot over the ground. It was a large aircraft, more powerful than the first; painted blue with a white stripe. Two men jumped out. The helicopter climbed back into the night sky and began to orbit the crash site with its searchlight illuminating the mountainside.

Jake rose to his feet. He was delirious, stumbling, and shivering, but inexplicably drawn toward the brilliant cone of light. He staggered a few more steps, light-headed and in pain, and searched for the object he'd seen stuck in the snow.

He was in a whiteout when he came to.

The helicopter was a hundred feet overhead and descending steadily, its powerful main rotor slicing through the air seven times a second. A man stared down at Jake from inside the aircraft, apparently unconcerned that the heavy machine would soon crush Jake beneath its skids. It drew closer, whipping snow into the air and stinging Jake's face and eyes. His heart beat furiously and his lungs gasped for air. He tried to run but his legs wouldn't move. His arms were frozen at his sides.

He felt paralyzed.

TWO

"KELLER IS ALIVE."

Misha was standing in the steam room, still kitted out in his mountain gear—everything except the boots. While weapons, drugs, and more prostitutes than a man could shake his stick at were routinely kept inside the chalet, shoes were not.

Ever.

Nikolai Kozlov was a man of absolutes.

The room was laid out like an amphitheater, with three rows of seating to accommodate the owner and his frequent guests. The walls were mosaics of smooth stone and glass that had been polished to look as if eons of waves had tumbled over them on some deserted beach in the South Pacific. Purple, green, and yellow LED lights embedded in the walls and ceiling changed colors in tune with the electronic dance music that was piped into every room in the house.

It felt like a cross between a primordial cave and a 1970s discotheque.

"How is this possible?" said Kozlov.

"He survived the crash," said Misha. "We found his footprints, but a rescue helo showed up before we could locate him."

"Were you seen?"

"*Nyet.*"

Kozlov stood, naked, and walked across the teak floor. Fifty-five years of age, he kept himself in peak physical condition, refusing to concede anything to the advancement of time. He opened a stainless steel freezer recessed in the wall, removed a bottle of Leon Verres vodka that cost as much as a nice house, and took a long pull.

"He must not find what he is searching for."

"The only thing he's going to find is a shallow grave," Misha said.

Kozlov took another drink and sat on his towel. "I need you focused on London."

"I'm focused," said Misha. "The advance team is there now, scouting routes and locations. I'll do preliminary recon as soon as Keller is in the ground and out of the picture."

Kozlov took another drink of vodka and lay down on the bench. Misha rolled his eyes. It might have been 115 degrees in the steam room, but he'd spent fifteen years in an elite military special operations unit where he'd routinely deployed to either the coldest place on earth or the hottest. Wearing his heavy mountain gear inside the steam room was like a fucking holiday.

"It must look like an accident," Kozlov declared just before the door to the steam room opened.

Misha turned to see a woman enter wearing a bikini made from what appeared to be a few pieces of string and three postage stamps. The tall Slavic beauty was young enough to be Kozlov's daughter but most certainly wasn't. She was part of a group of "massage therapists" who stayed in a nearby hotel for the month encompassing Orthodox Christmas and Russian New Year.

"Nadia," acknowledged Misha.

She ran her hand inside his jacket and over his equally impressive chest.

"You're hot," she said.

She walked over to Kozlov and lay down with her head in his lap. Misha took that as his cue to leave.

He took the elevator upstairs. The chalet was twelve thousand square feet of wood beams and locally sourced stone. Kozlov had built it three years earlier. He'd chosen Courchevel because of the French mountain town's natural beauty, expansive ski terrain, and large Russian expat population. Koslov counted himself among the group, having lived and conducted his business affairs abroad for eleven years, two months, and six days.

It was an easy date to remember, for it was the day the Russian president had taken power.

The president and Kozlov had been classmates at the prestigious Moscow State School 57. Both had been star students in math and science and fierce competitors on the school's elite chess team. They'd gone their separate ways during college but upon graduation each had been recruited to GRU, the nation's military intelligence directorate and external security service. The president had joined Second Directorate, focusing on intelligence analysis, while Kozlov had found his calling as an operations planner for the Main Directorate of the General Staff. Though their careers rarely intersected, the two men had rekindled their schoolboy friendship and become close. When the president departed GRU to run for local and then regional office, Kozlov had been an ardent supporter. Upon his ascension to the Kremlin, the president pulled Kozlov from GRU and put him in charge of a steel mill.

Though Kozlov was a chess grand master and a certified genius, all he knew of the steel industry was that the mill had been seized three months earlier by the Russian tax authorities. Yet, within a year, the once-failing mill became enormously profitable as inflated government contracts flowed in.

Kozlov channeled the initial profits back into the business. Other mills were acquired. More contracts were obtained. Competitors found themselves with legal trouble, labor problems, or supplier disruptions. A monopoly emerged. Kozlov funneled the profits through a Swiss bank with murky rules and ever-murkier ownership. For every ruble that was deposited, 25 percent went to a management company owned by Kozlov, 25 percent went to an investment portfolio owned by Kozlov.

And 50 percent went to the Russian president.

THREE

S THE LINE secure?"

"It's your equipment," said Misha.

"Don't be a wiseass. There's too much as stake."

"It's secure, but Kozlov isn't. He's worried about Keller."

"Put him on."

"He's . . . indisposed."

"I don't think you're taking this seriously enough."

"I just took down a commercial airliner—how much more serious do I need to be?"

Shadow said nothing.

"You're being paranoid," added Misha. "How much of a threat is Keller really?"

"He's barely thirty years old and he's already the best paramilitary officer I've ever seen."

"Except for me."

"It'd be a fair fight."

"Not if I'm involved."

"Don't be so goddamned cocky. Keller may be a Boy Scout, but every time we throw him in the deep end—Iran, Saudi Arabia, Somalia—he manages to thread the needle between doing what he thinks is 'right' and what the Agency actually needs. Once he gets his claws into something, he doesn't let go. I don't know what alerted him to you and Kozlov, but we can't have him poking around this close to the London operation."

"He's one guy."

"So is the president."

"And if Keller lives?"

"So does the president."

Misha snorted. "How is the golden boy now? He was in a plane crash. It's not a stretch to think that London might be over before he gets out of the hospital."

"He's alive. We don't have details."

"I thought CIA was in the intelligence business."

"Keller is on a leave of absence."

"I'm thinking I need to finish this on my end."

"Wait."

"Kozlov said the same thing. What's your problem?"

"What are you going to do, give Keller a little pillow therapy in the hospital? We took extraordinary measures to make this look like an accident. The Agency will put on a full-court press if he dies mysteriously after the crash."

"Fine, but I'm warning you. You know how Kozlov gets. He wants it to look like an accident but he also wants Keller dead. If we don't wrap it up soon, he'll call his GRU contacts, Keller will not-so-mysteriously die of polonium poisoning, and Russian fingerprints will be all over it."

"Be patient. Keller could be in a coma for all we know."

"You know he isn't. Get him back to Langley and find out what he knows."

"We'll keep him on a tight leash."

"Make it a noose."

FOUR

JAKE CLIPPED HIS access badge onto his jacket and walked across the CIA seal into the original headquarters building. The white marble lobby was dramatic, meant to inspire confidence and reflect enlightenment. Jake passed the Memorial Wall, where stars had been carved into the stone for the CIA employees who'd lost their lives in service to the country. In front of the wall was the Book of Honor. It held the names of the dead and blank lines for those who had lost their lives in times and places that could never be revealed. Many of the men had died in plane crashes. It was a hazard of an occupation that often demanded spur-of-the-moment access to dangerous places.

A well-known hazard.

Jake took the elevator down three levels to Ted Graves's office. Graves was Jake's boss and the shadowy chief of CIA's paramilitary Special Activities Center. He usually worked out of a nondescript building several miles away but also had an office at headquarters. He'd summoned Jake to the U.S. two days after the crash—on the very afternoon he'd been released from the hospital.

"They're in the conference room," said Graves's assistant.

They, thought Jake. Ted hadn't mentioned anyone else.

Graves was seated across the table, facing the door. Somewhere in his forties—everything about Ted was vague and mysterious—he was wearing a suit with no jacket or tie, and his sleeves rolled up to expose his muscular forearms. He prided himself on the two hours he spent in the gym every day in addition to the twelve to fourteen he spent in the office.

Next to him was Christine Kirby, his chief deputy at the center. A few years older than Jake, she was a former West Point swimmer and army helicopter pilot. Her unkempt strawberry blond hair and indifferent gaze camouflaged a sharp intellect and a provocative wit. She'd worked with Graves since he was Chief of Operations at CIA's London Station and was universally respected, if not particularly liked.

"Have a seat." Graves wasn't big on chitchat.

Jake lowered himself into one of the upholstered chairs.

"What's going on?" said Graves.

"The doctors said I'll need—"

"I don't care about your injuries. They'll heal. Where is your head at?"

Graves wasn't big on sympathy either.

Jake loved what he did. Protecting his fellow citizens and what his country stood for was what got him out of bed every morning. He had seen firsthand the evil in the world and felt it was his moral obligation to eradicate as much of it as he could, but he and Graves clashed mightily when Jake's conscience wouldn't allow him to execute a mission he felt was unethical, and the two men had reached an impasse a few weeks earlier while Jake was deployed to Africa.

In Graves's defense, he wasn't the one setting policy. The Special Activities Center executed orders that came from higher up the food chain—usually from the country's political leadership—and what was distasteful on a tactical level was often necessary on a strategic level. While Graves's methods were often harsh, he was exceedingly good at what he did. He'd pointed out that Jake's mission was only one small piece of the larger national security puzzle and that Special Activities would lose its effectiveness altogether if every field operative second-guessed his orders.

It had become heated.

Jake had countered that the end didn't always justify the means—especially when innocent lives hung in the balance, as they had in Africa, but Graves had insisted that Jake ignore the collateral damage and focus on the long-term goals.

It had ended with Graves, and a few people Jake trusted, telling him to take some time off and think about whether he still wanted to be part of the Special Activities Center. The trip to Courchevel was supposed to be the first week of a one-month leave of absence.

"I haven't made a decision," Jake said.

"One foot in and one foot out doesn't work for me."

"Don't lecture me, Ted. I've sacrificed everything for this job."

And while Jake loved what he did, it had cost him a great deal. Orphaned at fourteen after the deaths of his parents, he'd spent the next fourteen years rebuilding his life—only to have it all taken away during his first mission in the field. A foreign government had framed him for murder in an effort to discredit him and cut off CIA support. When it was over, Ted Graves had forced Jake to have plastic surgery, change his identity, and cut contact with everyone he'd ever known. At twenty-eight years old, Jake had started over in a career he couldn't discuss, traveling to the most dangerous places on earth, and routinely being placed in kill-or-be-killed situations. It had sucked the joy from his life and left him very much alone.

"People like us aren't meant to lead normal lives," Graves said without a hint of empathy.

"Jake," interjected Kirby, "tell me about the crash."

Like he'd flipped a switch, Jake ceased glaring at Graves and smiled at Kirby.

"I don't remember it. We were flying straight and level through a valley and the next thing I knew I was being winched into a rescue helicopter, strapped to a litter, and thinking I was paralyzed. The French doctors say I have post-traumatic amnesia."

"What about the weather?" asked the former aviator.

"Clear skies, no turbulence."

"Any indications of mechanical malfunction?"

"Zero," said Jake.

Kirby frowned. "Ted, we should look into this."

"Let's see what the French come up with before we kick the hornet's nest," said Graves. He glanced at his watch. "I've got another meeting upstairs."

Jake scowled. He'd had flown in from Europe for the five-minute meeting. Graves wasn't into face time or demeaning his subordinates—everything the man did was measured and planned—which meant that he'd summoned Jake across the pond for another reason, something as yet unspoken. Graves walked around the table, put his hand on Jake's shoulder, and looked him over from head to toe.

"Crazy stuff, that plane crash. I can't believe you survived."

Jake shrugged.

"Do me a favor," Graves continued. "Check in with me here every few days. I want to know the second that 'amnesia' of yours clears up."

FIVE

’LL WALK YOU OUT," Kirby said after Graves had left.

Jake had always gotten along well with Christine. Only once, when they'd been stationed in England together, had he questioned her motives. To be fair, she'd been wearing a balaclava and pointing a submachine gun at him at the time, but it turned out that she was there to save him, not kill him. Jake had watched in relief as she'd pulled off the mask and her tousled strawberry blond hair had cascaded across her shoulders.

"Sorry about Ted," she said as she took Jake's arm. "He's under a lot of pressure."

"I haven't exactly been relaxing on the beach."

"I know. What brought you to France?" she said.

"Skiing."

"Were you with anyone? I mean, you didn't lose anyone on the plane, did you?"

"No. I was alone. I do everything alone."

"You could have invited me," Kirby said with a flirtatious smile, but she watched Jake grimace as he descended a small stair.

"What are you doing for the pain?" she asked.

"The docs prescribed some oxycodone, but I just need to get back into the pool."

Jake had been a water polo player at Boston College, and though his workouts had been grueling, they'd also been cathartic. The sooner he resumed swimming laps, the sooner he would have a sound mind in a sound body and be able to make a decision about his future with CIA.

Kirby nodded. The former distance swimmer knew exactly what he meant. She pushed the button for the elevator.

"Jake, you'd tell me if you suspected foul play, wouldn't you?"

"I would if I remembered anything."

She squeezed his arm. "I'll talk to Ted about making some indirect inquiries."

The elevator doors opened and Christine ran her fingernails along Jake's bare forearm as he entered.

"You should really be in bed," she said.

The elevator doors closed.

Jake smirked. Kirby had a penchant for double entendres. He often wondered if she used them on everyone or if he was special, but the thought slipped from his mind as the elevator doors opened and he made his way back across the lobby. He paused again in front of the Memorial Wall and put a hand to the white marble. The stone was hard and cold.

Jake looked down at the Book of Honor. It was ordered chronologically, and an average year held one or two names, but there were more than a dozen entries since he'd joined the Special Activities Center two years earlier. The most recent ones belonged to a pair of CIA contractors who had died trying to rescue him in Somalia. Jake could still smell the gunpowder and still hear the mounted machine that had stolen the life from their bodies.

The entries were just a few weeks old.

"Those were our boys," said a familiar voice.

Clap was a paramilitary operations officer—a PMOO—just like Jake. A hair over five-foot, seven-inches tall, he was a compact mass of muscle. The former army Ranger and Delta Force operator had spent most of his career in the land of his ancestors, trying to keep the war-torn continent of Africa from tipping past the point of no return. He'd also been in command of the contractors in Somalia who'd died trying to save Jake. As Ted Graves was fond of saying, "Leadership isn't a reward. It's a responsibility," and Clap felt the loss of his men acutely. He valued his service to his country above everything else and it put a heavy strain on his mind and his marriage. Like Jake, he felt disconnected from reality when he was home, as if no one on the streets around him knew what the world was really like. To an outsider, running on pure adrenaline might have sounded exciting, but Jake understood that, like with any drug, withdrawal could be a bitch.

Jake looked over. "You all healed up?"

Clap had been injured in the same ambush and had flown alongside the bodies of his men to Germany, where they'd been shipped home, and he'd undergone surgery and rehabilitation at Landstuhl Regional Medical Center.

"I've got more pins in my body than a voodoo doll." Clap motioned to the wall. "I thought you might have your own star up there. Things weren't looking so good when I left."

"It was touch and go for a while," Jake allowed.

"Truth be told, you still don't look so good."

"Plane crash."

Clap raised an eyebrow.

Jake nodded.

"In that case, you look great."

"There is something going around this place." Jake gestured to all the freshly carved stars on the wall.

Clap shrugged. "It's a dangerous job."

SIX

A SCOWL RODE HEAVY on Jake's face as he walked out to the parking lot and climbed into his pickup. The 1967 Jeep Gladiator had once belonged to his adoptive uncle. After the uncle passed away, the entire estate had been willed to Zac Miller—the name Jake had been given by his parents at birth. After his uncle's will had been read, CIA had obscured the source of the money and seen to it that Jake got his inheritance, but the Agency had balked at transferring a dilapidated old pickup that could be easily traced by its vehicle identification number. But the truck was one of the few sentimental reminders of his old life, and Jake was nothing if not tenacious, so he'd purchased it for eight hundred dollars from the scrapyard to which it had been sold.

The door creaked loudly as he slammed it. Jake was keen to restore the truck himself, but his work at the Agency hadn't allowed for the consistent, sustained effort necessary to move it out of the "eyesore" category. In fact, aside from a new set of mud tires, he'd done nothing.

Jake winced as he turned the steering wheel, but it was more than his bruised ribs that were bothering him. The number of freshly carved stars in the Memorial Wall had left him unsettled. The Special Activities Center had always had the highest rate of officers killed in the line of duty; it was the nature of the paramilitary mission. But like everything at CIA, Jake's gut told him that there was more to it than what met the eye.

He was ten minutes from home when his cell phone rang. The number was blocked, but half the people he knew switched mobile phone numbers on a weekly basis. He put it on speakerphone.

"Yeah," said Jake.

"Nice attitude," said the voice on the phone.

Jake grinned. "I was expecting a robocall."

"No such luck. You stateside?"

"Yup."

"Glad to see my tax dollars at rest . . . lazy bastard."

"Is there a purpose to this call?"

"I'm polishing the brass over at the Pentagon for a few weeks. How soon can you drag your sorry ass out for dinner?"

"I'm free tonight," Jake said.

"Nice life. Text me the time and place. You're buying."

The line went dead.

Jake smiled. The last time he had seen Jeff was nearly six months ago, when the Delta Force troop sergeant major was recovering from a gunshot wound—a wound he'd suffered three feet from Jake's side while the two men were trying to prevent a war. They'd grown close in the aftermath, but the hectic paths of the army commando and the CIA paramilitary officer hadn't crossed since.

JAKE PARKED THE Jeep on the street in Washington, DC's, Georgetown neighborhood. The sight of the dilapidated pickup with two wheels up on the curb probably sent tremors through the hearts of the residents, but Jake hadn't come to make friends. He slammed the creaky door and headed east on foot. He'd walked less than a block when he spotted the person he was looking for. Anyone else would have seen the solidly built man with the sport coat, longish hair, and flecks of gray in his beard and thought him a professor at one of the many area colleges, but Jake recognized the type immediately. He saw it every day when he looked in the mirror. The man's eyes were in constant motion and laser focused, assessing everyone and everything on the darkened street.

Jake fell in thirty yards behind him on the tree-lined sidewalk and followed him into an upscale restaurant. The man passed the maître d' at the door, headed straight to the back of the restaurant, and into the men's room.

Jake followed.

The man was standing at a urinal when Jake entered and took the next one over. The man was staring at the wall in front of him.

"Nice watch," said Jake.

"It's from your mom," said the man, still staring straight ahead.

"It's good to see you, brother," Jake said.

"Don't be offended if I don't shake hands," said Jeff.

The dining room was paneled in dark mahogany and dimly lit. Most of the tables were already filled as the hostess showed the two men to their table.

"Nice place," said Jeff. "Very civilized."

"I wanted to make sure you wouldn't run into anyone you know. When did you get in?"

"03:00. Slept on the floor of a C-17."

"I thought you unit guys flew first class. How was Ukraine?"

"How did you know I was in Ukraine?" Jeff asked.

"Your wife talks in her sleep."

Jeff glared at him. "Is your life flashing before your eyes right now?"

"We're even after the crack about my dead mother. Productive trip?"

"Oh, yeah, it was great . . . ," said Jeff. "We were training their Omega unit. I speak about six words of Russian and my fine Ukrainian counterpart spoke about as much English, not including swearwords."

"How hard can it be? Point and shoot, right?"

"Try explaining the difference between a butt dial and a booty call to somebody who doesn't speak English. I'm not sure the subtleties of our latest counterterrorism doctrine made it through translation."

Jake laughed, but his bruised ribs caused him to wince in pain.

"What the hell happened to you?" Jeff said. "I thought I stumbled onto the set of a horror movie when I saw you limping behind me on the sidewalk. You forget to open your parachute again?"

Jake explained the plane crash.

"Skiing in France? Must be nice working for the Agency. I was sleeping on a stained cot and eating frozen MREs."

"I was on a leave of absence."

"That doesn't sound like a reward."

A waiter approached the table and Jeff segued to a personal conversation.

"We're expecting a third kid in July," he announced as Jake ordered a second round.

"I'm glad to hear a man of your advanced age can still make it happen."

"There's hope for you yet," said Jeff.

"So you'll be, what, seventy when this one gets out of college?"

"Sixty-six," Jeff said with a grin. "Jealous?"

"Envious," said Jake.

"What about you? Anyone special?"

Jake shook his head.

Jeff persisted. "No time or no interest?"

"An overabundance of interest . . . but the job doesn't lend itself to long, stable relationships."

"What about short, volatile relationships?"

Jake told his friend about the two women he'd loved since joining the Agency. One was dead and the other thought Jake was dead.

"That's not what I meant by short and volatile."

"I'm not getting any of that either."

"No wonder you're so angry."

Jake pointed his steak knife across the table. "Who says I'm angry?"

"Tell me more about this plane crash."

Jake spoke of the short flight from London to Courchevel, then regaining consciousness in the rescue litter.

"I don't remember the crash itself," he added, "but I've been feeling unsettled ever since."

"After plummeting into a mountainside stuck inside a steel tube? I think that's normal, dude. It's a miracle you survived."

"It's not that. Something in my subconscious is telling me this wasn't an accident, but the memory is just out of reach."

"Go see a shrink. Maybe he can hypnotize you or something. I'm sure CIA has people on retainer."

"CIA is part of the problem," said Jake. "There's a memorial inside the building to all the paramilitary officers who've died in action. I was looking at it today and it put me in a foul mood."

Jeff nodded slowly. "I was in Syria last year with some of your guys and they operate right on the edge. Not all of them came home."

"There's more to it than that. You know I was an intel analyst for five years before I took this gig and my brain still looks at events that way. It's telling me that the rate of paramilitary officer deaths is way too high."

"Statistically?"

"I know it sounds stupid, but something isn't right."

The waiter returned with another round of drinks and Jake and Jeff spent the next hour discussing the unclassified aspects of their lives. It was a lively conversation, punctuated by more ribbing and lots of laughter. The two men hadn't known each other long, but their friendship had been forged in fire.

It was close to eleven p.m. when they finally finished dinner and stepped outside.

Jeff was in a taxi and about to pull away when he lowered the window.

"All that anxiety you're feeling about the Agency and the plane crash?"

"Yeah?"

"Shake it off, bro. That was like four days ago."

SEVEN

JAKE LITERALLY TRUSTED Jeff and Clap with his life, but as was often the case with men who were very similar—in this case, type-A hunter/killers—their relationships had begun with friction and progressed to grudging respect before developing into admiration and friendship.

They were two of the finest men Jake had ever known.

Which was also a problem, because neither one of them shared his concerns about the spiking number of dead paramilitary officers.

Jeff and Clap certainly weren't naïve. They saw the good and the evil in the world on a regular basis and were driven to action. Like Jake, the force that propelled them forward wasn't about doing what was best for them as individuals; it was about doing what was best for others. Protecting those who couldn't protect themselves was the framework upon which they'd built their entire lives.

To a casual observer, a light aircraft going down in the Alps would be a tragedy, but certainly not unthinkable. The airport at Courchevel was one of the most dangerous in the world. The approach to land was made over cragged mountain peaks and through rocky valleys. The runway started six thousand feet up the side of a mountain and was shaped like a T. Immediately after touching down at the bottom of the T, the incoming aircraft climbed a 20 percent grade before the pilots were forced to turn left or right—or slide back down the mountain and tumble to their deaths in the valley below. There were no second chances.

But Jake knew that the elite group of pilots who were checked out to land at the Courchevel Altiport were experts in mountain flying. He had been riding in a Swiss-made Pilatus PC-12, a single-engine turbine-powered aircraft with seats for eight. The flight had been two hours out from London in light winds and visibility close to a hundred miles. At one point the captain had come over the intercom to point out the Swiss, French, and Italian Alps—all visible at the same time.

The large blue helicopter that had rescued Jake belonged to the *Peloton Gendarmerie de Haute Montagne*, the French mountain police. Widely respected for their abilities, PGHM aviators routinely plucked injured climbers and skiers from impossible crevasses and located lost hikers and avalanche victims whose only alternative was death. The medics had buckled Jake into a litter, hoisted him aboard, and flown him twenty minutes to the trauma unit at the University of Grenoble. The PGHM had undoubtedly saved his life, but it wasn't the big blue police helicopter that kept running through Jake's mind. There was something else.

He just couldn't, for the life of him, remember what it was.

EIGHT

JAKE LIVED IN Virginia farm country when he wasn't deployed overseas. The acres of open fields, the earthy smell of fresh-turned soil, and the hardworking people of the land were a calming respite from his high-pressure national security work. The carriage house he rented sat just inside the entrance to a well-kept gentleman's farm with fields, woods, and several outbuildings. The family who owned the farm used it primarily as a summer retreat from the chaos of Washington, DC, and had furnished the carriage house in the same high quality as the main house with custom mill-work, thick granite countertops, and a gourmet stove. They'd also given Jake full access to the forty acres of grounds and the barn to park his truck. He in turn had lied to them and shown them pay stubs from a CIA front company when he'd signed the lease.

Such were the trade-offs of the job.

Though he'd rented the carriage house because of its remoteness, its rural location was also outside reliable cell phone coverage, and as he drove home from his dinner with Jeff, something in Jake's subconscious alerted him that it was time to make a call before he was out of range.

He redialed the last number used.

"*Hey, babe,*" Jeff answered. "*I just finished dinner with that simpleton Jake Keller I told you about. I thought it would never—*"

"Hilarious. You free again tomorrow night?"

"*Sorry, man, I thought you were my wife . . .*"

"Tomorrow night. What time?"

"*21:00 hours,*" Jeff said, "*where you first picked me up in that piece-of-shit truck of yours.*"

JAKE STOPPED THE Gladiator outside Walter Reed Medical Center. Jeff hopped in.

"Why were you at the hospital?" Jake asked. "You injured again?"

"I challenge you to find some part of me that isn't."

During his twenty-two years in the army, with more than half of it in Delta, Jeff had put his body through hell. Not a morning went by that he didn't wake up in pain, but he got up each day without complaint and soldiered on.

"Is that gasoline I smell?" asked Jeff.

"There's a leak in the fuel line," said Jake.

"Sounds safe. Dude, when are you going to get rid of this truck? I'm from Wyoming and this thing would have been junked out there twenty-five years ago."

"It's a piece of Americana."

"It's a piece of something, all right."

A light dusting of snow covered the hospital's parklike grounds as Jake pulled away from the curb.

"So I don't see you for six months," said Jeff, "now it's twice in twenty-four hours. What's up?"

"I know you think I'm overreacting to the crash, but I'm starting to think that I was supposed to have a star carved on that wall too."

"Based on?"

Jake shrugged. "Gut feel."

"The plane crash sucks, but it's a stretch to think it was part of some overarching plot to wipe out the CIA. You were just in the wrong place at the wrong time."

"What about the others?"

Jeff sighed. "Look, boss, what we do is dangerous. I'm not going to tell you that it doesn't suck sometimes. I've got a bunch of numbers to nowhere on my personal cell phone, but it's part of the job. It's the same with your organization. You guys are on the front lines, or behind the front lines, with no support and up against some very bad people. You're going to lose people."

"The paramilitary officer who died in Syria, what happened to him?"

Jeff looked out the passenger window as they drove south through suburban Bethesda. Several couples and a few families wandered down the main street among trees decorated in holiday lights. It was all so very normal and so very strange at the same time.

"I guess it was fourteen months ago when it happened," Jeff began. "Your organization had two veteran paramilitary operations officers in-country for nearly a year, halfway between Damascus and Aleppo, in the city of Homs. These two guys were like deep-cover case officers and as dialed into the situation on the ground as any foreigner could be. They looked like locals, they spoke the language, they lived in town. They knew where they could go, who they could trust, and who was playing both sides of the fence. These were seasoned guys: One had been a master sergeant in the Unit and the other guy was Marine Recon with something like eleven deployments before he joined the Agency. The two of them were coordinating intel with French DGSE, who had a source inside Assad's organization. Assad saw the world as a zero-sum game and he'd unleashed the *Shabiha* death squads on the population. Some of these guys were Syrian militia units and others were basically street gangs, but the ops were all the same—making opponents of the regime disappear in the most brutal way possible. It didn't matter if it was the middle of the afternoon or the middle of the night. They'd roll up in a half-dozen vehicles, fire a bunch of rounds into the air just to make sure everyone knew what was going down, then crash the door and grab their target. They'd gang-rape his wives and children in front of him, then torture whoever was still alive. They burned people, hacked off pieces of their bodies, and forced them—"

Jeff interrupted himself. He was staring straight ahead with his hands balled into fists.

"I have seen a lot of shit in my career, but when the darkness finds me, it's memories of what I saw in Syria."

"Sorry, brother," Jake said.

Jeff nodded. "So the French had this Syrian source who was pure fucking magic. We all assumed he was either a top Assad aide or a commo guy, because he saw everything. I don't think any American ever knew who he was for sure, and it really didn't matter, because if this guy said something was going down, it went down."

"So what happened?" Jake asked.

"The two paramilitary officers figured out how ruthless the death squads were about two hours after they set foot in Syria. For ten months they'd asked Agency HQ to do something about it, to send them some military support to stop these sadistic animals from operating with impunity. The scuttlebutt was that the two guys pushed pretty hard and ruffled some feathers, but they were right, and they had this solid-gold intel from the French they could use to do something about it. Somebody in DC finally woke up, and after the obligatory National Capital Region ass-covering dance, a task force was finally formed under Title 50."

"You went in?"

"We got a green light to start hunting the hunters. Your guys were running the intel side and we supplied the assaulters. We were kicking down doors in no time. Quick hits. Lots of hits. Well timed and constantly changing. Sometimes we'd take these guys down on their way to grab somebody. Other times we'd take them on their way home. Once in a while we hit them where they slept. We tried to take them alive for the intel but we also used a lot of IEDs, UAVs, Javelins, and old-fashioned 5.56-millimeter mind erasers. We did a few joint ops with the French too—their CPIS special forces. We did everything we could to make each contact look different and obscure the source of the intel."

"To protect the guy the French were running?"

"Exactly. We were running flat out—sometimes two or three missions a day—and the intel just kept building on itself. The death squads were always our primary objective but we couldn't help but build a list of secondary targets. We'd been at it about six weeks when we got a lead on some high-value douchebag we'd been hearing about since we'd arrived. This guy was a *muallia*—a senior leader. He was juiced up on 'roids and absolutely crazy. He would roll into a neighborhood and slit women's throats and break kids' arms and legs—just to set the tone—before getting to the business at hand. DGSE's source learned that he was going to be at sunset prayers at a certain mosque on a certain day for some ceremony with one of his nephews."

"Did you go in?"

Jeff scowled. "Yes and no," he said. "Despite our best efforts to fly below the radar, Assad couldn't help but notice that a suspiciously large number of his pipe hitters were turning up dead, so his security people started taking some people out back and literally setting them on fire to see who would confess. The source the French had developed had balls of stone though. This guy kept feeding DGSE the same tier-one, solid-gold information he'd been providing all along—but he asked the French to halt operations for a couple of weeks so Assad would think one of the guys he'd already killed was the leaker."

"Makes sense," Jake said.

"It was a no-brainer," Jeff continued. "The senior paramilitary officer told CIA headquarters that we were going to dial it back and prosecute the list of secondary objectives until the coast was clear for the source."

"But HQ didn't like that," Jake said.

"They were furious. From their perspective, the lead paramilitary officer had ridden them since the day he'd arrived in-country, saying that they had to get into the fight—to protect the Syrian people from these fucking monsters—and now he wanted to pull back a month and a half after the task force was up and running? They thought it was embarrassing."

"What about Delta command?"

"It was a Title 50 op, so you fucks were running the show."

"No offense taken," said Jake.

"Look, man, I love you like a brother, but that's the problem with civilians running military operations. Shit changes and you have to adapt. DGSE kept passing the take to us with the expectation that we'd hold tight for a few weeks to take the heat off their guy."

"Couldn't you just tap the brakes without telling anyone?"

"Nope. Special Activities Center headquarters was seeing the intel the same time we were. Nabbing this *muallia* would validate the formation of the entire task force and probably get some desk jockey back at Langley a medal for his file, so they told us to shut up and hit the target."

"Knowing it would jeopardize the source?"

"They told us to make it low-key, but that was just ass covering so they could blame us if it went south. The target was going to be surrounded by family, guards, and maybe a hundred noncombatants as he left the mosque. It was in the middle of a pro-Assad neighborhood in an Alawite city. Ground vehicles would never make it through the checkpoints, so we had to use helos."

"What's wrong with helicopters?"

"It's pretty fucking tough to make it look like a coincidence when a stack of aviation assets shows up at your local mosque just as Syria's most wanted walks out the door. It would be pretty obvious to Assad's people that we had advance intel on the target's location."

"Which risked burning the source."

"And a lot of collateral damage. So the senior paramilitary operations officer went back to his boss and told him we needed to find another way to get the target, but Special Activities HQ wanted this guy bad. To his credit, the PMOO held fast. He basically told HQ that they didn't understand the situation on the ground and to stay the hell out of it."

Jake nodded. He'd had that same conversation with Ted Graves many times . . . and as recently as two weeks before the plane crash.

"Did headquarters back off?" Jake asked.

"They were 'evaluating' it."

"What does that mean?"

"Exactly. The decision was to not make a decision. Two days later, the paramilitary officer was walking through the local souk, dressed like a local, smoking those shitty local cigarettes, and chatting in Arabic with one of his local contacts, when a white Bongo van pulled up next to them. The side door slid open and two guys with Kalashnikovs opened fire. The PMOO and his contact were dead before the van drove away."

"So what happened next?"

"You know how it is: The mission goes on. The other paramilitary officer was sent home with his dead buddy, two new Agency guys showed up, and we launched on the mosque right on schedule."

"How bad was it?"

"We cut power to the neighborhood just as the target came out. Two Little Birds dropped into low hovers on the north and south sides and we set down east and west in two Black Hawks. It was loud, the helos were blowing trash into the air, and a bunch of guys with NODs and guns had just cordoned off the area. We hoped the show of force would knock some common sense into these fools but bullets started flying before the first American boot hit the ground. The target's protection detail looked like they were having a contest to see who could fire the most rounds into the crowd. They were literally shooting at us through the people in the square. We got our guy and threw him in the helo, but I'm telling you, there must have been thirty or forty civilians down from Syrian gunfire, which of course they blamed on us."

"What happened to the source the French were running?"

"The word on the street was that Assad's goons chained him to the ceiling and slowly lowered him into a bathtub of hydrochloric acid. I don't know if it's true, but I do know that our intel dried up, the task force was disbanded, and the death squads were back in business."

"And you don't think the paramilitary officer's assassination was suspicious?"

"Two guys with AK-47s in a van?" Jeff said. "That's just another day at the office in Syria."

"I meant the timing. It seems like the gunmen had intel on the paramilitary officer."

Jeff sighed. "Dude, it sucked, but we were in the middle of a war zone and you guys dance on the razor's edge for a living. You can't extrapolate from one incident and declare that there's a conspiracy out there to kill paramilitary officers."

Jake pulled to the curb outside Jeff's hotel. "I'm going to do a little digging."

"Yeah, well, good luck with that. The only people who know what really happened are the Syrians, and the only way you're going to get to them is if you've got a damn good source inside French intelligence."

NINE

SUNRISE WAS STILL two hours away when the two men departed the warmth of the chalet for the cold of the pine forest. The dim red glow from their headlamps and the rhythmic sound of their skis over the snow were the only signs of human presence.

It was one of Kozlov's rituals. While most of the chalet was still sleeping off the prior night's festivities, he rose each morning before dawn and ascended the mountain under his own power. The alpine touring equipment was comprised of carbon fiber ski poles, boots that were hinged to the skis only at the toe, and skis with climbing skins attached to the bottom. Much like cross-country skis, they glided forward smoothly, but bit into the snow as the skier pushed backward. The ascent was peaceful and cathartic, a time for him to strengthen his body and clear his mind before the day began in earnest.

Kozlov glanced over his shoulder occasionally as he and Misha moved swiftly up the mountain. Though Misha was younger and fitter, his boss was fiercely competitive and refused to show any sign of weakness. Misha had seen Kozlov's temperament manifest itself in cruel and capricious ways over the years, and he was content to follow him at a distance that made them both comfortable—Misha had proven himself long ago.

Kozlov stopped after an hour of hard trekking and shut off his headlamp. The light was no longer necessary as they were now above the tree line. Moonlight reflected like sequins off the dry white snow.

The oligarch took a drink of water. "This could be my favorite place, Misha. More than the yacht, more than the chalet—"

"More than Moscow?"

Kozlov chuckled. "Definitely more than Moscow."

Misha pointed up the mountain with his ski pole, at a windblown cornice that had formed on the leeward side of a peak. It looked like a tidal wave that had frozen atop the mountain.

"Do you ever worry about avalanches?"

"Not at this hour," Kozlov said dismissively. "Mother Earth creates the conditions for an avalanche, but ninety percent of the accidents are caused by man."

"What are the conditions?" asked Misha, warily regarding the giant mass of snow directly uphill from their position.

"A snowpack is like a tree. A slice will tell you a whole season's weather: when it snowed, when it rained, when it melted, when it froze. All those layers make it weak. Cold, moist snow is like cement: It binds the pack together. But this light powder we have today? It's terrible. Did you ever try to make a snowman with it when you were a child? It's impossible. The crystals are large and dry. They're beautiful but weak—like a woman."

"So these are good conditions for an avalanche?"

"Only if a heavy snow falls on top of the powder. It will have nothing to stick to, and with a little push, it will come sliding down. That is why I am always off the trail an hour before the lifts open."

"You don't trust your fellow man?"

Kozlov actually laughed.

"Most certainly not, but man alone does not dictate my timing. The probability of an avalanche increases as the sun warms the snowpack and changes its internal structure, so the ski patrol comes out after the sun is up, but before the lifts open, to clear dangerous snowpacks. Sometimes they use explosives. Sometimes they use propane cannons—"

"I like cannons."

"Either way, the concussion separates the different layers of snow and sends it all crashing down, like ice sliding off a roof."

Misha nodded thoughtfully. "How do you know all this?"

"My steel business has made me an amateur metallurgist. This is not so different."

Kozlov pushed off with his poles. "Come Misha, I'll race you to La Tania."

TEN

THEY WERE KNOWN as the Triplets.

Boris, Ilya, and Grigory weren't brothers, but the three men wore matching black jeans and black T-shirts, and they had matching black guns under their black jackets. When Kozlov needed to take care of something discreetly, he used Misha. When he wanted to send a message, he used the Triplets. Former heavyweight members of the Russian martial arts teams, they had been recruited to GRU as independent contractors once they were no longer Olympic prospects. Kozlov had hired them for an assignment soon after he'd acquired the steel mill, when its prior owner had threatened lawsuits and media exposure over what he perceived to be the illegal confiscation of his property. Tragically, despite living in a highly secure gated community in the affluent Moscow neighborhood of Rublykova, the former mill owner was found dead in the foyer of his home, the victim of twenty-two gunshots to the head and body.

The police ruled it a suicide.

And the Triplets were hired full-time.

They were in the ski room now, using their bulging muscles to clean and dry the equipment from the predawn outing. Kozlov was already upstairs when Misha propped his skis against the wall. Boris snatched them up as if they were feathers.

"Shit," Boris muttered. The palm of his hand was bleeding.

"Careful," said Misha. "I just had the edges sharpened."

Boris glared at him. The Triplets viewed Misha as a cocksure outsider who thought his vaunted special operations training made him better than them.

Misha agreed.

He smirked and walked upstairs past the kitchen. Though there were many outstanding restaurants in Courchevel, including a few with Michelin stars, dinner was always served at the chalet. The feasts often ran to five courses and fifty people during Russian New Year week, with locally hunted boar and venison and French wines and cheeses. Kozlov's wife frequently boasted that the chef they'd brought down from Paris knew his way around the kitchen better than any man alive.

Misha was just passing the walk-in pantry when he heard a crash and what sounded like a scream coming from Mrs. Kozlov. Misha threw open the pantry door. Pressed against the shelves, with her skirt hiked around her waist, was Mrs. Kozlov. Standing behind her, with his pants dropped around his ankles, was the chef.

Misha closed the door and continued up the stairs to the fourth floor, where Kozlov kept what he referred to as his "safe suite." The two-centimeter-thick titanium blast door had just opened and Misha could hear Kozlov berating someone inside.

"You stupid bitch. You have one job here and you can't even do that properly. Get out!"

Nadia emerged, flushed and fighting back tears. Misha reached out to comfort her but she pulled away and ran down the stairs. He continued into Kozlov's office. The oligarch was standing in front of his sofa, tucking in his shirt.

"What was that about?" asked Misha.

Kozlov fixed him with a cold stare.

"She needs to learn her place. You would be well advised to do the same."

Misha sat down. The room was decorated like the rest of the chalet except that behind the luxurious furnishings, its floor, ceiling, and walls were made from twenty centimeters of rebarred concrete to defeat physical attacks and lined with Ultra Radiant R-Foil designed to defeat electronic attacks. The safe suite had a bathroom, bedroom, food supply, weapons locker, and an extensive communications array—plus its own power source and air supply. It was reachable from Kozlov's office or the master suite, but only Kozlov had the access code, for while he often used the room to conduct sensitive conversations, he used it just as often to explore sensitive areas.

Usually Nadia's.

Misha's ears registered the increased air pressure as Kozlov pressed a button on his desk to close the door behind them.

"Where are we with the president's visit?" said the oligarch.

"His advance team has chosen three routes for the motorcade."

"Why three?" asked Kozlov.

"To make my job more difficult."

"Perhaps you should use the Triplets."

Misha grimaced. "Anticipating our enemies' moves requires brains, not brawn."

Kozlov frowned. He had subtly cultivated the rivalry between Misha and the three men, but it had become a problem lately. The friction hadn't yet led to blows, but it was starting to interfere with operations. Kozlov contemplated ordering Misha to include them in the London project, but there was a more pressing concern.

"What is Shadow saying about Keller?" said Kozlov.

"He's back in the United States and in good condition."

"Is he still looking for us?"

"He hasn't filed an official report, but if I were him, I'd redouble my efforts after somebody blew my plane out of the sky. I've got someone in the U.S. taking care of it."

Kozlov sat behind his desk. "A second accident will not look like an accident."

"Whatever," said Misha. "He'll be just as dead."

ELEVEN

DESPITE JAKE'S GROWING suspicion that the deaths of his fellow paramilitary officers were connected, his memory of his own near-death experience was still maddeningly out of reach. He needed to do something to clear his mind and jump-start his body.

His gym occupied one end of a strip mall a few miles from his home. It was more purposeful than posh, a tool rather than a toy. Almost as if it were indifferent to attracting members. If they wanted to show up, great, but the gym wasn't lowering itself to a fancy address or a lot of luxuries. About the only concession to the holidays had been made by the front desk staff, who'd decorated the lobby with a small tree and were still playing Christmas music well into January. A young woman wearing yoga pants and a George Mason University sweatshirt was sitting cross-legged on a chair behind the counter. Jake didn't recognize her, but turnover at the front desk was high. The club was always looking for help.

"Hi!" she said, her enthusiasm completely out of sync with the gray winter day. "Are you new?"

Jake showed his membership card and she handed him a cup of hot apple cider with a slice of orange and a cinnamon stick.

"I travel a lot," he said.

"That sounds exciting. Anyplace fun?"

"Definitely exciting, not always fun."

She watched anxiously as Jake took a sip of the cider.

"Delicious," he said.

Relief spread across her face. "It's my mother's recipe. Have a good workout!"

Jake finished the cider as he walked to his locker. The men's locker room could have been transported intact from any junior high school in the country, complete with industrial gray paint, tiny lockers, and an endless olfactory battle between mildew, cleaning supplies, and sources best not contemplated.

Jake changed into his bathing suit.

It was a weekday morning and there was only one other person in the twenty-five-yard pool, a woman swimming laps at a steady pace. Jake was lean and muscular, but he lowered himself into the water gently, mindful of the bruised ribs and leg injury he'd sustained in the plane crash. It was his first time putting any stress on his body and he planned on taking the session slow—just elevating his heart rate and stretching his muscles enough to help calm his brain and restore his memory, but the pain subsided after a few warm-up laps, and after a few more laps, it was gone altogether. Jake started to push. He launched out of his flip turns, fine-tuned his form, and poured on the speed.

He'd been at it for fifteen minutes when he began to feel lightheaded. Jake considered that maybe he'd driven himself a little too hard. He hadn't exercised since the crash, and it was possible that his muscles were diverting blood away from his brain to oxygenate themselves. He slowed his pace, but the light-headedness only worsened. Counterintuitively, his heart rate began to slow. His breathing became labored.

Jake was fit and strong, but muscle sank while fat floated, and he had to swim simply to keep his head above water. He was fading fast and five yards from the end of the pool when his remaining energy vanished. Jake's head sank below the surface. He tried to breathe but inhaled nothing but water.

He couldn't kick. He couldn't use his arms. He'd lost control of his body.

Just as he had after the crash, he felt paralyzed.

He sank farther below the surface.

Jake's mind was unfocused; his heart and his lungs were shutting down. His body's fight-or-flight response should have triggered a burst of adrenaline and enabled him to sprint for the safety of the pool's edge, but Jake felt nothing of the sort. There was no panic and no fear, no physical or emotional reaction at all. As he came to a rest on the bottom of the pool, he was perfectly at peace.

TWELVE

FOR THE SECOND time in as many weeks, Jake regained consciousness with no memory of how he'd lost it.

His eyes were little more than slits, but he could make out two paramedics kneeling over him. One was injecting something into Jake's leg; the other was calling out his vital signs. Jake couldn't move. His body wouldn't respond to commands. Even in his dense mental fog, he knew he was close to death.

A third man walked into view. Jake recognized him as the health club manager.

"What happened?" he asked the paramedics.

"Opioid overdose," said one of them.

No! Jake tried to say, but nothing came out.

"We gave him Narcan," the paramedic continued. "It binds to the opioid receptor cells in the body and blocks the drugs. He's had three doses so far."

"Is three a lot?" asked the manager.

"One dose is bad. Two is critical. Three is Hail Mary territory."

"He looks pretty fit for a drug user."

The paramedic pointed out bruises from the plane crash and scars from past adventures.

"This guy has known pain in his life. Maybe he decided he didn't want to deal with it anymore."

"Suicide?!" said the manager.

"Or a creeping dependency on painkillers. The body builds up a tolerance to opioids, so users need more drugs to get the same effect. It's insidious."

Jake was sweating and shaking, and his heart was racing, but he still couldn't speak or control his movements.

"What's happening to him?" asked the manager.

"Withdrawal. His heart and lungs are trying to get oxygen to his brain."

"Will he survive?"

The paramedic studied Jake's vital signs. "He's got a chance."

JAKE WAS IN a hospital room, alone again except for a few machines that were monitoring his vital signs.

A nurse stopped by wearing scrubs that indicated they were at the Prince William County Medical Center, near Jake's home.

"How are you feeling?"

"Depleted," Jake said. "What happened to me?"

"You overdosed. The paramedics gave you Narcan, but it only lasts an hour or two. Given the large quantity of drugs in your system, you could overdose again when it wears off. We'll need to keep an eye on you."

Jake was about to protest that he hadn't taken any drugs, but the nurse had probably heard a hundred similar denials. Worse still, if the nurse did believe Jake, then they were talking about attempted murder, and Jake didn't want to involve the local police until he knew what the hell was going on.

"What happens after the overdose risk has passed?"

"You'll feel completely normal in a few hours, but you should get some counseling. You were in acute respiratory distress and nearly in a coma when the paramedics reached you."

"What . . . did I take?" The question probably wasn't as rare as it should be.

"The tox screen said liquid oxycodone and Xanax. You can't mix those two, ever. It's a death sentence. You were very lucky."

"Lucky? I almost died."

"But you didn't," said the nurse.

"You're a glass-half-full kind of guy, aren't you?" Jake said.

"You have to be when lives are on the line."

Jake pondered that one for a moment. He'd always been an optimist at heart, but his years in the Special Activities Center had turned him into something of a cynic. That change in perspective was another unwelcome development he needed to confront as he contemplated his future with the Agency.

"Is there someone you can call to pick you up? Friends, family, maybe a coworker?"

Jake shook his head. He'd made it through most of his life alone. He could handle this.

"I'll take a cab."

"Don't forget to stop by the health club and thank those people for what they did."

Jake grimaced. "You can be sure of that."

THE NURSE WAS right about Jake's recovery.

Four hours after Jake had looked into the abyss, he felt perfectly normal. The drugs and the antidote were out of his system, his heart rate and his breathing had returned to normal, and the unpleasant effects of withdrawal were gone. Jake took a cab home and told the driver to wait while he got dressed. Five minutes later, Jake was back in the cab with a pistol on his belt and a knife on his ankle.

He pushed open the door to the health club. The young woman in the college sweatshirt was gone, replaced by an equally young guy Jake recognized as one of the trainers.

"Where's the girl who was working the desk this morning?"

"Courtney? She's gone, man. Went home sick or something."

"Is the manager still here?"

"Yeah. Everything all right?"

"I need to talk to him. Now."

Jake said it in a calm voice, but his eyes told a different story. The trainer picked up the phone and a minute later the club manager emerged from his office. It was the guy who'd been talking to the paramedics. He'd worked there since Jake had joined.

"Oh, thank God," he said upon seeing Jake. "You're OK?"

"Fine. Is Courtney around?"

"I gave her the rest of the day off. She was pretty upset."

"I'll bet," Jake said. "Do you have any more of that hot apple cider?"

"No, she brought that from home. Sweet kid. It's her mother's recipe."

"Her mother must be quite a woman. Do you have Courtney's address? I'd like to show her my appreciation."

"I can't give that out, but why don't you come back to my office and we can call her? I'm sure she'll want to know you're OK."

Jake followed the manager into a small shared office and memorized the ten-digit phone number as the manager dialed. He gestured for Jake to take a seat as the line rang and rang.

"No answer," said the manager. "Strange."

"Shocking. I need to get my things out of my locker."

"Of course. By the way, what's your name? She never checked you in this morning."

"Jake Keller. I showed her my card."

"Maybe she forgot. She only started working here a few days ago. Nice kid though."

"I'd really like to see her—after what she did."

"That's very nice. I'll let her know you're OK."

"Do that. Tell her I hope to see her real soon."

JAKE RETURNED HOME and stood at his kitchen counter. With one hand, he ate a sandwich he'd picked up on the ride home, and with the other, he did a quick internet search of Courtney's telephone number on his laptop. Not surprisingly, it belonged to an untraceable prepaid phone. Whoever she was, she was probably already out of the state if not out of the country.

The nurse was also right about Jake's brush with death. He had been lucky. And as he contemplated the two close calls he'd had in just a few weeks, he thought of those who hadn't been so lucky—the men whose stars were chiseled into the Memorial Wall—and decided to do something about it.

THIRTEEN

IT WAS AN hour before sunrise when Jake pulled the Gladiator to the side of the road in Old Town Alexandria. Clap climbed into the pickup, wearing a worn canvas jacket and holding two cups of steaming-hot coffee.

"I don't drink coffee," Jake said.

"I don't trust people who don't drink coffee," said Clap.

"That's airtight logic, but we agreed that you'd pick up breakfast."

Clap pulled two foil-wrapped bacon, egg, and cheese sandwiches out of his pocket and threw one on Jake's lap.

"Choke on it."

Jake's ribs still hurt when he laughed—but a little less than the day before—more like an ice pick than a dagger.

"Does this thing have a heater?" Clap said as he scrutinized the fifty-year-old dashboard.

"It's on," Jake said.

"No cupholders either?" Clap muttered as he searched the cab. "So why did you drag me out of my nice warm bed and away from my nice hot wife on this god-awful morning?"

"You didn't seem surprised about the plane crash."

"You expect me to faint?"

"Do you know a lot of people who've been in plane crashes?"

"I've been in a helicopter crash."

"Doesn't count. Someone took my plane down on purpose."

"How?"

"I don't remember the details—the doctors said I have post-traumatic amnesia—but I know."

"Wait and see what the investigation turns up."

"I'm not sure I have that luxury. I overdosed on pain meds yesterday."

"You have to watch that stuff. It creeps up on you."

"Except I didn't take any pain meds."

"Listen to me, Jake. Everybody deals differently with returning from deployment. I get ADD—adrenaline deficit disorder. When I was in the army, I'd come back to the States and ride my motorcycle a hundred fifty miles per hour at three a.m. just to kill the boredom."

"I didn't take the pain meds, Clap."

"OK. I'm just saying, if you did, it would be a good idea to talk to somebody before it happens again. It's not weak—it's smart. All that stuff we see and do doesn't go away just because you're not thinking about it. You're going to have to deal with it at some point—better that it's on your own terms. My CO sent me out West to a place called Big Sky Bravery in Montana to deal with it. It definitely saved my marriage and it probably saved my life."

Jake wanted to punch the steering wheel. No one believed him about the drugs.

"What about all those new stars on the Memorial Wall?" Jake asked.

"The enemy gets a vote too."

"But the numbers are spiking. They're too high and too close together. I think someone is targeting paramilitary officers."

Clap was looking out the window. Even in January, joggers were out pounding the brick sidewalks, their breath condensing in the frigid morning air. He clutched his coffee in both hands and took a sip.

"You're not suspicious at all?" Jake said.

"No, I'm not. You saw what happened to us in Somalia and I was with one of the other guys when we lost him too. It sucks, but it's not a conspiracy."

"Tell me about the other guy," Jake said.

Clap looked over. The men weren't supposed to discuss classified operations with anyone not specifically cleared for them, but as it was with human beings everywhere, personal trust sometimes transcended the rules.

"We were part of an op in the Central African Republic. It was anarchy down there—weak government, fourteen militias competing for power, and zero rule of law. The citizens had no way to defend themselves and they were dying like flies. So why do we care? It's in the middle of Africa," Clap said sarcastically. His ancestors had been emigrated from the continent two hundred years earlier and he'd spent his entire career at the Agency risking his life to make it better for those who were still there.

"Well," he continued, "despite about a million alerts from State, the advice of ten thousand UN peacekeepers, and warnings from every local they'd ever spoken with, a couple of bright-eyed twenty-something idealists from UNICEF decided to show the world that we can all coexist peacefully if we just try . . . They decided to visit the Boali waterfalls two hours northwest of Bangui. It's the Central African Republic's version of Niagara Falls."

"Good trip?" asked Jake.

"They made it halfway."

"Never even saw the falls?"

"Dragged off the bus at gunpoint, but the local authorities assured UNICEF that they'd only been kidnapped, so that calmed everybody right down. Unfortunately, no one ever reached out to the family or the UN with ransom demands."

"What was the local response?"

Clap took another bite of his sandwich and looked out the window.

"That's a good one," he said. "There's a unit down there called FORSDIR. It stands for the Force for the Protection of the Democratic Institution, but everyone just calls them FORSDIR, and it was obviously named by somebody with a sense of humor because its sole mission, aside from lining its own pockets, is to keep the current dictator in office. The local intelligence service is almost as bad but they act as a counterweight to the FORSDIR because they're both competing for the same bribes. Anyway, it's all moot because the government forces are generally afraid to leave the capital."

"So there was no 'local response.'"

"Correct," said Clap. "UNICEF was pleading with the White House for something to be done, so the hostage response group kicked it to us."

"I'm sure the UNICEF staff are big supporters of CIA."

"We're like the cops. They hate us until they need us, then they complain we're not doing enough."

"What about letting the volunteers live with the consequences of their actions?"

"Not PC, bro," said Clap. "Bad stuff is always somebody else's fault."

"So what was the plan?"

"Our team leader started throwing money around and we got a hot lead within a couple of days, but pretty soon we hit a dead end, and then our source asked for more money so he could acquire more information. It soon became obvious that this was a business for them. They kept dribbling out information, asking for more and more cash, until they couldn't string us along any longer. We'd identified the group that'd grabbed the couple from UNICEF, the guy who was running the show, and where the hostages had been taken after they'd left the bus—but they'd been moved in the interim, and we didn't know where."

Clap took another sip of his coffee.

"Don't get me wrong. We weren't just relying on paid informants. We were gathering our own intel too, but every time we brought something to FORSDIR or the *Police Judiciare*, they claimed they'd look into it, but we wouldn't hear anything back unless we greased everybody in sight. I thought our local sources were soaking us, but the government officials were the all-star team of bribe taking. They eventually told us they'd 'discovered' where the couple from UNICEF was being held."

"How much?"

"A million dollars . . . They said it was to 'support us' with the rescue."

"Isn't that their job?" Jake said.

"The local commander said it was a bargain. He knew there were U.S. and UK special ops teams in other parts of the country and explained to us how moving the allied teams into position for a rescue attempt would be risky since Russian mercenaries and spec ops troops were also operating in-country . . . or we could make it all go away for a cool million. Our team leader was against it, but he ran it up the flagpole and somebody in DC swallowed it hook, line, and sinker."

"So we paid the million?"

"A duffel bag full of cash—old-school CIA shit. Hell, we used to change whole governments for a million bucks and now we're dropping that kind of dough to recover a couple of dumb kids."

"Lousy inflation . . . ," Jake said.

"Anyway, the next day our eight-man team loaded up along with twenty FORSDIR troops 'handpicked' by our government contact—probably his cousins—and set off on a four-hour slog over rutted jungle roads to the place where the UNICEF workers were being held. We decided to attack in the daylight because the FORSDIR troops had never trained for night ops, or day ops for that matter, but we figured we'd be safer with the sun up."

"Fun drive?"

"It was something else. I've spent my whole Agency career in Africa and I've never seen anything like it. Those people had probably never had a drink of clean water in their lives. It was like the land that time forgot—and not in the way that people always romanticize—these people were starving. They had zero access to medical care, no ability to defend themselves, and were at the mercy of the armed gangs who roamed the countryside looking to pick up sex slaves and child soldiers. It was literally kill or be killed. One of the UN people told me the Central African Republic has the lowest male life expectancy of any country in the world—forty-nine years."

"Did you find the UNICEF folks?"

"The only thing we found was a fucking ambush. The camp was filled with militiamen, mounted machine guns, and RPGs. The FORSDIR troops had led us right into it. It was about a hundred of them against eight of us, plus two."

"Plus two?"

"The two MQ-9 Reapers we had overhead. We didn't trust the FORSDIR troops so we never told them about the drones, but we were in direct comms with the operators and had them scout the route ahead of us. They'd seen the camp and the enemy formation an hour before we got there, but we decided to let it play out in case the hostages were actually there. But our FORSDIR support melted into the jungle as soon as we started taking incoming fires, so the mystery of what was going down was over. The Reapers lit up the camp while we were still a couple hundred yards out. Half a dozen Hellfire missiles sent it back to the Stone Age."

Clap continued. "I can't really say it was a surprise. We sort of figured that the FORSDIR officers were involved in the initial kidnapping, based on some signal intercepts we'd seen. The head kidnapper used a nom de guerre that we voiceprinted and tracked back to our contact at FORSDIR."

"So why did you follow them into the jungle?"

"We figured it was just the business they were running. They knew the U.S. wouldn't pay a ransom, so they framed it as compensation for all the 'work' they'd put into helping us find the UNICEF workers. Anyway, that's why we kept the Reapers in our back pocket."

"Were they surprised when the missiles hit?"

"Like the hand of God had come down from the sky. They bolted. We didn't take any casualties, but HQ was furious that we'd been double crossed."

"Didn't your team leader advise them not to pay?"

"Yes. So now they looked like idiots. They told us to get the money back. We asked and threatened the locals, but they refused. Our contact claimed that he'd fulfilled his end of the deal, brought us to the hostages, had no idea about the ambush, etcetera. Then, to top it off, he claimed that we killed the hostages during the air attack."

"How'd that go down at Langley?"

"About as well as you'd expect. SAC HQ told us to send a

message—to let people know that screwing over the United States was not OK. The thought was, if there were no consequences to kidnapping a couple of Americans and then stealing a million dollars from their government, then it was just going to keep happening. We needed to establish a credible deterrence."

"I can't say I disagree," said Jake.

"Same here," said Clap, "but the devil was in the details. HQ told us to eliminate our contact at FORSDIR and the entire team he'd assembled for the ambush."

"Execute them?"

"'Drown them in a pool of their own blood' was the unofficial order."

"Did headquarters have a finding to take these guys out?"

"That part was a little vague. Our team leader asked if we had the legal authority to go crash these dudes and no one responded. The inference was that it was a question that never should have been asked. Two days later, we were literally on our way to the airport to exfil when we got ambushed again, but we weren't as lucky the second time. Our team leader and our linguist were killed immediately."

"What about the Reapers?"

"Our air support had been terminated that morning."

"That sound like a coincidence to you?"

"Sometimes shit just goes sideways. Look, Jake, you're probably still shaken up from the plane crash. Take it easy on the pain meds and don't start chasing shadows or you'll drive yourself crazy."

The two men drove in silence for several minutes until Jake dropped Clap several blocks from his apartment in Old Town Alexandria. As Jake turned for home, he thought carefully about what Clap had said and the jumble of disconnected data points that were swirling around inside Jake's mind.

He wasn't being paranoid.

Someone was killing the Agency's paramilitary officers.

There had been attempts on his life before the plane crash. But in each case, he understood the context and had seen the situations evolve. He knew the players and comprehended their reasons for trying to kill him.

In each case, but one.

It had been Jake's first mission in the field and it had gone wrong from the second he'd set foot in-country. There were at least twenty countries and hundreds of nonstate actors who would readily kill a CIA officer to establish their bona fides with their own constituencies, but Jake didn't have the perspective to know if that initial attempt on his life was linked to what was happening now.

But he knew someone who did.

FOURTEEN

JAKE DIALED A number on his cell phone as the pickup rumbled over the cobblestone streets.

"Hello," said a woman.

"Bravo alpha, four zero zero," said Jake.

"Hold one moment . . ."

It was closer to five minutes. Similar calls in the past had been routed to embassies in the Middle East, jets over the world's oceans, and once to a ship in international waters that was on a cruise to nowhere with a dozen passengers of uncertain legal status.

"I can't talk," a pained voice said through the phone. *"I'll call you back."*

Jake clicked off without saying another word. He didn't want to get anyone killed, especially his most senior contact at CIA.

Half an hour later, Jake's phone rang. The number was blocked.

"Everything OK?" Jake asked.

"Far from it. I just watched the Nutcracker *for the eighteenth time in six years. If you ever have a daughter, don't let her take up ballet."*

"Don't they usually do that before Christmas?"

"A quarter inch of snow canceled the performance . . . By the way, what's that noise? It sounds like you're riding in the back of a cargo plane."

Jake frowned. He'd restore the pickup when he was good and ready.

"Can you give me ten minutes?" he said.

"Can you come to Arlington?"

"I'll be there in twenty."

"See you then."

Peter Clements had been chief of station, London, and Jake's first boss at the Agency. He was now associate director for intelligence and a very big deal at CIA, but the two men had remained close through Clements's climb up the company ladder and Jake's transition from desk analyst to field operative.

Clements was sitting on a park bench wearing a down jacket and drinking a cup of coffee when Jake walked over. It was one of their many meeting spots, two miles from Clements's home and a good place for a private conversation. They rarely met in the office because most people at the Agency recognized Clements on sight and it was safer for Jake if no one knew of their association. While Clements had been Zac Miller's boss in London, there was no reason for him to know Jake Keller. It would be game over for Jake if the wrong person put it together.

"You look terrible," said Clements.

"Not for someone who's nearly died twice in the past two weeks."

"I suppose everything is relative."

Jake filled him in on the crash and the overdose while Clements drank his coffee. He knew better than to bring one for Jake.

"You think they're connected?" asked Clements.

"No question."

"Based on what?"

"Someone took down the plane and I didn't take any drugs."

"I thought you had amnesia."

"It's like a dream I can't quite remember. I know what happened. I just don't have the details."

"That should hold up well in court. Why did you want to see me?"

"I think my recent troubles are part of a plot to target paramilitary officers and I want to talk to you about what happened to me in Iran."

"That's next to Iraq, right?"

"Did you ever learn why I was arrested?"

"I think it had something to do with you exposing their top secret nuclear missile program."

Jake smirked. "They grabbed me long before that."

"Either way, the Agency never pursued it."

Jake's usually stoic face conveyed his surprise. "You didn't even look?"

"You 'died' a few weeks later," said Clements. "The worst thing that could've happened would have been for word to get out that CIA was investigating the death of Zac Miller. It wouldn't be too hard for a careful analyst to tie Zac's death to Jake's appearance a few months later."

"Did it ever cross your mind that the Agency might have a leak?"

"Of course," said Clements, "but it was a high-risk operation and you'd gone in with thin cover. We decided not to pursue it because of the risk to your safety."

"Who decided?"

"I did," said Clements, "along with Ted Graves."

Jake frowned.

"It could have been something as simple as turning on your phone," Clements continued. "We know the second an Iranian SIM card starts looking for a network on U.S. soil and they have the same capability. Maybe the ayatollah wanted a public relations victory to counteract his staggering unpopularity at home, or maybe, even though you're convinced you did nothing to reveal your mission, you were acting like a spy."

"What does your gut tell you?"

"My gut has nothing to do with it," said Clements. "I go by facts. And the fact is, it was a single point in time two years ago and I wasn't with you when you were arrested."

"Only one person was."

"Then that's who you should be talking to."

FIFTEEN

JAKE CAUGHT THE next red-eye flight to London.

The city had been the launching point for the Iran operation, and as he'd done in a dozen countries since then, Jake melted into the crowd as soon as his feet hit the ground—just one of the more than two hundred thousand passengers who would pass through Heathrow Airport that day. Walking with purpose through the terminal, he stopped only to purchase a prepaid phone—with a UK SIM card—to make his obligatory check-in call to Graves. For reasons he didn't entirely understand, Jake didn't mention the incident at the health club.

He rented a gray Volkswagen Golf and spent ninety minutes crawling through morning traffic before pulling onto a wide boulevard just south of Kensington Gardens. It was a highly desirable section of London, and he was forced to circle the block several times to find a particular parking space. Though it was marked "Residents Only," on the spectrum of risks in Jake's life, a parking ticket didn't even register.

The five-story building at Number 18, Queen's Gate Terrace was one of many townhouses and embassies in the area, but one of the few private residences—most of the others had been converted to apartments or condominiums. Even on a gray January day, its brilliant white paint and nineteenth-century architecture seemed to brighten the street.

But Jake wasn't focused on the brick or the balustrades or the balconies.

He was watching the front door.

And he didn't have to wait long for it to open.

The target stepped out wearing a calf-length wool coat and headed west toward the shops on nearby Gloucester Road. Wearing a hat and sunglasses, Jake grabbed a package from the seat next to him and fell in behind her on foot.

The woman stepped into a small Middle Eastern food market. Jake followed her inside and spent a few minutes browsing the shelves while she greeted the staff by name. In the reflection of a pane of glass, Jake spied a clerk retrieve an item from behind the counter and place it in the woman's small shopping cart. She moved slowly through the front of the store, carefully selecting specific items from each aisle.

Jake waited until she was alone in the back of the store before making his move. He approached her from behind and deftly placed the package he'd brought in her cart.

The woman was about to put a small container of tabbouleh in the shopping cart when she noticed the package.

She looked at Jake over the top of her reading glasses.

"Is this yours?"

He removed his hat and glasses. "It's yours."

She scrutinized him.

"I'm quite sure it's not," she said. "I may be old, but I'm not senile."

"Open it," Jake said.

She lifted it out of the cart.

"A brown paper package tied up with string? How quaint. Are you going to sing to me too?"

She looked into Jake's eyes.

"Do I know you?"

"The package will explain everything," he said.

The woman unwrapped the package. It was an eight-by-ten-inch painting of a British Spitfire fighter plane over London during the Battle of Britain.

"My father flew . . ." Her voice trailed off as her mind worked overtime.

"I remember," said Jake. "You told me on our flight."

Lady Celia Parker was quiet for a moment. The septuagenarian stared deeply into Jake's eyes once again, then started pushing her shopping cart down the aisle. Jake fell in alongside her.

"So you're alive," she said as she placed a few sprigs of mint in the cart.

"Thanks to you."

Celia nodded once.

The two had been seatmates on the commercial flight that inserted Jake into Iran a year and half earlier. While Celia had departed none the worse for wear, Jake had been arrested within minutes of landing, caught in the middle of political infighting at CIA, and left out in the cold. Though he'd never seen her again, she'd later been instrumental in his safe return home.

"I did warn you not to take those pictures," she continued.

Jake smiled.

"The painting is lovely. Will you hang it for me? I live just around the—" Celia interrupted herself. "But of course, you already know where I live, don't you? Maybe I am senile."

She took the painting and walked out of the market.

"Would you like me to carry your groceries?" Jake asked, motioning to the cart she'd left inside.

Celia frowned. "Don't be barbaric. It's all put on my account and delivered."

IT WAS WELL-KNOWN in London that the Metropolitan Police and the UK Security Service used real-time facial recognition software to analyze the feeds from the tens of thousands of closed-circuit television cameras around the city. Jake donned his hat and sunglasses as he followed Celia outside.

"Still in the game, then, are you?" Celia said.

Jake didn't reply, but she had her answer.

"We'll talk inside," she said.

The entrance to the townhouse was flanked by a dozen sculpted boxwood plants and two stone bulldogs. Celia's housekeeper took their coats and brought them tea in the second-floor study. Jake closed the French doors after she'd left.

"Do you still go by Zachary?" Celia said.

"It's Jake Keller now. The name came with the plastic surgery."

"I suppose it was your only option after all that adverse press. Can you tell me what happened?"

"I was hoping you could tell me," Jake said.

"Of course I'll tell you what I know, but why now?"

Jake smiled. The woman didn't miss a thing.

"There's been a suspicious increase in fatalities inside my organization."

"And you're wondering if you have a leak . . . I teased you earlier about taking pictures, but you weren't the only one using his phone and the Iranians had a body double on the flight to Singapore. That's not the kind of thing one conjures up on the spot. I don't think there's any question about it. They were expecting you. You were either just fortunate enough or just determined enough to survive."

They sipped their tea in silence for a few minutes.

"You know, I recognized your voice and your eyes in the market," she said, "but I couldn't put it all together until I saw the painting. It's quite lovely. Thank you."

"It's the least I could do," Jake said.

"But your eyes, they've gotten harder. I suspect they've seen a great deal since we last saw each other."

"The work is rewarding, but the new identity cost me a great deal . . . Everyone I'd known, everything I'd done. I had to give it all up."

"You must be terribly lonely."

"The love and the joy have been sucked out of my life," Jake conceded.

"Then why do you do it?"

"Because I need to protect those who can't protect themselves."

"Says the little boy who lost his parents . . ."

"Excuse me?"

Jake was incredulous. He'd been just fourteen when they'd died. Home alone while they'd gone out for dinner, he'd been awakened in the middle of the night and informed of their deaths by a police officer. Jake had curled up on the kitchen floor and cried himself to sleep, but they were the last tears he'd ever shed over the two people he'd loved more than anything in the world. When morning came, something had changed inside him. His life flashed before his eyes: not backward, as some people experience before they die, but forward. An only child, he was suddenly alone. It was an inflection point, a sharp one, with consequences both good and bad. He swiftly concluded that there was ultimately only one person responsible for his well-being: himself.

"You're trying to save the world because you couldn't save your parents," Celia continued. "It's completely daft, if you ask me."

Jake was speechless. Of course, Celia was right in one sense: The loss of his parents had cultivated a protective instinct inside him. It had driven him to CIA, and then to the Special Activities Center, where he felt he could do the most to protect the country he loved, but the psychological edge that enabled him to detach himself from the horrors he'd experienced had also come at a great personal cost. He'd barricaded himself behind an emotional wall.

"Your parents died because of a drink driver, right?" she said, using the British phrase. "You were a child. You're not responsible for their deaths and you're not responsible for saving the world."

"What does that—"

"You're making yourself miserable, striving toward an unattainable goal. It's a worthy goal, but you have to accept that you'll never achieve it. Good people will suffer and bad people will succeed. That's life."

"I shouldn't care?" Jake said.

"Of course not. That would be inhuman and your compassion is what makes you special, but you can't neglect yourself. Do you remember when we were sitting next to each other on the aeroplane?"

"Vaguely . . ." Jake rolled his eyes. Celia had been as forthright and opinionated then as she was now.

"Well, what do they always say during the safety briefing? 'In the event oxygen is required, put your own mask on before helping others.' Do you know why they say that?"

"Because if you don't take care of yourself, you won't be able to help anyone else."

"Exactly, and then your hopes and dreams and secret missions will all be over, because you'll have a breakdown or be dead, and you'll never save another person. Just like protecting this way of life can't be done alone, life can't be lived alone. We all need support, whether from our God, our families, our friends, or our colleagues."

Jake nodded slowly.

"So, what are you going to do about it?" said Celia.

"About what?"

"About anything. About feeling sorry for yourself, about being lonely, about the fact that someone betrayed you? Finding the leak in your organization isn't going to cure the emptiness inside you. No one is going to hold your hand and tell you it's going to be all right. You're an adult. Fix it. Chop-chop."

She stood.

No one had spoken to Jake like that, ever, but the slap across the face was exactly what he'd needed. At thirty years of age, he was finally admitting that man was not designed to be alone. He'd seen the opposite, and envied it, in his peers who'd been in the military. Nothing was more important than the person right beside them. Jake felt that way in the abstract—a need to protect others—but such connections had eluded him on a personal level for most of his life.

Jake had never shied from action, but he'd always taken it on behalf of others. He realized now that Celia was right. Now he needed to do something for himself.

And Paris was only ninety minutes away.

SIXTEEN

ANOTHER CAR. Another country. Another stakeout.

Jake drove slowly along the tree-lined Champs-Élysées in a rented Mercedes sedan, looking to the world like just another affluent French commuter on his way home from a late night at the office. Though the streets were deserted, he drove the speed limit, signaled every turn, and obeyed every traffic law. The last thing he wanted was to show up on the authorities' radar. Not only was the target of his surveillance an employee of the Directorate-General for External Security, or DGSE as the French equivalent to CIA was commonly known, but Jake had some history in France.

He was wanted for murder.

Technically, Zac Miller had been the target of the nationwide manhunt, but Jake didn't need an aggressive cop and a bad piece of luck undoing the two years he'd spent building his new identity and landing him in jail. It had gone down during the Iran operation and left him with no way out aside from plastic surgery and a name change. Ted Graves had assured him that the U.S. National Security Agency had altered the fingerprint records in the French and the

INTERPOL databases, but Jake and Ted had always had an adversarial relationship and, after two attempts on Jake's life in the past few weeks, trust was a commodity in short supply.

He turned the sedan onto a cobblestone alley in the Eighth Arrondissement and slowed as he passed the rear entrance to a private townhouse. There were two reserved spaces but only one car, a large Peugeot sedan. Jake passed the Peugeot and spent the next twenty minutes conducting a surveillance-detection run along the local streets before returning to the alley. He crept along the rough pavement until he found an empty parking space and backed in.

The rented Mercedes was a model used by high-end car services everywhere and Jake was fluent in French, the product of years of schooling and a visiting college professor who'd taught him the finer points of French culture. If asked why he was parked in a reserved space, he would respond with a perfect Parisian accent that he was simply waiting for a client. He'd even worn a suit and a tie.

It was 0630 the next morning when the townhouse's rear door opened. A gentleman in his sixties with thinning gray hair and a finely tailored suit emerged carrying a briefcase and drove off in the Peugeot.

Jake watched him leave.

The man wasn't the target.

The home belonged to the parents of the DGSE operative, whose own address was hidden from public search records. Jake could have located it through CIA, but every keystroke at the Agency was logged and monitored, and the instinct and the training that had kept him alive in some of the most dangerous places in the world was telling him that he needed to keep this operation off the books.

Jake was still waiting when the gentleman in the Peugeot returned twelve hours later. There were a few explanations for the lack of other activity: His wife was away, his wife had left him, or his wife was dead. But it was more likely that his wife simply didn't use the back alley because the front of her home opened onto a beautiful Parisian street. Truth be told, Jake didn't really care about the parents' comings and goings, but he knew that if the DGSE operative were to visit, it would be by car. Jake returned to the rental agency, picked up a different vehicle, and returned to the alley.

And so it went for two more days: switching cars, switching parking spaces, switching his schedule—all so he wouldn't arouse suspicion or stick out in anyone's memory.

It was just past eight p.m. on the third day when Jake returned from the rental agency with an empty bladder, a full stomach, and a midsized BMW sedan. He drove slowly through the alley and noticed that the interior of the townhouse was brightly lit and a small Porsche SUV was parked in the empty space next to the Peugeot.

The target had arrived.

Jake parked at the end of the alley and walked indirectly toward the Porsche, audibly dropping his key as he passed by. He bent down to retrieve it with one hand and used his other hand to discreetly affix a GPS transmitter inside the Porsche's plastic bumper using two-sided tape.

Two hours later, Jake was waiting at the end of the alley when the Porsche drove by. Even in the dim light of the streetlamps, he glimpsed a woman with long dark hair behind the wheel.

Her name was Geneviève.

Despite a great deal of time and distance, she'd never been far from his thoughts. At substantial risk to her career and her life, she'd helped him flee across France and had ultimately wished him fare winds and following seas at the edge of the English Channel. He'd vowed to call as soon as he'd made it to safety, but never did.

In his defense, he was dead.

At least officially.

The sensational nature of the murder warrants against him ensured that his apparent death was well publicized, and for the past two years Geneviève believed that he'd died a horrible, violent death. Given her role in a foreign intelligence agency, CIA had forbidden Jake from telling her the truth. It was a commitment he had taken seriously, and it had cost him no small amount of personal anguish, but he was nothing if not loyal—at least to his job.

But much had changed between then and now. The connection Jake felt between the attempts on his life and the dead paramilitary officers was growing by the day. He owed it to his country and himself to find whoever was responsible and bring them to justice. And though his trip to England had started with a question about his arrest in Iran, and the visit to Paris was supposed to be personal, it was all inextricably intertwined. Celia had ended up giving him deeply personal advice, and Geneviève was his sole contact at DGSE—the only agency that really knew what happened to the dead CIA officer in Syria.

Like Celia, Geneviève had never heard of Jake Keller. Two women, one old, one young. Each had heroically come to his aid and never heard from him again. Celia had been pleased upon hearing the news that he was alive. Somewhere in her late seventies, she had seen and experienced much. She'd lived abroad, she'd had grandchildren, she'd become a widow. She was at a point in her life where the highs weren't as high and the lows weren't as low.

The pit in Jake's stomach told him Geneviève wasn't going to be quite so stoic.

The Porsche rumbled down the cobblestone alley, blipped the throttle at the main road, and made a quick right and an even quicker left before roaring off into the night.

Jake smiled. He'd never catch her without speeding through Paris, and if Jake was honest with himself, he might not catch her even then. Geneviève was a skilled driver and a fast one. She'd unashamedly told him how she routinely avoided speeding tickets with a smile, an apology, and a few bats of her eyelashes.

It was France, after all.

She was heading northeast. Jake started the rental car and followed at a leisurely pace, keeping one eye on the GPS tracker resting on the passenger seat. He'd been on the road for eight minutes when the signal vanished. Jake arrived at the site of the last transmission, an apartment building in the Tenth Arrondissement. He would have missed the elegantly camouflaged parking garage had it not been for the graded curb in front. The door was down and the lights were off.

She was in for the night.

Jake parked around the corner and returned on foot. As expected, Geneviève's name wasn't listed on the building's list of residents. He returned to his rental car and set an alarm for five o'clock. He closed his eyes, but anticipation and anxiety kept sleep at bay.

It was just after seven a.m. when the garage doors opened and the Porsche emerged into the brilliant morning sunshine with Geneviève behind the wheel—and a man in the seat next to her.

SEVENTEEN

JAKE WATCHED THEM drive away.

The GPS beacon he'd planted under the Porsche's bumper began transmitting.

Jake had certainly considered that Geneviève might be involved with someone else. She was brilliant, kind, and beautiful. Women like her didn't lack for attention. But he had severely underestimated the angst that consumed him from seeing her with another man. Was he her live-in boyfriend? Maybe her husband? Jake hadn't expected her to mourn him for eternity, but he felt as if he'd been punched in the gut.

Jake started the rental car and glanced at the GPS.

To the left was the airport; to the right was Geneviève.

Jake cursed and turned right.

While he might have lost what he could never get back, Geneviève was also his only link to DGSE—and DGSE was his only link to Syria. He would have to put aside the personal loss if he was going to unravel the loss of a dozen Agency paramilitary officers.

Jake followed the GPS tracker until he caught sight of the small

SUV entering the Nineteenth Arrondissement. Geneviève wasn't making it easy. Her heavy foot and the rush-hour traffic kept Jake several car lengths behind until she pulled into the right lane to make a turn onto Boulevard Mortier. Jake cursed aloud as he realized where they were headed. Two kilometers down the road was a complex that one might have mistaken for a university campus if not for its high walls, coils of concertina wire, and the men with automatic rifles guarding the entrance. Known colloquially as the CAT, the *Centre Administratif des Tourelles* was the headquarters for the French spy service.

And the Porsche turned inside—with both its passengers.

Geneviève's love interest was in the game.

Jake passed the center. There was no way he could reveal that he was still alive and ask about a top secret intelligence operation in Syria in front of another DGSE officer. Any inclination Geneviève might have to help would be scuttled immediately—especially if her boyfriend/fiancé/husband deduced that she and Jake had once been romantically involved.

But it wasn't in Jake's nature to give up, and a plan formed in his head as he drove. It would require another car, a change of clothes, and a few accessories, but it might be his only shot.

He spent a few hours assembling the items on his list and checked into a hotel. He tipped the valet twenty euros to park the black Mercedes-AMG out front, went to his room, and scribbled a note on the hotel stationery. Five minutes later he lay down on the bed, wearing jeans and a blue-and-red jacket from the Paris Saint-Germain Football Club.

Jake set the GPS tracker to alert him when the Porsche started moving, and took a nap.

It was just past five p.m. when the tracker began to beep. Jake put on his sunglasses, took the elevator to the lobby, and handed the valet another twenty euros. The GPS beacon showed Geneviève's Porsche moving west, back toward her apartment, at a high rate of speed.

Jake did the same, but he'd chosen a hotel two blocks from her apartment to give himself an unbeatable head start. He drove the Mercedes to her apartment in a low gear, keeping the twin-turbo V8 nearly at its redline for the entire trip. By the time he reached the entrance to her garage, the motor was hot. He shut down the engine, raised the hood, and opened a liter of motor oil that he'd bought earlier in the day. Jake glanced at the GPS tracker. Geneviève was thirty seconds away. He poured the oil over the four-hundred-degree engine block and threw the empty container in a nearby trash bin.

By the time the Porsche arrived, the Mercedes was engulfed in a cloud of dense blue smoke—and blocking the entrance to Geneviève's garage. Jake stared at the car as smoke billowed from its open hood.

Geneviève's passenger immediately stepped out. With close-cropped hair and an athletic build, the man did a quick scan of his surroundings and walked directly to Jake.

"What happened?" said the man in French.

Jake's first thought was *soldier*, but Geneviève joined them before Jake could answer the man's question.

"Laurent?" she said.

Jake nearly lost his balance. She was standing ten feet away, wearing a winter coat and waving noxious smoke from her face, and she looked even more beautiful than he'd remembered.

"I'm sorry," she said upon seeing Jake's face. "My brother has the same car and the same jacket."

"I hope your brother's car works better than this one. I left the Relais Pigalle service station and two minutes later it did this."

The man grimaced and walked into the cloud of smoke. Jake took off his sunglasses and stared at Geneviève. She scrutinized his face. The Agency's plastic surgeon had done a good job, but Jake's eyes hadn't changed, nor had his voice.

"Do you live in the building?" she said.

"No," Jake said. He glanced down at her hands and didn't see a ring. "I'm heading to Dieppe, then sailing to England."

Geneviève looked perplexed as the boyfriend returned.

"Did they put oil in your car at the Relais Pigalle?" he said.

Jake nodded. "Two liters."

"Fools," said the beau. "They overfilled it. There's nothing wrong with the engine. The smoke will stop in a few minutes once the extra oil burns off. Back up so we can pull into the garage."

He walked back to the Porsche, leaving Geneviève alone with Jake.

"Good luck with your trip," she said tentatively. She paused before turning back to her car, but the boyfriend was impatient. Jake discreetly slipped the note into her pocket. Geneviève hesitated for an instant, struggling to understand what she was seeing and hearing, but she kept moving—back to her car, back to her boyfriend, and back to her life. She pulled the Porsche into the garage and Jake watched as the door slowly closed between them.

EIGHTEEN

JAKE STRIPPED OFF the red-and-blue jacket and sat on the bed in his hotel room with a disposable phone in his hands. It rang three hours later. The incoming number was blocked.

"The last time I saw you, you were on your way to London," said Geneviève. *"Tell me about the trip."*

"I sailed across the Channel in a storm and it nearly killed me," Jake said.

"But apparently it didn't. How can I be sure?"

"Who else knows that you loaned me your brother's jacket and drove me across the country in his car?"

Geneviève was silent for several seconds. There was street noise in the background, as if she'd gone out for a walk.

"Where did we meet?" she said.

"At a rest stop—"

Jake could feel her smile through the phone. *"Where did we first meet?"*

"In Brussels," Jake said. "You were wearing a blue suit and had your hair pulled back. You were staring at me—"

"*You were staring at me.*"

"We need to talk," Jake said.

"*Sacré-Coeur, the chapel in the back.*"

"I'll be there in twenty."

THE TWO DOZEN tourists who'd braved the cold January evening to admire the famous basilica gazed mostly at the shining golf-leaf mosaic of Jesus on the ceiling above the altar. Hardly anyone ventured behind it to the more sedate chapel of the Virgin Mary.

Jake had been sitting in a pew for ten minutes when Geneviève knelt down three rows in front of him. Although Jake was an unemotional and battle-scarred veteran of numerous overseas deployments, his heart ached as he looked at her.

The defense-industry conference in Brussels where he'd first seen her was still etched vividly in his memory. Roughly his age, she'd been a study in contrasts. She'd been wearing a solid blue business suit, but it was finely tailored and highly flattering to her tall, athletic figure. Her hair was luxurious and dark, but it was pulled back in a simple ponytail. Her eyelashes and eyebrows were sculpted and alluring, but she wore almost no makeup. He'd found her incredibly sexy. They'd exchanged a few lingering glances, but nothing more.

A few months later he'd seen her at another industry conference in London. Having chastised himself many times for letting her slip away in Brussels, he'd immediately excused himself from his group and introduced himself. She'd teased him a little, pretending she didn't remember him, but eventually they'd exchanged phone numbers.

As he watched her now, barely ten feet away, he swore it could have been yesterday.

She stood and walked out without making eye contact. Jake fol-

lowed her outside and down the grand staircase to Louise-Michel
Square.

"The jacket and the car were good," she said once they were alone.

"I needed to be sure you'd get out of your car."

"How did you find me?"

Jake raised an eyebrow as if to say, *I'm still with the Agency . . .*

She nodded.

"This is a lot to process," she said. "You know they built that
basilica in honor of the last man to rise from the dead."

"I couldn't tell you I was alive."

"You could have. You chose not to. You prioritized your career."

Jake said nothing.

"An anonymous phone call, a cryptic note, anything," she said.
"I had nightmares, wondering if you'd suffered."

Jake was silent.

"Here, walking along in the dark, listening to your voice, it's all
flooding back," she continued. "The joy, the fear, that last kiss on the
streets of Dieppe, and then you were gone forever. Why now? Why
are you doing this to me now?"

Jake hesitated. The timing was complicated.

"One of our paramilitary officers was assassinated by Syrian intelligence."

She froze.

"I thought—" Jake began.

"Tell me you're not upending my life over your career again."

"It's not about my career. It's about a man who was gunned down
in cold blood. We were conducting an operation to take out a senior
figure in the death squads when the officer was killed. DGSE has
an agent in place inside the Syrian government. I was hoping—"

"Not a word for almost two years, *two years*, and now this? Maybe
the man I knew really is dead, because I have no idea who you are."

She started walking back toward the basilica. Jake jogged to catch her and held her elbow. She wheeled around, looking as if she might kill him.

"Don't touch me," she snapped.

"This isn't easy for me either," Jake said. "This isn't how I envisioned our reunion. I hadn't planned on the car, or the jacket, or pretending to have a breakdown in front of your building, but—"

"I've moved on and so should you."

"Give me your number," he said. "I'll call you."

"I've heard that before, and even if I did believe you this time, how would I know it's you? I don't even know your name."

She stormed off.

"It's Jake," he said, but no one was listening.

NINETEEN

JAKE FELL ASLEEP in his hotel room bed with the phone clutched in his hand, waiting for Geneviève to call.

She never did.

In the morning, he booked a flight back to the States. He'd just finished packing when the phone rang, but it wasn't the French drop phone. It was the one he'd bought in the UK. It was Celia calling, inviting him to a dinner party that night in London. Though she'd never been directly involved in the espionage business, the worldly septuagenarian hooked Jake with a tantalizing clue about what had happened to him in Iran.

Her final line before hanging up was, "I'm serving a taste of Persia."

Jake canceled his ticket to America and booked a Eurostar train to London. The train had just pulled out of the Gare du Nord station in Paris when Jake opened his laptop and began to research the Syrian death squads. If his access to Geneviève and DGSE was cut off, he would have to find another way to uncover who'd killed the CIA paramilitary officer who'd been working with Jeff. Jake's Arabic skills were excellent, the product of CIA's language institute and extensive operations in the Mideast, so he began reading Syrian opposition websites in Arabic, hoping to get a view of what was happening on the ground that was untainted by Western media bias.

The images were gruesome. Jeff hadn't been exaggerating when he'd spoken of the atrocities committed by the regime-sponsored squads. Jake had been working for about twenty minutes when he noticed the man next to him peering across the armrest at Jake's laptop. The man promptly turned away each time Jake looked over, but quickly resumed stealing furtive glances.

Jake scowled.

There were several ways it could play out. 1) Maybe the man spoke Arabic and was actually reading the site. 2) Maybe he was fascinated by the grisly photographs. 3) Maybe he thought the solidly built, dark-haired man sitting next to him was a terrorist. The opposition website Jake was on had the bare-bones look of a jihadi website, with simple graphics and uncensored photos of extreme gore.

Jake didn't want a nervous citizen to spark a terror warning as the high-speed train approached the Channel tunnel—especially while they were still in France, where Jake had once been wanted for murder.

He put the laptop away and began to read an old *Sunday Times* newspaper that someone had left in the seatback in front of him. He was still on the first section when the man seated next to him began looking over once again. It quickly became obvious that the right answer to Jake's earlier question was: 4) The man seated next to him was a prying, nosy boor.

Jake found the newspaper's crossword puzzle, stared at it for a single minute, then used a pen to fill in every answer, doing the horizontal clues first, then the vertical. He folded the newspaper in his lap, put the pen in his pocket, and closed his eyes. Jake had scribbled nothing but gibberish in the puzzle squares—he'd barely read the clues—but the seemingly astonishing feat managed to neutralize the meddlesome man in the seat next to him.

The train pulled into St. Pancras International in London two hours later. Jake passed under the station's arched ceiling and made his way to South Kensington where he checked into a boutique hotel. Knowing and fearing Celia, he dressed in a jacket and tie for dinner and took a long walk through Kensington Gardens.

He arrived at Celia's precisely at seven p.m. Soft lighting illuminated the boxwoods and the two stone bulldogs flanking her front door. The housekeeper greeted Jake and informed him that Lady Celia would be down in a moment. He poured himself a twelve-year-old scotch and perused Celia's bookshelves, eventually taking down a hundred-year-old volume called *The Standard Dictionary of Facts*. He was reading it at her desk when she arrived a few minutes later.

"Do make yourself at home," she said as she crossed the room and placed his glass on a coaster.

"There's a section in here on giants," Jake said. "Did you know the Roman emperor Maximan was nine feet tall?"

"Yes, we used to play tennis together. How was Paris?"

Jake closed the book and stared at the floor.

"Unproductive."

"You mean she hadn't built a shrine and taken a vow of celibacy?"

"She was angry."

"How very selfish of her. After all, all you'd done is come back from the dead after she'd spent two years mourning you with a broken heart. You'd think that sort of thing happens all the time."

Jake took a sip of his scotch.

"She's probably in shock," Celia continued. "We may fall in love with the person inside, but we associate it with the person we see."

Jake started at her blankly.

"Let me see if I can put it in terms a man can understand. Your favorite sports car is stolen. For two years you hear nothing about it. Then one day, completely by surprise, it's parked in front of your home. At least you think it's yours, but it's been painted a different color and it doesn't handle the same at all. You wonder if maybe it was in a bad accident—something that can't be fixed. So now you have to decide whether to keep it and spend a lot of time and energy trying to repair it, or put it in your past and move on with your life."

Jake drained the rest of the scotch and poured himself a second.

"And I'm not just talking about your face. She's probably deciding whether it's worth upsetting the life she's finally put back together to figure out how much of the man she once loved is still there."

"It was a waste of time," Jake said. He walked to the windows and looked out over the street.

"Quite right. Spend more time feeling sorry for yourself," said Celia. "It's wonderfully productive. Whatever you do, don't go back there and show her how much you still care."

"It's not that simple. She's—"

"Do you still love her?"

"Yes."

"Did you tell her?"

"No."

They were interrupted by the doorbell, which was just as well, because as tough as Jake was mentally and physically, Celia's emotional game was on an entirely different level. She'd make one hell of an interrogator. She took Jake's arm, gave him a reassuring smile, and walked to the door.

Sir James Houghton was standing in the foyer. Roughly Celia's age, lean, with thinning gray hair, and over six feet tall, he was dressed immaculately in a three-piece suit and handmade shoes. His driver handed the housekeeper a bag with four bottles of wine, thanked her by name, and bade Celia a polite "m'lady" before departing.

James introduced himself to Jake and the two men shook hands.

"Shall we have a drink, Celia, or is it time for supper?" said Sir James.

"Is it just the three of us?" asked Jake.

"Hoping to skip out early?" James said. "Has Celia been giving you one of her famous 'pep talks'?"

Jake grinned. "I saw the four bottles of wine."

Sir James leaned in close.

"It's mostly for her. I enjoy an occasional taste, but she's a real tosspot."

"You may have that backward, James," said Celia.

"Good heavens, she's right."

They adjourned to the candlelit dining room and feasted on a beef Wellington prepared by Celia's housekeeper. True to character, James kept everyone's glasses filled with the 2009 Château Pauillac he'd brought, and the discussion meandered from books and history to politics and current events. After dessert, they moved to the library and finished a third bottle of wine by the light of a dozen candles and a wood fire. It was nearly midnight before anyone noticed.

"Thank you for coming, gentlemen," said Celia as she stood. "It's been truly grand, but I'm going to bed . . . and don't either of you dare think about leaving."

She'd been gone about a second when James met Jake's eyes. The conversation at dinner had been pointed, but not personal. The two men looked at each other for several seconds more before James started speaking. He told Jake about his forty-year career in the UK Foreign Office, about the many countries he'd visited, all the friends he'd made and lost, and the family he'd raised along the way. It was a winding tale, poetically told, and by the end, there was no question in Jake's mind that Sir James was a British spy.

The older man tended the fire, opened the last bottle of wine, and ceded the floor. It had been Celia's agenda all along, of course. The dinner party for three, the four bottles of truth serum, and the promise of a taste of Persia. It had been her way of telling Jake that the two men had something to discuss.

Jake told him everything.

When he'd finished, James raised his glass in salutation.

"It seems as if you've kept your wits about you," said James.

"I've kept my head attached to my neck."

"That's half the battle, my boy."

"What's the other half?"

"I suppose that's why we're sitting here. Celia sees some mystery that needs to be solved or some bridge that needs to be built, and she thinks you and I have the power to do it."

Jake was staring into the fire when he spoke again.

"Someone has penetrated the Agency, but I can't prove it."

James finished his wine and poured two glasses of scotch.

"Well, then, let's start with what you know."

TWENTY

NIKOLAI KOZLOV WAS nothing if not disciplined.

He split each day into distinct segments, and while the afternoons were devoted to work and the evenings to play, the mornings were unequivocally dedicated to sport.

Twice each week, his predawn ascent of the mountain on alpine touring skis was followed by four hours of intense downhill training in the company of his *moniteur*—as the French ski instructors were known. Today, Kozlov was practicing on the giant slalom racecourse used each season for World Cup competition, and though France was ostensibly the land of *égalité*, Kozlov had paid a considerable sum to keep it closed to anyone but himself.

The Russian oligarch stood in the starting house wearing a padded race suit laser-cut to his body, carbon-fiber arm guards, a spine protector, and a professional race helmet. The skis and boots were the same used by professional racers—unavailable to amateurs—or at least amateurs without Kozlov's means.

He took several quick breaths as the race timer began a series of five low-pitched beeps. With his arms outstretched and ski poles planted forward of the starting line, Kozlov bent his knees and arms, tilted his upper body forward, and compressed his body like a spring. As soon as the starting timer emitted its final, high-pitched beep, Kozlov exploded. His powerful legs straightened, his upper body shot forward, and he kicked up his heels until only the forward tips of his skis remained on the snow.

Kozlov grunted as he used his poles to pull himself forward, swinging his legs across the starting line and starting the course timer. The fifty-five-year-old billionaire continued pushing off with his poles and skated forward on his skis with the drive of an Olympic contender.

He skied past the first gate and accelerated quickly as he compressed his body into a more aerodynamic shape. His hands and poles were out in front, driving him forward through the course. Still accelerating, Kozlov rolled his skis to the side so the tips would bite into the snow and propel him through the turn. By the time he rounded the third set of gates, the Russian was traveling over forty miles per hour down the giant slalom course. As he approached the fourth turn, he leaned over so far that his body was nearly parallel to the slope and his elbow kicked up a rooster tail of snow as it brushed the surface.

Kozlov's edges carved deep ruts through the snow. One-tenth of a second after he finished the turn, he shifted his weight from the left edges of his skis to the right as he prepared to round the next gate. Constantly in motion, he routinely experienced twice the force of gravity as he compressed and extended his body through each turn.

The oligarch was three gates from the finish line when he crossed a patch of ice he hadn't planned for. His edges sounded like jackhammers as they chattered across the frozen surface. He leaned over farther, putting more pressure on his inside edges, willing them to bite into the ice.

But it was not to be.

Fully loaded with speed as he rounded the gate, Kozlov's skis broke free from the ice and shot into the air. In an instant, his inertia carried him sideways, tumbling fifty feet over the ground and slamming into a plastic snow fence. Scattered across the slope behind him was a trail of lost skis and poles.

Kozlov rose to his feet and reclaimed his equipment. He skied slowly down the mountain and stopped just past the finish line, next to the *moniteur*. The man had once coached the French Alpine World Cup team and Kozlov paid him handsomely each season, with a leather satchel filled with cash.

"It is not good conditions today, Nikolai," said the instructor. "The ice will soften up once the sun hits it. Perhaps we should try again tomorrow."

"Afraid of killing the goose that lays the golden egg?" said Kozlov.

The instructor shrugged. The Russian didn't mince words.

"Again," said Kozlov. He headed for the lift.

On the next run, Nikolai Kozlov approached the ice patch going even faster than the first time, and his skis betrayed him once more. Once more, he ended up tangled in the plastic orange snow fence. Once more, he tried again.

On the third run, Koslov carved through the patch of ice like a figure skater: elegant, fast, fluid. With the finish line in sight, he compressed his body into an aerodynamic tuck that he'd practiced over the summer in a wind tunnel normally reserved for Formula One race cars. Kozlov knew the proper position for every part of his body and he accelerated past sixty-five miles per hour as he crossed the finish line.

"Excellent, Nikolai," shouted the *moniteur*.

The Russian skidded to a stop. "There was too much lateral movement from the last gate to the finish," the oligarch said as he looked up at the digital racecourse timer. "It cost me at least three one-hundredths of a second."

The coach nodded. Kozlov had also scrubbed too much speed taking the wrong line around several gates, but why aggravate the man? He was competing against no one but himself.

TWO HOURS LATER, after falling three more times and shaving four-tenths of a second off his initial run, Nikolai Kozlov skidded to a stop outside La Soucoupe. Situated just below the dramatic Col de la Loze peak in Courchevel, the rustic stone restaurant was his favorite slope-side eatery. His *moniteur* arrived a moment later, diplomatically accommodating his client's need to finish first at everything he did.

The two men walked inside. Several of Kozlov's friends and entourage were seated at a long table in front of the stone hearth. The *moniteurs* had their own table to the left. On the right was a third table filled with a uniquely Russian combination of wives, girlfriends, and prostitutes.

Misha arrived ten minutes later and clunked over the rough wood floors wearing his ski boots—like nearly everyone else in the restaurant. He spotted Nadia seated at the next table wearing a tight white sweater and even tighter white ski pants. She caught his gaze as it explored the curves of her figure and settled on her fur-trimmed suede boots. She'd taken the chairlift up for lunch.

Misha smirked.

"How was the skiing?" he said.

She held up her middle finger, flashing him a diamond ring the size of a walnut.

"Icy," she said.

She ran her other hand up the back of his thigh.

Misha extricated himself and took an open seat next to Kozlov. On the table was a thousand euros' worth of caviar in a crystal bowl with a mother-of-pearl spoon and a platter of miniature blini pancakes. Identical bowls were on the other tables.

Misha waited for the waiter to finish pouring from a magnum of vintage French champagne and leaned in close to Kozlov.

"Keller is in London," said Misha.

Kozlov leaned in closer.

"Shadow?"

Misha nodded.

"One month before the president's visit?" said Kozlov. "That's not a coincidence. What else did Shadow say?"

"Keller hasn't filed any reports at CIA, but apparently that's not unusual. He's something of a lone wolf."

"This could put us in a difficult position."

"Difficult?" said Misha. "I don't know what first twigged him to us, but if he finds out about London, we're fucked. Aren't you the one who always says never do anything halfway? Let me kill Keller and get on with London."

Kozlov nodded. "Take the Triplets."

"Those apes? They won't fit in. At least I speak the language."

"The English might debate that," said Kozlov.

"I can handle Keller on my own."

"I have seen no evidence to support this claim you so boldly make."

"He survived a goddamned plane crash," Misha whispered angrily. "It wouldn't have looked much like an accident if we'd shot it down with a surface-to-air missile like Boris had suggested."

"Nevertheless, Boris will go with you, as will Ilya and Grigory."

"Nikolai, they're incompetent."

"Says the man who assured me the poison-in-the-pool would work."

"Keller got lucky."

"A man can be lucky once, maybe twice. Perhaps he is better than you."

Misha seethed.

"You will take the Triplets and you will do the job correctly," said Kozlov.

The waiter approached to take Misha's order.

"He's not staying," Kozlov said to the waiter.

Misha glared at his boss, dug his soupspoon into the glass bowl, and scooped out the entire glob of caviar.

He ate it in a single bite.

AN HOUR LATER, he'd collected the Triplets and was riding in one of the chalet's black Mercedes Geländewagens to the Altiport. The twin-engine helicopter was warming up on the tarmac with its rotor turning and its side door open. It would be a thirty-minute flight to Chambéry Airport, where one of Kozlov's private jets would take them to London.

TWENTY-ONE

THE TWO AUDI sedans were parked at either end of Queen's Gate Terrace. The men inside were watching the house with the stone bulldogs.

"*Anything?*" Misha said into his encrypted radio. He and Ilya were at the east end, facing west.

"*Nothing,*" said Boris. He and Grigory were at the west end, facing east.

Misha could see the townhouse as well as the others. He just wanted to make sure the two idiots in the other car hadn't fallen asleep, which was a real risk, as it was close to two a.m. before anything happened.

"*The front door just opened,*" Misha said into the radio.

"*Da,*" said Grigory.

A man stepped out of the townhouse and did a quick scan of the street, but the block was saturated with luxury cars and his eyes skimmed right over the two black Audis.

"*It's Keller,*" said Misha.

"*We make killing now,*" Grigory said. He pulled a suppressed pistol from under the dashboard and tucked it inside his black leather jacket. Boris started the car.

"Not here," said Misha.

Grigory cursed. The Triplets didn't like operating under Misha and he didn't like relying on them. Misha had taken Ilya in his car because he'd served in the Russian military and at least had some semblance of training and discipline. The mission to kill Jake Keller had been tense since they'd left the chalet.

A gray Jaguar sedan pulled up in front of the townhouse. The driver stepped out and opened the rear door.

"We do now," said Grigory, *"before he go."*

"Wait," Misha commanded.

Sir James emerged from the townhouse and exchanged a few words with Jake. The older man stepped into the Jaguar and it pulled away. Though Misha wanted to handle Keller himself, he and Ilya were positioned to follow the Jaguar.

"We've got the old man," Misha said into the radio. *"Stay with Keller."*

Ilya started the car and followed Sir James around the corner onto Gloucester Road.

Jake walked at a relaxed pace toward Boris and Grigory's Audi.

"I have him," Grigory said. *"We do now."*

"Listen to me, you idiot," Misha growled into the radio. *"It can't be tied to the old lady. It has to look like an accident."*

"So he will 'accidentally' be run over," Grigory said to Boris. From London to Moscow, the Triplets had beaten and killed more rivals than they could count and subtlety had never been their trademark. "Let's go."

Boris pulled away from the curb and began to accelerate, but Jake turned onto a side street and out of their path.

"Bah," said Grigory as he pointed one of his sausage-sized fingers at Jake. "He take Gore Street."

The quaint residential road was barely three hundred feet long. Keller would spot the Audi the moment it turned.

"What do I do?" Boris asked Grigory.

"Pull over," said Grigory. Outfitted in his trademark black jeans and a black jacket, he holstered the suppressed pistol inside his jacket and exited the car.

"I am on my feet," Grigory said over the radio.

"You mean you're 'on foot,'" said Misha. *"Stay alert. Keller is a trained operative, not some Chechen gangster."*

Grigory cursed in Russian. Kozlov said that Keller must die, yet that arrogant bastard Misha was attaching all these conditions on how to kill him. If there was one thing Grigory knew how to do, it was how to kill a man, and one day he would show Misha how good he really was, but Kozlov had put the prick in charge and Kozlov was paying the bills, so Grigory turned up the collar of his leather jacket and fell in a hundred feet behind Keller.

"Boris," said Misha. *"Turn right on the main road and be ready to intercept Keller."*

"Da." Boris sped out to the main road, aimed the Audi toward the intersection where he expected Keller to emerge, and shut off his lights.

"I am ready."

Jake ambled along the quiet street, taking in the cool night air as he walked.

In an uncharacteristic display of forethought and teamwork, Grigory advised his partner, *"I count down now. Keller will cross intersection when I say 'one.'"*

Grigory began counting down from ten. When he reached "five," Boris accelerated away from the curb. He was doing forty miles per hour by the time Jake stepped into the road.

Like most civilized people, Jake looked left as he entered the crosswalk.

"Kill him!" Grigory shouted in Russian.

Boris floored the accelerator and the turbocharged Audi leapt to fifty miles per hour. He turned on his high beams to blind his target.

Befitting a man who'd drunk two bottles of wine and a few glasses of scotch, Jake's reaction time had slowed, but he caught his mistake two steps into the crosswalk and looked right, toward oncoming traffic.

He spotted the Audi bearing down fast.

Boris had his target in sight. The American was barely fifty feet away—less than a second from the speeding Audi. But despite Jake's impaired reaction time, he still had the reflexes of a professional athlete, and he leapt forward into the median of the divided road.

The car's tires screeched as Boris swerved toward his airborne target. Jake landed on the median and rolled onto his side. The Audi jumped the curb and flattened a road sign as it raced by just inches from Jake's head. A hundred feet down the road, the car screeched to a halt, and Boris stepped out with a suppressed pistol of his own.

"Talk to me, guys," said Misha.

"I miss with car," said Boris. *"Will not miss with gun. I shoot him now."*

"That car is registered to Kozlov. Get it out of there before someone makes the license plate!" said Misha. *"Grigory, what's Keller's location? Ilya and I can box him—"*

Grigory reached into his jacket and switched off his radio.

Too much talking, he said to himself.

He raised the pistol and fired two snap shots at Jake from a hundred feet away. One ricocheted off a light post with a metallic clang and one thudded into the side of a car parked across the street.

Jake, being well acquainted with the sound of suppressed gunfire, took off running.

He fled south until he reached Cromwell Road. The normally busy street was deserted at the late hour and Jake slowed his pace as he turned onto Stanhope Gardens road. It was a stately block, bordered on one side by townhouses and expensive flats, and on the other by the private garden that gave the street its name.

Grigory was quick despite his bulk, but he lost sight of Jake on the dark street. The Russian cursed as he looked around, then decided that he would have gone into the poorly lit garden if he were trying to hide. He vaulted the fence and drew the gun from his jacket. He held the weapon waist high, in both hands, as he skulked along the trails. He made his way to the far side of the park and cursed again. Down a narrow alley he saw the bright lights of Gloucester Road, but there was no sign of Keller.

Grigory switched his radio back on. *"Keller is gone."*

"Where have you been?" Misha snapped.

"I am in Stanhope Gardens," Grigory read from a nearby sign.

"Well, if you'd listened to the briefing I gave on the flight over instead of playing games on your phone, you'd know that the Gloucester Road tube station is one block over and the goddamned Piccadilly Line is running all night long because it's Saturday. Keller is gone all right, right in front of your stupid nose. Leave your radio on, idiot. Ilya and I will stay on the old man."

TWENTY-TWO

MISHA AND THE Triplets stashed Kozlov's matching Audis in a warehouse owned by a local Russian *mafiya* boss and rented less-conspicuous vehicles. Boris and Grigory were in a blue Volkswagen SUV posted outside Celia's townhouse while Misha and Ilya followed Sir James in a black Opel sedan. Misha shook his head in disbelief as he realized that the two old coots were his only hope of quickly reacquiring the man who could destroy all of their well-laid plans.

It was midday when the gray Jaguar dropped James at a brick townhouse in Knightsbridge. Misha and Ilya parked around the corner in the black Opel. Twenty minutes later, they spotted Jake walking toward the townhouse.

"*I have Keller in sight,*" Misha said over the radio. "*He's on foot, heading south on Sloane Street.*"

"We're going to lose him," Ilya said.

"No, we're not," said Misha. "I know where he's going."

Jake entered a nearby park with a cotton duffel bag over his shoulder.

And then he was gone.

Patience . . . Misha told himself, but it was easier advice to give than to take. Kozlov had been furious that the previous night's mission had failed. The Triplets had later encouraged the oligarch to use his extensive *mafiya* connections in England to assassinate Keller in a gangland-style shooting, but Misha had argued that such a brazen display of force would bring unwanted scrutiny on all Russian activities in the city—which was the last thing they needed in the final weeks before the London operation.

Misha had won out—for now.

Though Kozlov had started in military intelligence, he'd become an oligarch during Russia's transformation from communist state to kleptocracy. It was a period when commercial disputes were settled not by competition or by courts but by violence. Intimidation, beatings, and murder were the negotiating tactics of the era and Kozlov attributed his success to his own cunning, aggressive action, and men like the Triplets.

Of course, Kozlov knew that the Russian president had given him his start—he could hardly forget it when he paid the man half his profits every month—but with Kozlov's ill-gotten riches came arrogance and the belief that more violence was the solution to every problem. Unlike the Russian president, whose tactics had evolved to rely heavily on misdirection and subterfuge, Kozlov preferred simple blunt instruments.

Which made Misha something of an experiment; an interloper among the more numerous goons. The spec ops veteran was constantly educating his boss on low-visibility operations, about achieving goals without attribution back to Kozlov, but they were concepts the oligarch struggled with. Whether it was his wealth, his women, or a dead man lying in the street, Nikolai Kozlov wanted everyone to know that he was the force behind it.

The difference in styles kept Misha on shaky ground. Though he'd successfully integrated Kozlov's GRU and *mafiya* connections— and brought with him a source inside America's CIA—he was still seen as an outsider.

And always would be.

Misha relaxed a little as Keller came around a street corner and entered the brick building on Herbert Crescent.

"Forget the old lady," Misha said over the radio. *"Meet us at the Special Forces Club."*

TWENTY-THREE

THE SPECIAL FORCES Club had no sign out front, but the redbrick building was well-known to those in the community of soldiers and spies. Founded at the end of World War II by the chief of Britain's Special Operations Executive, it was a place where men and women could eat, socialize, and change the course of world affairs.

The cost of initiation was paid not in coin but in blood.

Sir James was seated in the Donovan Room when Jake arrived. The classically furnished space was still except for a fire in the fireplace and a man on the other side of the room reading a printed newspaper—whether it was the thick walls or active jamming, no one would say, but mobile phones never seemed to get a connection inside the building.

Jake and James greeted each other warmly. Though they'd met only the prior evening, they'd forged a strong male bond over a long night of stories of adventure, philosophizing, and heavy drinking. Jake had gone for a run—his first since the crash—in Hyde Park that morning to burn away the alcohol but Sir James looked none the worse for wear. He ordered two snifters of brandy and escorted Jake to seats in front of the fireplace.

"I made a few inquiries about that couple from UNICEF you mentioned last night," said James. A wry smile crept across his face. "Unfortunately, their outing to the waterfalls of the Central African Republic appears to have been the ultimate terminus of their travels."

Jake nodded politely. Truth be told, he really didn't care about the missing couple. They'd shown enormous hubris and zero common sense by rejecting the advice of everyone around them. Anyone with half a brain could have predicted the outcome, and good men had lost their lives trying to rescue them.

"However," James continued, "whilst I was making said inquiries, a fellow I've known for some years told me SAS were in-country the same time your boys were."

"Did he know anything about the ambush?"

"We didn't get into specifics," said James.

Jake nodded politely again. The fireplace and the brandy were nice, but he'd come for details. Someone was killing his teammates.

"Is there any chance I could speak to him directly?" Jake said.

"Brilliant idea. Ian, do you have a moment?"

The man seated on the other side of the room folded his newspaper and walked over.

"Jake Keller, this is Ian Hunter of the Security Service, or MI5 as you chaps call it."

In his late thirties, with a crew cut and a thick scar across his jaw, Hunter gave a curt nod, pulled up a chair, and waited with his thick hands resting on his knees.

He and Jake stared at each other for a few seconds, each assessing the other.

"Sir James tells me you're Agency?"

Jake nodded.

"All right, then. Given that we're sitting in the Donovan Room, and you blokes paid for it, I suppose I can answer a few questions."

Jake smiled. Several rooms in the club were named in honor of foreign intelligence operatives, including "Wild" Bill Donovan, who led the Office of Strategic Services—the predecessor to CIA—during World War II. It was customary for the honored individual's home country to chip in to decorate the room. In addition to the leather chairs and game tables, there were dozens of original black-and-white photographs of Donovan and other OSS operatives working with their British SOE colleagues during the war.

"How much do you know about the Central African Republic?" Jake said.

"It's your basic shithole," said Hunter.

"You've been?" Jake said.

"Yeah. I was SAS until about a year ago. We were in the north, trying to keep Boko Haram on the other side of the border."

"What do you know about the UNICEF workers who disappeared?"

"Fucking wankers went missing while I was there. Suicide by stupidity, I'd call it. It's bloody dangerous down there, mate, and everybody knows it. Our fully kitted-out SAS troop wouldn't have taken the bus from Bangui to Boali."

"Did you know an Agency team was sent to recover them?"

Hunter nodded.

"Do you know what happened?"

Hunter nodded again, but this time, it was accompanied by a scowl.

"Do you think they were ambushed?" Jake asked.

"Twice, from what I heard. Word on the street was that they'd hooked up with a crooked FORSDIR officer—though I suppose that's redundant—who was working with one of the local militias.

Your boys fought their way out of the first ambush, but the second one was a different story."

"Why is that?"

"They were up against Russian mercenaries."

"Russians?"

"Yeah, that's right—Russian private military contractors, mostly ex-Spetsnaz. They're all over Africa. Christ, they even have air support: 'MiGs for mercs' we used to call it. Russian soldiers and Russian aircraft, but no insignias on their sleeves or on their wings so the government can deny it. The local militias wouldn't lay a brick without Russia's permission, much less attack a team of Americans. No question about it."

"Did anyone else know the Russians where behind it?"

"Everyone knew. Your Special Forces laid waste to the place after the CIA team evacuated."

"To avenge the ambush?" Jake said.

"That's right. A couple SF teams went to Bangui with air support and destroyed a FORSDIR base. I think they wiped out close to fifty locals."

"But no Russians?" Jake said.

"Not that I know of. Everything's done through proxies down there to keep the big boys in neutral corners."

Hunter glanced at his watch and handed Jake a business card. "Look, mate, you're wading into a giant bog of shit, but call me if I can help. I love bogs of shit."

Hunter had been gone for an hour when Jake and James finished lunch. Jake grabbed his duffel bag and the two men walked out to the street. Sir James's gray Jaguar was nowhere in sight.

"My car is around the corner," James said. "My driver works at Scotland Yard when he's not working for me, but you never know who is watching."

"Is he armed?"

"Good heavens, what for?" said James. "This isn't Chicago."

"Someone took a shot at me last night."

"Do you think you were targeted?"

"His partner tried to run me down with his car."

"That's unlikely to be a coincidence. Did you make out the number plate?"

Jake shook his head.

The old spy motioned toward the park next to the club. Jake smiled. It was the same route he'd taken to get there. Even with the differences in their ages, the two men had thought the same way.

"Give you a lift?" James said once they'd reached his car.

"I don't want to put you in any danger. I'll take the tube."

"Nonsense. We'll give you a ride to the station."

Jake got in. "I came into Knightsbridge Station."

"Then you'll go out through Sloane Square."

James glanced at his driver in the rearview mirror, the driver nodded, and the gray Jaguar pulled away from the curb.

Half a block behind it, the blue Volkswagen did the same.

TWENTY-FOUR

JAKE AND JAMES were riding in the back of the Jaguar.

"Did you know the Russian president was in Iran the same time you were arrested there?" said James.

"I did not," Jake said.

"He was in Tehran, meeting with the ayatollah to discuss a cooperation pact. It's likely the Russians exposed you as a gesture of goodwill. Three months later, the Iranian foreign minister spoke at the Valdai Discussion Club in Moscow and praised their growing collaboration."

"And you think they meant me?"

"Quite possibly."

"Ian said Russia was also behind the attack in the Central African Republic."

James nodded. "You're thinking this is all wrapped up nicely, aren't you?"

"I was until you said it like that."

"My dear boy, you're going to run into Russia everywhere America is. It's like yin and yang."

"They've penetrated the Agency."

"I'd be surprised if they hadn't. You've penetrated them."

"But they're killing our officers."

"A tragedy to be sure, but what's the common thread? Without that, you'll never find the leak inside CIA."

"I don't have anything else to go on."

"What about Syria? Celia mentioned you're close with someone at DGSE."

"I was," Jake said. "Past tense."

"Dead or burned?"

"Is there something worse?"

James raised an eyebrow.

"Well, young man, I'm afraid the French are your only hope in Syria. Our GCHQ and your NSA have all sorts of signals intelligence, but the only ones with actual humans inside the Syrian government are DGSE."

Jake scowled.

"Don't despair," said James, "You're making progress, but a coincidence is not a conspiracy. You need something more than a hunch to connect the deaths."

Jake's scowl deepened. The old spy was right.

James's driver turned the Jaguar onto a busy road one block from the Sloane Square tube station.

"What you must do," James continued, "is either find the connection to understand why, or understand why to find the connection. Then you'll have your mole."

Jake was trying to figure out what the hell James meant when the blue Volkswagen SUV in front of them slammed on its brakes. Almost simultaneously, the black Opel sedan behind them tapped their rear bumper. It was a classic chain reaction accident.

Except for the guys with the ski masks and the guns.

The first one jumped out of the Volkswagen, dressed all in black, and walked through traffic back to the Jaguar. He raised his pistol and waved it at the driver. Jake looked over his shoulder and saw a second armed man get out of the Opel. He approached the Jaguar and looked in the back seat. The man saw Jake and raised his own silenced pistol.

Jake pulled the handle and launched his shoulder into the car door, driving hard with his legs. It swung open violently and knocked the gunman into the path of an oncoming car whose driver had no time to stop and no room to maneuver in the heavy traffic. The oncoming car plowed into the man with the gun, but the black-clad goon was nimble for his bulk. He tucked his body into a ball and rolled off the side of the car's hood—losing his weapon in the process but staying alive. Another driver laid on his horn as he was forced to swerve around the man in black. The gunman rose to his feet in the middle of the road and slammed his fist down on the passing car's roof as it drove by.

Jake dove for the loose pistol lying in the road, narrowly escaping the path of an oncoming truck as he grabbed hold of the weapon and rose to his feet.

The gunman from the forward vehicle spotted Jake with the gun and fired three quick shots from his own weapon. The bullets flew across two lanes of oncoming traffic, smashing the windshield of a passing car and shattering a shop-front window across the square.

Jake was unharmed, but he didn't have a clean shot at his attackers. The square was packed with moving cars and running pedestrians, and Jake would rather let his assailants escape than kill an innocent bystander.

The man from the Volkswagen had no such problem.

He fired another three rounds as fast as he could pull the trigger. One of the bullets struck the driver of a passing minivan, who lost control of his vehicle and smashed into a parked car.

The goon who'd been hit by the car staggered toward Jake, undaunted by his brush with death. He was big and in shape—maybe even the man who'd shot at Jake the night before. Jake raised his pistol and the man ducked behind a passing delivery van for cover.

It was chaos in the upscale square. Cars were swerving and honking, people were running and screaming, and staccato blasts of gunfire ripped through the air.

A distant siren began to wail.

The man from the VW fired again, but Jake was in constant motion—drawing the attack away from Sir James and the crowded sidewalk just beyond.

Another siren sounded from a different direction.

The Opel's driver did a high-speed U-turn across traffic, picked up the man who'd been hit by the car, and drove off in the opposite direction.

The sirens grew louder.

The gunman from the Volkswagen fired blindly down the city street to cover his escape as he ran back to his vehicle. Jake took aim from a hundred feet away and put two rounds into the SUV's rear window just as the gunman climbed inside. A few blocks away a police car turned onto Sloane Street. Jake spotted its flashing blue lights in his peripheral vision. As he watched, the VW sped away.

By now the square was mostly empty and Sir James's driver sped back to Jake's position.

"Do get in," said James through the lowered rear window. The Jaguar had absorbed a few ricochets, but James and his driver were all right.

Jake climbed into the sedan and James's driver turned abruptly onto King's Road.

James looked at his driver. "Can you handle this?"

"A gunfight in Sloane Square?" asked the off-duty policeman. "You might have to call some people if a camera caught him firing that gun."

"Airport?" Jake said.

"Train will get you out of the country faster," said James. "You have travel documents in another name?"

Jake nodded. They were sewn into the liner of his coat.

"Give me your hotel key. We'll sanitize the room."

Jake fished it out of his pocket and handed it over.

"You may also want to leave that with me." James motioned to the gun in Jake's hands. "Security do frown upon them."

Jake handed over the 9mm SIG Sauer. Sir James expertly dropped the magazine, ejected the live round, and visually inspected the chamber and the barrel. Satisfied, he reseated the magazine, racked the slide, and placed the loaded weapon inside the Jaguar's armrest.

He noticed Jake watching him, impressed.

"Like riding a bicycle, I suppose," said James. "What are you going to do next?"

"Take the train to Europe."

"No, dear boy. What are you going to do to pull this all together: your dead colleagues, Russia, CIA, the men who just tried to kill you?"

Jake was quiet as the Jaguar stopped outside the train station.

"Give your contact at DGSE another try," said James. "It may be your only hope."

TWENTY-FIVE

THREE HOURS AFTER the gunfight in the middle of Sloane Square, Jake's train pulled into the Gare du Nord in Paris. Going on nothing but the parting advice of a man he'd met less than twenty-four hours ago, Jake chose to return to the country where he'd been framed for murder, survived a plane crash, and discovered the woman he loved was now with another man.

A rational person would have sworn to never set foot inside the country again.

Jake, on the other hand, stepped out of the station and into a nearby butcher shop. The *boucherie* was filled with choice cuts of beef, pork, veal, and the meats of several game animals. Jake nosed around for a few minutes, asked about a gift for a friend, and walked out with a hand-carved mahogany cutting board and an all-purpose kitchen knife.

Out on the street, he dumped the cutting board in the trash.

Jake proceeded to a men's clothing store and discarded what he'd been wearing in London. He left the shop wearing a forgettable gray suit and a pair of sunglasses. It was all basic tradecraft, techniques he'd learned and executed countless times before, but none of his training had prepared him for the next item on his to-do list.

Jake stood on the sidewalk facing Geneviève's apartment building. Though it was only five stories tall, it suddenly felt more imposing than he remembered, as if he were staring up at a skyscraper. He handed the doorman a sealed envelope. The note inside contained his phone number and Jake's old initials because, as Geneviève had pointedly explained, she didn't know his new name.

Jake checked into the upscale Nolinski hotel on the Avenue de l'Opéra, ate dinner alone in his room, and sparred with his brain. He ran through countless scenarios: who would have the information necessary to kill Agency paramilitary officers, who would benefit from their deaths, and who would suffer, but every time he reached an impasse, every time his brain paused for even a millisecond, he thought of Geneviève. He'd told himself that he would be just fine without her—but he slept in fits and starts until the phone rang at eight a.m. the next morning.

"You left in the middle of our first date. Where were you going?"

"Singapore," Jake answered.

"Meet me at Père Lachaise Cemetery at ten thirty. Balzac's grave."

The line went dead.

At 10:29 he was at the final resting place of the renowned French novelist. At ten thirty, Geneviève called and directed him across the cemetery to another grave, and then a third, to ensure he was alone.

He was standing on the hill next to Bizet's mausoleum when she approached.

"Why the runaround?" he said.

"You still don't appreciate how difficult this is." Geneviève pointed to a woman walking through the cemetery a hundred feet away. "What if she walked up to you on the street one day and said she was me. Would you believe her?"

"Not everything has changed."

"I haven't seen you in two years, and even if I had, I'm sure CIA or GRU has some way of replicating someone's eyes and voice."

"Then why did you call me back?" Jake said.

"I don't know." She shook her head.

"This hasn't been easy for me either. My entire life was erased two years ago and I was assigned a new one by the Directorate of Operations."

She stared at him for a few seconds.

"I go by Jake now. Jake Keller."

"Everything has changed," she said as she resumed walking.

It was a warm day in Paris and the park was filled with couples strolling arm in arm or holding hands—except Jake and Geneviève. They walked two feet apart and stared straight ahead. She interrogated him with more questions about how they'd met and their time together. Jake answered each question with as much detail as he could recall, but she kept asking increasingly specific questions until he was certain that even she didn't know the answers.

She eventually launched into another round of questions about what he'd been doing since he'd disappeared from her life: the circumstances surrounding his escape, his "death," and his role at CIA—but no inquiries about his personal life. The inquisition lasted for twenty minutes and Jake answered every question that was asked—most of which was top secret and some of which was code word classified.

They walked in silence for a few minutes.

"Thank you for finally trusting me the way I trusted you," she said. "I know this could get you fired."

"I need you to understand I'm serious."

"Serious about what?"

"All of it. I thought about reaching out to you a hundred times, but I couldn't."

"You could. You didn't."

"I swore an oath to the Agency."

"So what's changed?"

"The Agency," Jake said. "It's not the same place I joined."

Geneviève nodded.

"I see it in your eyes," she said. "They used to be warm and inviting. Now they're hyperalert. It's like you're glaring at the world, waiting for the next danger to emerge so you can put it down."

"I've been a little on edge lately."

"Is that why you're carrying the knife under your sleeve?"

Nothing escaped her.

"When we met at Sacré-Coeur," Jake began, "I asked about Syria because I didn't want to scare you off by getting personal right away. You've obviously moved on."

"Ask me whatever you want."

Jake told her about the Central African Republic and the Russian mercenaries and how he thought it might be connected to the assassination of the paramilitary officer who was hunting the death squads in Syria.

"I'm trying to find out who outed our officer to the Syrians—to see if there might be a Russian connection."

"And what does that have to do with me?"

"DGSE has an agent in place—"

Geneviève stopped walking and stared at him.

"You told me to ask whatever I wanted," said Jake.

"You're unbelievable," she said. "When you said you'd finally come to me because the Agency had changed, I assumed you meant your priorities had changed, not because you needed my help. I thought you were going to ask about me, about my life in the past two years, about what I want, about what I need."

They walked in silence for several minutes with Geneviève

seething and Jake afraid to speak, lest he put his foot in his mouth again.

"What makes you think DGSE even knows what you're looking for?" she said.

"The death squads were a mishmash of civilians, military, and internal security, and your source had advance intel on all of their operations. He was above all of them—maybe in Assad's inner circle."

"Why didn't the Agency make an official request of DGSE?"

"The source had asked the task force to stand down for a few weeks."

"And the Agency refused?"

Jake nodded.

"So CIA paid for their arrogance," said Geneviève.

"A man paid with his life."

"And now they sent you here?"

"This is personal."

"No, Jake, you and I are personal. This is business."

"I'm having trust issues with the Agency."

"You always have."

They walked through the park for a few minutes. The grass sparkled as the early-morning sunshine melted the frost that had accumulated overnight.

"The Agency isn't blameless," said Jake, "but good men's lives are at stake."

Geneviève shook her head. "Against my better judgment, there's someone I can ask."

"Thank you."

She stopped walking and looked Jake in the eyes.

"I'm only doing this because one of those good men is you."

JAKE RETURNED TO his hotel on the Avenue de l'Opéra. He didn't need the private terrace that came with the room and he certainly didn't need the king-sized bed, but the Nolinski had a pool, and the former water polo player needed to burn off some stress. He bought an overpriced bathing suit in the gift shop and started grinding out laps. He soon found a decent rhythm. He was nowhere near his old pace, but he was breaking up the scar tissue of his accumulated injuries, both physical and mental. By the time he got out of the pool, he felt sharper than he had in weeks, and hungrier. He ordered room service and took a poor man's ice bath—standing under the cold shower in his room—until he was shivering so bad that he could barely turn off the water.

The room service dinner had arrived while he'd been in the shower and Jake frowned as he looked at the small table next to the window, covered in a white linen tablecloth. While he would be eating alone again tonight, the server had set the table for two based on the amount of food Jake had ordered, including two complimentary glasses of wine. Jake started with raclette and Viande des Grisons, a platter of melted cheese and dried meats, before devouring a petit filet, both glasses of wine, and a chocolate mousse.

He climbed into bed but sleep would not come. He tossed and turned as he wrestled with indigestion and the long list of unknowns in his life. He'd practically kicked the covers off the bed by the time someone knocked on his door two hours later.

Jake threw on a robe, grabbed the knife from the butcher shop, and looked through the peephole.

It was Geneviève.

She entered the room but stayed near the door.

"How did you know where I was staying?" he asked.

"You're not the only one in the intelligence business. It took me thirty seconds to triangulate your phone."

"There are four hotels on this block."

"But only one with a pool," she said. The faintest hint of a smile appeared on her face. "A man at the front desk gave me your room number when I told him I was here to surprise you."

"Thank you for coming in person."

"This isn't the kind of thing we could discuss over the phone. Your man was targeted by Russian military intelligence. GRU provided the Syrians with a photo and a location of the man they wanted killed."

"They were after a single man . . . not the whole team?"

Geneviève nodded.

"Do you know if the source passed this information on to DGSE?" Jake asked.

"Only after the fact. There was a mole hunt going on inside Assad's organization and he thought it might be a trap."

Jake grimaced. "Do you trust *your* source?"

Geneviève gave him a dismissive look.

"I'm serious," Jake asked. "I need to know if this is the official line or what actually happened."

"I trust him . . . on this."

"The man I met outside your apartment?"

Her face reddened. "That's not your concern."

"He was there?"

"He asked a friend," said Geneviève.

She turned and looked out the windows. The lights of the Place de l'Opéra bathed the hotel room in a warm light. Jake looked at her and smelled her perfume. She wore almost no makeup and had her hair pulled back in a simple ponytail—just like the first time they'd met. His mind drifted back to the times they'd shared before every-thing had changed.

He failed to notice her looking at the dinner table set for two and the bed that looked as if it had hosted a wrestling tournament.

"I love you," he said.

Geneviève turned, her face twisted in disbelief.

"I'm sorry. What did you say?"

"I still love you," Jake said. "I was thinking—"

She left without saying a word.

TWENTY-SIX

MISHA WAS CLIMBING the stairs while Nadia was taking them down. She was dressed in a Gucci tracksuit and he was wearing jeans and a T-shirt with a pistol holstered on his hip—a new accessory around the chalet since the gunfight in Sloane Square. With each failed attempt to kill Jake Keller, Kozlov and his team became increasingly anxious.

"Why is Boris's arm in a sling?" she said.

"Because he's an idiot. He got hit by a car but he's fine. The sling is window dressing so Nikolai doesn't fire him."

She looked at the floor. "Everyone is so on edge."

Misha reached out gently, lifted her chin, and looked in her eyes. "Are you scared?"

She nodded. "Why didn't you ski up the mountain this morning with Nikolai?"

"Not invited."

They sat on the stairs. The chalet was mostly empty. It was snowing heavily outside, and Kozlov had taken Ilya up the mountain for the predawn ascent then met his *moniteur* to work on the racecourse. Mrs. Kozlov was in town with a few friends having a day at the spa before the evening's party.

"There's nothing to worry about," said Misha.

"Then why are you carrying a gun inside the chalet?"

He didn't answer.

She threaded her arm inside his and leaned against his strong shoulder. The chalet was silent. Even the ever-present electronic dance music had been turned off.

"Why did you join up with Nikolai?" she asked.

Misha sighed and squeezed her arm gently in his.

"I was working for someone else when we first met, but we had some common interests, so we kept in touch. Eventually he decided that my skills and connections would be valuable to him, so he offered me ten times what I was making."

"You quit the other job?"

"After a while," said Misha. "How about you—"

He caught himself at the last second. "Sorry."

"It's OK. Not a day goes by that I don't think about it. I started running with a fast crowd in Moscow when I was fifteen. I was young and beautiful and naïve and I thought that parties, clubs, and drugs were everything a girl could want. I ended up owing some very bad people a lot of money and this is how they wanted me to pay them back. It wasn't an accident. It happened to a lot of girls. They would give us fancy vacations and drugs, and then after a while, they would tell us it was all a loan and that they needed the money immediately. We knew they were gangsters but we didn't care when they were buying us champagne and cocaine and taking us to the islands. I met Nikolai about two years later and he must have paid them off or something because they released me from my debt."

"I've never seen you do drugs," said Misha.

"Those days are long past," she said. "In a few years I'll have enough money saved that I'll never have to touch another man."

Misha looked at her.

"For money," she said with a sheepish grin.

"I guess he bought us both," said Misha.

"We aren't that different, you and I," she said. "Maybe one day—"

The empty elevator descended through the glass shaft toward the ski room on the ground floor.

Kozlov had returned.

Nadia leapt up from the stairs.

She smiled awkwardly and went downstairs without saying another word. Misha watched her leave and resumed climbing the stairs. He reached the fourth floor just as Kozlov emerged from the elevator.

"Office," said the oligarch. He'd become decidedly cooler after each failed attempt to kill Jake Keller.

The two men entered the safe suite and Kozlov sealed the door behind them. He unrolled a paper map of London across the table and weighted the corners with marble coasters. Though they used multiple layers of virtual private networks and encrypted email for routine internet traffic, Misha had advised him to avoid using the internet for anything related to the London operation. The Western spy agencies were simply too good.

"Show me," said Kozlov, pointing at the map.

"I can't," said Misha.

"Misha," Kozlov boomed. "I have not invested all this time and money only—"

"Relax, Nikolai. The route hasn't been decided yet. The local police and the president's security team won't make the final call until a week from the visit."

Misha took a yellow highlighter and outlined two routes from memory.

"But I have done some preliminary reconnaissance and these are the only two ways the motorcade can go from the airport to the palace. I'll have a primary and a secondary plan for each route."

"Have you decided how you're going to do it?"

"Yes."

Kozlov waited a moment.

"You're not going to tell me?" he said, his temper rising again.

"It's better you don't know. Plausible deniability."

The oligarch nodded slowly.

"But you're certain it will work? Your record lately is not so good."

No doubt the Triplets had been chirping in the boss's ear that the Sloane Square shoot-out had been Misha's fault.

"We can't have Keller's death tied to the old woman because CIA knows about her, and if he dies on her doorstep, the Agency is going to start digging. Right now, it's only Keller who seems to have picked up our scent. Trust me, you do not want CIA and the UK Security Service to make a full-court press three weeks from the president's visit."

Kozlov stared at Misha for a moment before opening the door and motioning for him to leave.

"I need a massage," said the oligarch.

Misha started to leave, then hesitated in the doorway.

"Does your wife mind Nadia spending so much time at the chalet?"

The oligarch shrugged. "It is not her concern."

"She spends a lot of time in the kitchen for a woman who doesn't cook."

Kozlov regarded him coolly.

"That is not your concern."

TWENTY-SEVEN

WITH PULSING LIGHTS, artificial smoke, and thumping dance music, it could have been a nightclub in New York or Moscow—except for the two hundred guests wearing cashmere slippers with the letter "K" monogrammed in gold and silver thread.

The party in the chalet's basement discotheque had been raging for three hours by the time Misha arrived. He passed a waterfall of champagne flutes and pushed into the crowd—couples and groups—all drinking heavily and pulsing to the music. The air smelled of cologne and perfume and human sweat. As he neared the dance floor, a man whose consumption had exceeded his ability to dance stumbled toward Misha with a drink in his hand. Misha sidestepped deftly and watched unamused as the man crashed to the floor. Off to the side, on a table in one of the booths, one of Kozlov's cronies was snorting lines of cocaine off the bare midriff of one of the "massage girls."

He was halfway into the disco when an enthusiastic voice called out.

"Misha!"

He turned to see Mrs. Kozlov. Fifteen years younger than her husband, she'd replaced the original Mrs. Kozlov when the oligarch had decided that the mother of his children no longer fit in with his newfound wealth and fancy friends.

A former concert pianist, with short dark hair and a trim figure, her wide eyes conveyed desire and a staggering amount of mischief. She wore a tight silk blouse that revealed every contour of her surgically enhanced breasts—which she pressed firmly against Misha as she leaned in to be heard over the music.

"You never come to the parties!"

"I'm looking for your husband," said Misha.

"He's probably with one of the whores. Dance with me."

She slid her hand down the outside of his pants and practiced a set of scales on his organ. Misha turned and saw Boris standing ten feet away, watching.

"Fuck me," Misha muttered to himself.

"It's a date!" shouted Mrs. Kozlov as he walked away.

Misha pushed farther into the crowd and passed two people kissing passionately at the bar. He recognized them as the wives of two of Kozlov's business associates from Moscow. Misha threaded his way through the pulsing mass of ass to the back of the club where Kozlov was seated in an elevated booth overlooking the dance floor. Misha stopped short when he caught sight of Nadia hanging on Kozlov's arm in a short dress. She looked stunning as she laughed at something the oligarch had just said. She and Misha made eye contact and she quickly turned away, pretending to look at something across the room. Her smile vanished.

"Shadow said Keller is in Paris right now," he said to Kozlov. "Let me finish this."

"No," said the oligarch. "It feels like a trap."

"It's ninety minutes away by helo. He'll be dead before breakfast and we can focus on the other thing."

"I will think about it," the oligarch said as he pulled Nadia closer. "Now is not the time."

Misha walked away. He was halfway to the door when he spotted a commotion on his left. Most of the guests were generally well-behaved out of deference to Kozlov, but the combination of drugs, alcohol, and sexual tension was frequently enough to make people forget the limited social graces they'd acquired. Security at the parties was handled by the Triplets, whose sheer size and menacing appearance were usually enough to remind troublemakers that Kozlov was not just another nouveau riche jackass, but a man with deep ties to organized crime and the Russian president.

Not that there was much of a difference.

Misha watched Grigory yank someone from the ground. There was broken glass and a spilled drink on the floor, but no fight, no one throwing up or urinating in a corner—nothing that would seem to justify the Triplet's ferocious response. It was one of the massage girls. She looked as if she'd had too much champagne and was clutching her shoulder where Grigory had nearly dislocated it.

The big Russian followed it up with a brutal slap across the face. The girl was slim and half his weight and the blow sent her back to the ground, where she landed on the broken glass. Grigory yanked her to her feet a second time and pinned her to the wall with his left hand clamped around her throat and his right hand clamped under her miniskirt. The girl's arm was bleeding and her eyes were wide with terror when Grigory suddenly released her.

The big Russian stumbled backward, his arms flailing.

With Misha right behind him.

His arm was locked around Grigory's neck, his biceps and forearm forming a V that pinched the larger man's carotid arteries and cut off the flow of blood to his brain. The larger man struggled for a few seconds before reaching inside his jacket and grabbing an expandable baton. He flicked his wrist and the weighted steel weapon extended to its full twenty-inch length.

Misha saw the weapon deploy and knew it could do a lot of damage, especially if Grigory connected with Misha's head or shins. He instantly rotated his grip on the larger man's neck so the pressure was no longer on the sides of his neck—compressing his arteries—but on the front of his neck—compressing his windpipe. In less than a second, Misha had switched from a nonlethal sleeper hold to a potentially fatal choke hold.

The former martial artist recognized the difference immediately and understood the choice he'd been given. Grigory dropped the baton and lowered his hands.

Misha released him.

The big Russian turned around slowly, his head lowered in defeat, and snapped a punch at Misha's face.

So predictable . . .

Misha dodged the strike and stepped forward. He fired three quick punches into Grigory's exposed ribs, then whipped his torso to the left and used his body weight to land a titanic elbow strike to the big Russian's nose. Grigory looked as if someone had smashed a packet of ketchup on his face, but the veteran street fighter stayed on his feet.

"I'll kill you!" Grigory shouted.

Misha punched him in the throat and sent him to the ground.

The big man would live, but only because Misha let him. If he'd thrusted a little harder and a little deeper, Grigory would have gone down for good.

A dozen partygoers stood around the two men, holding their drinks and watching the action as if they'd bought tickets to a Vegas prizefight, only to have it end in the first round.

Misha took the girl by the arm and led her out of the disco.

TWENTY-EIGHT

THE STORM SAT over Courchevel for two days, blanketing the Three Valleys under a meter and a half of fresh snow. The flakes were dry and fine—the kind of high-altitude powder that skiers dream about—and Kozlov was out the door before sunup with Ilya and a *moniteur* in time to cut fresh tracks up the mountain.

Misha was a competent skier, but he wasn't insanely competitive about it the way Kozlov was. While Misha had spent his twenties and thirties traveling the world as part of one of the world's premier special-mission units, the oligarch was still trying to prove his physical prowess in his mid-fifties. He saw his body as a source of pride.

Misha saw his body as a weapon.

He spent an hour in the gym while the others were ascending the mountain, alternately jumping rope and lifting weights. Once a week Misha went to Aquamotion, the village's aquatics center, which had multiple indoor Olympic-sized pools, where he could do a distance swim, but today was a speed workout, which he did in the chalet's smaller indoor pool. He'd swum almost forty laps when the sliding-glass doors opened and Nadia entered. With each breath, he caught sight of her walking to the pool's edge and dangling her legs in the water.

Misha stopped.

"Don't stop," she said softly.

Misha obliged, not swimming any faster or any slower than before, just pushing through the water at a constant pace and doing his flip turns at each end. Out of the corner of his eye, he saw Nadia grinning each time he passed by.

"I like watching you. It's so peaceful," she said once he'd finished.

Misha swam to the side.

"It's as much for my brain as it is for my body," he said, and then he laughed. "Although I lost track of my lap count when you showed up."

"Sixty-four since I arrived," she said. She rested her feet on his shoulders. "The square of eight, the cube of four, and two to the sixth power."

Misha smiled.

"I always loved mathematics," she said. "It's so much simpler than life."

"Math is simpler?"

"Everything has a right and a wrong answer. If you make mistake, you know it immediately."

"And you can start over," said Misha.

Nadia reached across the teak deck to hand him his towel as he climbed out of the pool.

"Careful with that," he said.

"Is it dangerously fluffy?" she asked with a smile.

He unfolded the top half to reveal the pistol he'd tucked inside.

Her mood soured.

"I'm sorry," he said. "Things won't be like this much longer."

They sat on a sofa behind the pool, overlooking the distant mountains through a wall of one-way glass.

"Thank you," she said.

"For what?"

"What you did for Tatiana."

"Fucking Grigory," said Misha.

"He's always leering and grabbing and being rough. I know he doesn't scare you, but he scares everyone else. Nikolai should get rid of him."

"He should get rid of all of them, but Nikolai thinks a little fear is healthy around here."

Nadia clutched her knees to her chest. She didn't need to be told.

Misha continued. "He's pissed at me because he needs the Triplets for something, but Boris still has his arm in a sling and Grigory can't breathe through his nose without whistling."

"So much violence . . . ," Nadia said.

Misha nodded. "I won't lie to you. I enjoy the action—but not the killing."

"You could stop."

"I'm not qualified to do anything else."

Nadia closed her eyes. A tear ran down her cheek.

Misha gently brushed it away with his thumb.

"I could stop doing what I do and you could stop doing what you do," she said. "We could start over."

"Like a math problem we got wrong?"

They sat silently for a minute. Misha put his arm around her shoulders and pulled her tight.

Nadia stopped crying and looked into his eyes. The sun rose over the distant peaks, bathing them both in warm sunlight through the plate-glass window. She pushed her mouth closer to his. Misha leaned in to meet her lips when Kozlov's voice boomed over the intercom system.

"Misha, my office now."

Nadia recoiled as if she'd been struck.

Misha put on his robe and headed upstairs. He liked Nadia a great deal—maybe even loved her—but he'd lied to her when he said he didn't enjoy the killing.

He enjoyed it quite a bit.

TWENTY-NINE

MISHA STARED AT the hidden camera in the wall outside the safe suite. The titanium blast door opened automatically and he stepped inside. Kozlov was there with Boris standing behind him. The sling was gone from his arm.

Kozlov pressed a button on his desk and the door closed and latched.

"Where you have been?" he said, looking at Misha.

"I was unavoidably detained."

Boris snorted. "Did the lifeguard give you mouth-to-mouth re-satisfaction?"

"The word is 'resuscitation,' idiot."

"I have reconsidered Shadow's information," said Kozlov. "You should go to Paris."

"I've made other plans. Ilya and I are going to the UK."

Kozlov glared at him.

"I'm sorry, Nikolai, but that intel is stale. The time to act was three days ago when I brought it to you. Keller is already back in the United States."

"Our missteps are making his job easier."

"I'm not even sure Keller knows what he's after. Shadow thinks he's hunting us like a dog that's picked up a scent, but I'm not convinced. There's no way he could have found out about London."

"Who says he's hunting us because of London? There are plenty of reasons for a man like Jake Keller to want us dead."

"Our operational security has been airtight," said Misha.

"And if you're wrong? The entire London operation is at risk."

"If I'm not in Scotland tonight, there is no London operation," said Misha. "I'll take care of Keller when I'm back."

"Time is a luxury we do not have, Misha. Boris will handle Keller."

"Boris can't handle Keller."

"*Yob vas,*" said the goon. "He'd been dead already if you weren't such a pussy."

"Perhaps Boris is exactly what we need," said Kozlov. "I would send Grigory as well, but he's . . . indisposed at the moment."

Boris stepped around the desk and pointed one of his meaty fingers at Misha. "Try that with me and you'll be dead."

"She's half his size," said Misha. "The idiot could have killed her."

"She's a whore," said Boris dismissively.

Misha was halfway across the room when Kozlov spoke up.

"Stop!" shouted the oligarch. "Everyone knows Misha has a soft spot for the girls."

"It's because he's one of them," said Boris. "They sit around and braid each other's hair and talk about their periods."

"Enough!" said Kozlov, rising from his chair. "We are about to execute the most significant operation of our lives, a CIA operative is closing in on us, and you two are acting like children. Focus on your jobs."

Misha stared at the two Russians. In an eerily calm voice he said,

"You hurt the girls, you go down. If you want to prove how tough you are, prove it to me."

The warning was as much for Kozlov as it was for Boris. Neither man said a word.

Misha sat down and put his wet feet on Kozlov's desk.

The oligarch brushed them away. "When do you leave for the UK?"

"One hour. The helo is at the Altiport."

Kozlov nodded. "Talk to Shadow and find out where Keller is right now. Boris is going with you."

Misha leapt to his feet.

"Just to London," said Kozlov. "Then Boris is catching a flight to America."

THIRTY

MISHA PULLED OFF the gravel track and shut off the Land Rover's engine. He and Ilya were tired and stiff after the ten-hour drive up from London in gusty winds and heavy rain.

They stepped out and took in the Scottish Highlands. The rain had stopped, but a low ceiling of dark gray clouds hung over the treeless brown hills, blotting out most of the sunlight. A cold black river snaked through the valley floor, burbling over a rocky bed. Even at midday, it felt as if the dead of night was just minutes away.

A man walked over wearing a waxed-cotton coat and calf-high rubber boots.

"Misha," he said.

"Andy."

Misha opened the Rover's rear gate and showed the man an open duffel bag.

"Fifteen thousand pounds, plus two more for delivery."

Andy reached for the bag.

"Not until we test it," said Misha. He put the bag back in his truck.

Andy led the others to his own truck, another Land Rover, but forty years older, with its own scars and bruises from a life well lived.

"Where are we doing this?" Misha asked.

"Right here along the mighty River Findhorn. In another month, it'll be dotted with salmon fisherman, but the only people around today are maybe a few wing shooters chasing pheasant and partridge, or maybe a hunter hoping to put a deer in his sights. Either way, a few shotguns and rifles will provide good cover for us."

Misha nodded. The two men had crossed paths a decade earlier during their military careers before each had gone his own way—and off the reservation.

Andy spoke again. "Tell your friend with the pretty muscles to help me with these."

"I talk English," said Ilya.

"More or less," observed Misha.

The men carried three footlocker-sized crates to a patch of gravel a hundred feet from the road. Andy jammed a crowbar under the lid of the first crate and pried it off.

"Careful with that," said Misha.

Andy looked up at him and smiled.

"Mate, you could run a fucking tank over this thing and not hurt it."

Andy opened the first crate and removed a heavy tripod. Inside the second crate was the body of the weapon. Three feet long and eight inches in diameter, the hardened steel receiver smelled like oil and required two men to lift and mount atop the tripod. Along its right side was a movable bolt handle that slid forward and back to accept the shells. Andy attached a synthetic rifle stock and a high-power scope, then screwed the barrel into place. To the muzzle end of the barrel, he screwed a wide, flat device with half a dozen vents angled back toward the shooter.

"What's that?" asked Ilya. The Triplet had served in the Russian army, but he'd been a demolitions expert, not a rifleman.

"It's called a muzzle brake," said Andy. "It counteracts the recoil, sort of like a thrust reverser on an aeroplane. It channels some of the expanding gas from the gunshot back toward the shooter, so it's pulling the gun forward at the same time that the bullet is pushing it backward."

Andy continued. "The weapon would be unusable without it. At a minimum, the recoil would dislocate the shooter's shoulder. It might even kill him."

Misha looked sideways at Andy. "Have you shot it yet?"

"Where the fuck am I going to shoot it? I live in Brixton, mate, not Baltimore."

The Englishman returned to his truck and came back with five empty paint cans.

"Range to target?" he asked.

Misha hesitated. Operational security was so ingrained in his training that he was reluctant to reveal even the slightest detail of the mission.

"C'mon, mate. It's me, Andy. What's your zero?"

"Two hundred meters," said Misha.

Andy whistled. "These things move eight hundred meters per second. Are you sure you want high-explosive rounds?"

Misha said nothing, so Andy headed off downrange. Like any experienced marksman, he knew how many of his strides equated to a fixed distance and he stopped at two hundred meters. He set the paint cans twenty feet apart atop a natural berm and filled them with sand and rocks.

"How many rounds you got?" asked Andy.

"Ten," said Misha. He opened a box to reveal two rows of five shells. The 30mm x 113mm high-explosive cannon rounds were designed to be used by American Apache helicopters to destroy armored targets.

"Should be plenty. Let's zero it in."

Zeroing a rifle was the process of aligning the scope and the barrel so the round hit where the shooter wanted it to. Subsequent shots were taken at other distances and conditions to create a simple database of how much adjustment was needed to compensate for the effects of things like wind and gravity. Though zeroing a rifle was a straightforward process, it was a highly precise one because of the distances involved. A one-millimeter change at the scope could translate into a hundred-meter miss at the weapon's maximum range.

Andy showed Misha how to unlock the heavy bolt, load one of the cannon shells, and lock the bolt back into place. Despite its weight, the action was smooth and fast.

The three men put in earplugs and Misha aimed at a large rock on the side of a hill roughly two hundred meters away.

He fired.

The weapon's report was fierce. The ground shook and debris blew into the air as the round launched downrange. Its supersonic motion through the air created a shock wave, called bullet trace, that could be seen with the naked eye, and Misha watched it through the scope as the cannon shell flew toward the target.

The round impacted the hill about two meters high and four meters to the right of where Misha had been aiming.

He removed the turret caps from the Schmidt & Bender scope and moved the crosshairs to the spot he'd hit. It was hard to miss because it had made a three-foot-wide crater in the side of the hill.

Smoke and heat billowed into the air as Misha yanked back the heavy bolt and ejected the empty cannon round. He loaded a second shell, aimed at the rock once again, and fired.

The noise, concussion, and flying debris were the same as the first time, but the second round hit the lower-right corner of the big rock. Misha adjusted the scope once again, and his third round was dead center. He fired a fourth, and then a fifth, and all three were within a few inches of one another, although that was really just an estimate because the rock itself had been blown to pieces by the high-explosive, armor-piercing warheads.

Misha ejected the spent shell casing, stood back from the weapon, and worked his jaw from side to side to equalize his ears. Each time he'd pulled the trigger, the pressure wave from the muzzle brake was like getting hit in the face with a mallet. Firing it from an enclosed space would be impossible—but that was a problem for another day.

"Time for some target practice," said Misha. He knelt down beside the gun, loaded another shell, and aimed at the first paint can.

The breeze was mild, maybe five knots from the southwest blowing up the river valley, and the temperature was in the low forties Fahrenheit—almost identical to the conditions he could expect in London.

Misha pulled the trigger. One quarter of a second later, a cloud of dirt and dust rose into the air two hundred meters downrange.

But the paint can was still there.

"Six inches low," said Andy, who'd been observing through a magnified spotting scope.

Misha made a minor correction to the riflescope, ejected the spent case, and loaded another round. He pulled the trigger and the first can disappeared.

"Good hit," said Andy.

Misha destroyed three more cans in quick succession. There was one can left.

Misha took off his shooting glasses and his hearing protection and gave Andy a thumbs-up.

"I'm out of ammo but she shoots like a dream."

"It's a good scope too," said Andy. "It'll hold zero forever."

"Has anyone else seen it?" asked Misha.

Andy shook his head. "I machined every piece myself."

"And no serial numbers?"

"Tattoos are for girls, not guns."

Misha grinned. "You want a hand picking up the paint cans?"

"You have yourself a rest," Andy said with a grin. "Labor is included in the purchase price."

The Englishman set off downrange, more focused on the seventeen thousand pounds he'd just made than the weapon's intended purpose. He was halfway to the remaining paint can when Misha pulled another round from his pocket.

THIRTY-ONE

THE MEN LEFT the Scottish Highlands half an hour after the cannon's final shot. Misha drove the rented Land Rover with the disassembled weapon and Ilya drove the old Land Rover with the disassembled Andy.

They deposited the armorer's body parts in a rubbish bin along the motorway and left his vehicle in the long-stay parking lot at Glasgow Airport. By the time Misha and Ilya reached London, they hadn't taken more than a catnap in twenty-four hours.

But there was no time for rest.

Misha parked along the Pall Mall road between St. James's Street and Trafalgar Square. The limestone-covered seven-story building was some of the most expensive commercial real estate in the city. Misha had first laid eyes on it three months earlier, after one of Kozlov's many intelligence sources had notified him of the president's visit to London. Well before any public announcement, the security man informed Misha of the president's itinerary, the guest lists, and the motorcade routes.

It was the last item on the list that was of particular interest to Misha.

Kozlov had given him a tight timeline and a loose budget, and Misha had gone to London two days later, equipped with a false identity, a network of layered shell companies, and a dozen accounts at banks around the world.

He'd gone to rent a property that had just come on the market. Upon meeting the building's agent, Misha had taken an immediate dislike to the man. Several years younger than Misha and devoid of any muscle mass, he'd arrived wearing fluorescent socks and a skintight suit whose pants ended above his ankles. He'd proceeded to chirp incessantly about the fiber-optic data lines, new elevators, and the other parties who were interested in the property. Misha briefly considered snapping the man's neck so he could think in peace, but the man had droned on about the building's prime location. He'd talked about its proximity to Trafalgar Square, St. James's Park, and Buckingham Palace, how many great restaurants were in the area, all the nearby shopping, and a whole bunch of other crap. The space was three thousand square feet, on a high floor, at the intersection with Marlborough Road, and the owner required a five-year lease.

Misha had agreed to it on the spot. Though he didn't particularly care for the real estate agent, the man was indisputably right about one thing.

The location was perfect.

Misha had used cutouts to hire an interior designer and local contractors to build out the space as soon as he'd signed the lease. He'd divided the rectangular floor plan into two identical offices for the fictitious partners who owned the firm, with a much smaller third office in the middle for a shared secretary. On each side, he'd specified the same wood paneling, matching furniture, and identical thousand-liter fish tanks. Misha had the interior designer take the building manager through the space to show the progress they'd made, then immediately changed the locks and installed a layered high-security alarm system while he outfitted the space for its intended use.

BUT THAT WAS months ago.

Misha and Ilya attracted little attention as they moved the cannon into the office. Early-morning laborers were not unusual in the busy metropolitan hub and the nondescript crates going up the freight elevator could have held anything from building supplies to computer equipment. The sun was just rising over the horizon by the time they'd finished and Misha stood for a moment in front of the floor-to-ceiling windows gazing down Marlborough Road.

He looked at the Mall.

Constructed in the 1600s as a park, the half-mile-long Mall was lined with London plane trees. The hearty hybrids had been planted throughout the city two hundred years later, as they were one of the few species that could survive the dense soot of the Industrial Revolution. Two hundred years after that, the Mall changed again, this time from a park to a majestic boulevard. The trees had been trimmed and the ground had been paved until it had taken its current form, running from Admiralty Arch at one end to Buckingham Palace at the other.

But in the months since Misha had signed the lease, the pleasant blue sky had turned a cold gray and even the hardy leaves of the London plane tree could not survive the onset of winter. The limbs were bare for as far as the eye could see.

From Misha's perspective, the view had only improved.

He walked to the back wall and pushed the top and bottom buttons of a digital light switch at the same time, then depressed the middle button for three seconds before pushing the top and bottom buttons once again. A floor-to-ceiling panel next to the fish tank opened silently on two hydraulic rams. What had been called the "secretary's office" in the plans was in fact a secret room hidden between the two large offices.

The six-foot-wide space was dark except for several red LEDs along the floor.

"Give me a hand with the crates," Misha said to Ilya. The two men moved the cannon into the small center room.

Operating such a powerful weapon in an enclosed space had presented Misha with a significant problem: The muzzle blast from the weapon would blow out his eardrums and maybe even his eyes. The massive increase in noise and pressure inside the small room would simply be too great for such soft tissue.

He'd negated the weapon's recoil by having the contractors pour a slab of concrete in the middle of the small room. Roughly the size of a casket, it weighed four thousand pounds and had a movable pintle mount embedded in its center. He and Ilya attached the cannon to the thick steel pintle, but even the two tons of concrete and all the steel in the world would not address the explosive increase in pressure caused by the muzzle blast. Not only would it damage his body, but it would also shatter the windows and give away his position.

Which was why he'd installed the fish tanks.

Like most special operators, Misha was adept at improvisation. He'd been pondering the problem of the cannon's damaging report since the day he'd commissioned it, but the solution had come to him, of all places, while watching a television documentary about the American space program.

Misha had seen the film clips many times before. The Apollo

space launches and their enormous Saturn V rockets. He'd watched their eight million pounds of thrust sprayed with a torrent of water at liftoff, generating giant clouds of steam that billowed into the surrounding air. Yet much to Misha's surprise, the narrator explained that the deluge system, as it was known, was not intended to dissipate the heat generated by the five liquid-fuel engines, but the noise.

It had given Misha an idea.

He was still listening to the narrator when he'd begun to sketch a new muzzle device for the cannon, with ports on either side of the barrel—just like the muzzle brake—but instead of venting the exploding gas into the room, the ports would channel it through stainless steel pipes on each side of the barrel—and into the fish tanks.

The cannon round itself would still make a terrific crack as it broke the sound barrier on its way to the target, but the water would absorb the noise and concussion at the firing position—and keep all eyes focused on the president's limousine.

MISHA CLIMBED ONTO the concrete casket and looked through the scope. He'd chosen the Schmidt & Bender PMII because it had been designed for high-powered rifles, and it had proven itself worthy in Scotland, where it had held zero for ten—*eleven*, Misha corrected himself—of the brutal 30mm x 113mm rounds. Nonetheless, he and Ilya had been exceedingly careful with the precision optic to avoid doing anything that might knock it out of zero, for it wouldn't matter how accurate the cannon was if it was pointed in the wrong direction.

THIRTY-TWO

ONLY AFTER GENEVIÈVE had left had Jake noticed the two place settings left by room service and the rumpled bed and realized that she'd probably thought he'd been with another woman. Jake had called and texted her through the night, but received no response. He'd flown home to America the next morning.

Yet, as discouraging as the trip had been personally, it had been highly productive from an intelligence perspective. A Russian thread, thin and tenuous, was emerging in the deaths of the Agency paramilitary officers. They were targeted killings. As Sir James had said, Jake needed to understand why certain officers were being assassinated and others were not. Only then, as a pattern emerged, could Jake hope to locate the mole inside CIA.

It wasn't something he could do on his own. He needed to speak with Jeff and Clap. While neither man saw a connection between the deaths, Jake knew that if the three of them sat down and shared what they knew, the pattern he was looking for would emerge.

JAKE PULLED HIS phone from an electromagnetically shielded bag and reinstalled the battery as he rode home from the airport in a taxi. It was standard procedure when operating covertly to avoid tracking by foreign governments—or his own. There were several messages, including one from Sir James indirectly explaining that his man at Scotland Yard had successfully purged Jake's images from the CCTV records of what the British tabloids were calling the Sloane Square Shoot-Out, and that it was safe for Jake to return to Britain whenever he so chose. There were also two messages from Jeff. The first was an invitation to get a beer; the second—left several hours later—was a profanity-laden tirade chastising Jake for not returning the call and letting him know that Jeff had to head back to Fort Bragg for a few days. There were also several messages from Ted Graves conveying his displeasure that Jake had skipped his check-in again. The calls had come in with increasing frequency and agitation while Jake was in Europe. Jake dialed Clap's number but it went straight to voice mail.

Jake shut off the phone.

He still didn't know how the Russians were getting their intelligence and, though he had no firm recollection of the plane crash, subsequent events had left no doubt in Jake's mind that someone was trying to kill him. He had the taxi drop him at the barn and he retrieved a hidden handgun once the cab had left the property. Jake checked the perimeter of the carriage house, checked the locks, and checked the alarm. All was as he'd left it. He entered the house, relocked the door, reset the alarm system, and pulled his trusty Delta Level Defense short-barreled rifle out of his gun safe. The compact weapon, chambered in .300 Blackout and outfitted with a stubby DeadAir suppressor, didn't leave his side for the rest of the day.

Jake slept fitfully that night, his mind constantly exploring hypotheticals as it struggled to understand what was happening and why. With so many variables combining in endless permutations, Jake found sleep only once he'd resolved to focus only on what he could control.

UNLIKE THE HEADQUARTERS buildings, which were situated on a large and secure campus, much of CIA's staff was located elsewhere inside the National Capital Region. If identifying America's intelligence operatives had been as simple as using satellites to scan license plate numbers in the headquarters' parking lots or faces as they entered buildings, America's enemies would have done it long ago.

The building that housed the Special Activities Center was part of an office park consisting of four identical seven-story towers, all clad in reflective glass, although inside the glass facade, the walls of one of the buildings had been built without windows to prevent electronic, acoustic, or visual surveillance.

There was no sign out front or anything in the lobby that identified it as a government agency, but after entering the guarded parking garage, Jake passed through several additional layers of security before reaching Graves's floor, where a pleasant-looking woman in her late thirties was seated behind the wide desk. Though she appeared to be a receptionist, the woman was a highly trained CIA protective service officer with a submachine gun hidden beneath the bulletproof desk. Only after she cleared Jake to enter was he allowed through a nondescript door and into a mantrap. Another officer, safely behind the Kevlar-clad and copper-lined walls, verified Jake's identity with facial recognition software before allowing him to enter.

Graves was out, doing something unspecified with persons unknown, so Jake strolled over to see Kirby. She was sitting cross-legged in her chair with her strawberry blond hair wrapped in a bun around a pencil.

"Hello, Jake Keller," she said without looking up. "Did Ted know you were coming?"

"It was supposed to be a surprise," Jake said.

"We all know how much Ted likes surprises."

"He told me to 'get my ass in here' ASAP."

Kirby smiled. "Well, your ass is mine now. When did you get back?"

"From where?"

"From wherever you were. I assumed you were out of town because you never checked in."

"Is Ted keeping tabs on me?"

"Like you're his teenage daughter," said Kirby.

"I got back yesterday."

Christine gave him a slow-motion once-over. "You ready for that drink now?"

Jake smirked. "I'm not sure Ted would approve."

"Then it's right up your alley."

"I suppose it is." Jake smiled. "I'll call you."

"When, Jake? I'm a busy girl."

"It's on my list."

"You're putting me on a list?"

"Right near the top."

"I want to be on top."

"Of course you do."

"You'll call me this week?"

"This week."

"I'm clearing my calendar."

"Tell Ted I stopped by?"

"Right after you call."

"Stay close to your phone. The next call could be from me."

"I'll set it to vibrate."

Jake grinned as he walked to the elevator. He was pretty sure Christine was just flirting, but there had been some natural chemistry since they'd first met in London, and reading women certainly hadn't been his power alley lately. Either way, she was witty and sharp and he enjoyed the banter. She would have made a good case officer if Graves hadn't needed her at headquarters.

But Jake's smile faded as walked to his pickup. Jeff was out of town and Clap wasn't answering his phone. It was a cold January day and the light snow had turned into a mix of sleet and freezing rain. Jake spent the morning running errands and stopped by his gym in the strip mall for an afternoon swim.

He left his pistol locked inside the pickup but kept the knife he'd strapped to his ankle as he entered.

"Is the manager here?" Jake asked the new receptionist, a kid who looked as if he'd come straight from seventh-period geometry.

"Can I tell Mr. Zilligen what it's about?" he said.

"You can tell Mr. Zilligen that Jake Keller would like to talk to him."

The manager appeared a minute later.

"Jake! It's good to see you. How are you feeling?"

"Any word from Courtney?"

"It's strange. She never picked up her paycheck."

"That is strange. Do you have her address? I could drop it off."

"I can't give that out. Privacy laws, you know."

"I notice you're not serving hot apple cider anymore."

"The cider was Courtney's idea," said the manager, as if she deserved all the credit.

"Right—her mom's recipe."

"Yes! We haven't seen you since the, uh, accident. Are you here to swim?"

"I sure am."

"Great, great. Maybe I'll come down and watch, just for, uh, you know . . ."

"Liability reasons?" Jake asked.

Zilligen smiled. "Better safe than sorry, right?"

TRUTH BE TOLD, Jake didn't mind the club manager looking over his shoulder during the workout. Given Jake's growing penchant for attracting trouble, having someone watching his back while he had his head down was just fine.

The freezing rain worsened while Jake was in the health club, and he was forced to spend several minutes warming up his truck and scraping ice from the windows. The roads were slick and getting worse. Once the sun dropped below the horizon, the freezing rain and sleet turned to ice the moment they hit the pavement. Jake man-handled the pickup's transfer case into four-wheel-high and slowed down. In the span of four blocks, he saw one fender bender and two cars that had lost control and slid off the road. A thin layer of frost formed inside the Gladiator's windshield as the truck's apathetic heater and semiretired air conditioner were outmatched by the weather.

Jake watched a tractor trailer slide helplessly through an intersection a moment before he turned off the narrow streets and onto the wooded county road that led back to the farm. The wind picked up and the wintry mix fell harder until the road, the sky, and the air all blended together into a swirling gray mass.

In front of the pickup, its high beams lit nothing but two cones of snow and sleet.

Behind it, the road was empty—except for a distant pair of head-lights.

THIRTY-THREE

THE LIGHTS IN Jake's rearview mirror grew larger. Widely spaced and high off the ground, they looked as if they belonged to a heavy-duty pickup or a large SUV, but Jake could barely see fifty feet in front much less two hundred feet behind him. They were the only two vehicles in sight.

Jake had driven the county road countless times in the two years he'd lived in the area, and he knew that the long, sweeping turn they were approaching was dangerous even in good weather, bounded as it was on both sides by a deep ditch and thick woods. But the other vehicle kept coming, traveling far too fast for the conditions.

They were halfway through the turn when the vehicle behind him began to accelerate. Jake eased the old pickup toward the side of the narrow county road but the pavement was covered from edge to edge with snow and ice. The fifty-year-old Jeep had left the factory long before antilock brakes and electronic stability control were invented, and even with four-wheel-drive, the Gladiator demanded his constant attention and both hands on the wheel to keep it from sliding off the road and tumbling into a ditch.

The SUV's driver turned on his high beams and steered toward the center of the road to pass.

He didn't quite make it.

Jake heard a crunch and felt a jolt as the pickup started to spin. He turned into the slide and gave it some throttle, but even the new tires couldn't bite into ice, and the pickup kept sliding. Jake's headlights washed over the vehicle that had hit him. It was a dark-colored Chevy Suburban—as much a part of the Washington, DC, landscape as the cherry trees—and the driver had finally slowed down, but too late to save Jake.

The pickup slid sideways over the ice-covered road at thirty miles per hour until its rear end plunged over the steep shoulder. The back of the truck fell away as if it had been dropped out of an airplane, and for a moment, Jake was starting straight up into the night sky. He glimpsed the sleet and snow falling straight down through the beams of his headlights.

But inertia and gravity were forces not to be denied, and the truck's tailgate slammed into a ditch. The truck flipped like a coin tossed in the air. Jake had no idea how many times—at least three or four—because he was too busy clinging to the wheel so he wouldn't break an arm. Pieces of steel and sheet metal sounded like a string of explosions as they smashed into the ground. Glass shattered in the front, sides, and rear. Snow and sleet blew through the interior as if driven by a blizzard.

There was a deafening crash as the pickup hit a thick pine tree and stopped. A moment later, the truck tumbled sideways and came to rest on its roof, with all four tires in the air.

Up on the road, the SUV's reverse lights came on.

The Suburban pulled abreast the wreck and the driver stepped out. He was large but athletic, and he took short, cautious steps across the icy ground, bracing himself against the SUV with one hand. He lowered himself to his hands and knees to see inside the pickup but the wrecked truck was down a steep embankment and he could see nothing but bent axles and the vehicle's still-spinning wheels. The pickup's lights had gone off in the crash. The man grunted and crawled the final few feet over the icy road. He slid down the shoulder on his black jeans and scanned the interior.

JAKE WAS BARELY conscious, sprawled on the truck's ceiling. He felt a hand come through the broken side window and grab his chin. He felt an arm snake through the shattered rear window and wrap itself around his head.

He knew what was coming next.

It was a technique he'd used in desperate situations before—to snap a man's neck.

Jake became lucid in an instant. He reached behind him, found the man's face, and plunged his thumb into the man's eye socket.

Jake dug harder as the man tried to pull away, driving his thumb through the vitreous gel of the eyeball to the back of the socket. Screaming in pain, the goon released his grip. Jake scrambled out and came up in a fighting stance. The man was on his knees, leaning against the wreck, but far from dead. He reached inside his jacket and pulled out a pistol.

Jake had no time for a weapon of his own. His right leg exploded forward and the heel of his boot caught the man in the face, obliterating his nose and launching his skull backward into the pickup's steel frame. The five-thousand-pound truck shuddered from the impact.

The man slumped forward.

Jake searched him for other weapons but found nothing.

The Suburban was still idling up on the county road.

Jake took the man's gun and scrambled awkwardly up the shoulder, still dazed from the crash. He opened the SUV's tailgate and cleared the interior. It was empty. Jake staggered back to the overturned pickup, retrieved his personal effects, and hefted the would-be assassin onto his back. The man was large and muscular, and Jake's injuries from the plane crash mixed unfavorably with his injuries from the rollover as he crawled up the shoulder. Only a surge of adrenaline got him to the road with enough strength to shove the man into the back of the SUV.

Jake used the man's belt to hog-tie his hands and feet. He was unconscious now, but that could change in an instant, and Jake had a few questions he needed answered. He'd decide what to do with the goon once they were finished.

Jake drove the SUV to a nearby shopping mall, parked far from any lights or surveillance cameras, and found the owner's manual in the glove compartment. He found the wiring schematic and pulled the fuses for the vehicle's GPS and cellular systems. He also found a cheap cell phone in the Suburban's center console. The call history had been deleted, so Jake removed the battery and stuffed the phone in his pocket.

Jake took a deep breath, calmed his nerves, and began the most intricate surveillance detection run he'd ever made.

His would-be killers had brought the fight to the U.S. and Jake couldn't risk leading them to the carriage house if they didn't already know about it. The icy roads were deserted, and over the course of the next ninety minutes, he passed a total of five cars, three snowplows, and two police SUVs. When he was certain he was clean of a tail, Jake returned home, stepped out among the swirling snow to slide open the big barn doors, and parked the Suburban in the back by the ATVs.

Even in the semidarkness of the barn, Jake could see that the serial numbers had been filed off the assassin's cheap 9mm semiautomatic pistol. He unloaded the weapon, wiped his prints from it, and hid it in a drawer. Jake preferred the HK VP9 pistol he had holstered inside his waistband, just to the right of his belt buckle.

Jake checked on his prisoner. The man was still unconscious, with a shattered nose, a missing eye, and a large quantity of blood streaming down his face. Jake stripped the body and searched the man's things, but found only an unmarked hotel key card. Jake searched the Suburban and found the SUV's rental agreement in the glove compartment. It had been rented under the name "Thomas Colgan"—a trite alias if Jake had ever heard one—but it listed an incoming flight number from London. It wasn't much to go on, but the English city's large community of dubious Russian expats and the man's ethnic Russian features were more data points in Jake's analysis.

Jake had interrogated prisoners before—some under controlled conditions, where he could take his time and build trust—and some under duress, where lives had been at stake and more draconian measures had been required. The man lying on the barn's straw floor had thrust himself into the latter category and could fully expect more unpleasant surprises when he came to.

Jake checked his breathing. It was shallow and weak. If he wasn't in shock, he might be soon. Jake taped a gauze bandage over the man's bloody eye socket and covered him with a horse blanket. Jake was about to close the barn doors and head to carriage house when a pair of headlights turned down the driveway.

Jake had to make a split-second decision. The barn doors were large and heavy, and the vehicle's driver would spot Jake as he slid them shut. With the attempts on his life growing in frequency and in boldness, Jake chose instead to hide with pride. He drew his pistol and ran into the woods the behind the barn.

The vehicle continued down the driveway, moving slowly, cautiously, as if it was searching for something or someone. It passed in front of the lights of the carriage house and Jake recognized it as a Ford Explorer, but the push bar on the front bumper and the half dozen antennas on the roof told him that it wasn't another assassin.

It was a cop.

THIRTY-FOUR

JAKE HOLSTERED HIS pistol under his jacket and walked out of the woods. The police officer was fifty feet away when he lowered the Explorer's window and lit Jake up with the side-mounted spotlight.

"This your place?" said the cop.

"I rent the carriage house," Jake said.

"You Mr. Keller?"

"I am."

The cop stepped out of the SUV amid the swirling wind and snow. He was in his middle forties with short-cropped hair and a nylon police windbreaker over a fleece jacket. The snow crunched underfoot as he approached.

"Prince William County Police. You got any ID?"

Jake handed over his license. "What's this about?"

"You own an old Jeep pickup?"

"I do."

"A highway department crew found it wrecked on the county road but didn't find anyone in the vehicle. I came to see if you're all

right or if we should be searching the woods before you die of hypothermia. You're not supposed to leave the scene of an accident."

"I'm sorry to drag you out here. I should have called but I couldn't
get cell service after the crash."

"And later?"

"A passing car gave me a ride. I guess I just forgot."

"Were you drinking?"

"No, Officer. I'll take a Breathalyzer if you'd like."

"It's 'Detective.' Were there any other vehicles involved in the
accident?"

"Just mine," said Jake, somehow forgetting to mention the Suburban that was parked two hundred feet away in the barn.

"Any injuries?"

"I got my bell rung pretty good, but I'll live."

"Where'd that come from?"

Jake's heart skipped a beat as he looked down and spotted what
was easily a pint of blood smeared across his jacket.

"Bloody nose," Jake said, "from the crash."

"That's a lot of blood. It's a miracle you didn't pass out."

"It stopped pretty quick."

"And no bruising on your face. Incredible."

The police officer stood there for several seconds.

"So what are you doing out here at midnight? Seems odd for a
guy who was just in a major accident."

"Just going for a walk," Jake said. "I'm trying to stay awake in
case I've got a concussion."

"And the gun?"

The detective had spotted the weapon printing through Jake's
jacket.

"Coyotes."

"Uh-huh," said the cop. He glanced toward the barn for a moment, then back at Jake. "By the way, that's an old wives' tale about falling asleep. You'd barely be able to stand if your concussion was that bad."

He reached into his windbreaker and pulled out a business card.

"I'm Detective Rooney. Call me in the morning and I'll get someone to take your statement."

The police officer stared at Jake for a solid five seconds before he climbed back into his truck and spoke through the open window.

"Good luck with the coyotes."

THIRTY-FIVE

JAKE CURSED AS he watched the police car's taillights disappear onto the main road. It had been a close call, with the man who'd tried to kill him lying unconscious in the barn, behind the truck he'd used to run Jake off the road.

At least that's how Jake saw it.

Detective Rooney would probably get wrapped up in esoteric legal phrases like "assault," "kidnapping," and "felony grand theft auto." But without knowing whom he could trust at CIA, Jake couldn't come clean with the cop. By intercepting his vehicle on a deserted stretch of road, the unconscious assassin in the barn had demonstrated extensive knowledge of Jake's pattern of life. It was a level of detail that teams of surveillance professionals often took weeks to build. Given that Jake had just returned to the United States, the man wouldn't have had the time or the resources to pull off such a well-timed plan on his own. Such precise information implied local help.

Insider help.

Agency help.

Jake closed the barn doors and made his way to where the man lay under the horse blanket. It was time to get some answers. Jake shined a flashlight on the man's face and was pleased to see that the bleeding around his eye and nose had stopped. However, Jake's enthusiasm was tempered somewhat by the realization that the flow of blood had stopped because so had the man's heart.

Jake felt disappointment but not remorse.

The man had tried to kill Jake, and while the immediate threat had been neutralized, Jake harbored no illusion that the danger had passed. The dead man was surely part of an organized effort. Over six feet tall and maybe 240 pounds, he was thick all around, like a heavyweight wrestler—probably hired muscle and not the brains of the operation. He looked as if he could have been one of the masked gunmen from London, but was he a foreign national, maybe even a contractor hired by CIA?

Jake examined the body carefully. The man had Slavic features, with blue eyes, a high forehead, and a thick brow, but no distinctive tattoos or anything that would definitively indicate his nationality. Jake pried open the man's mouth—rigor mortis sets in early in the jaw—and shined a flashlight inside.

Jake counted seventeen fillings—stainless steel by the looks of them—and two missing teeth. There was no doubt the man was Russian—oral hygiene in the country had been notoriously bad when the man would have been a youth. The dead body was another data point, but also a liability. A competent medical examiner would notice the manner of death and the crude dentistry. Questions would follow about a dead foreign national. The investigation would lead to the missing rental car, the man's empty hotel room, and probably something somewhere with Jake's name or picture on it.

Detective Rooney would come knocking again, this time with a SWAT team.

Jake grabbed his cold-weather gear from the carriage house and returned to the barn. He disconnected the lights on one of the ATVs and draped the Russian across the back like he was on a horse in an old Western movie. Jake rode into the snowstorm, navigating across the property under night vision goggles until he'd reached a shallow ravine halfway between the main house and the property line. The low clouds, dense forest, and heavy snow blocked out the moonlight like a blanket. The only noise was the howling of the wind and the creaking of the trees.

Jake untied the body and a shovel he'd brought, and thrust the rounded spade into the earth. The first inch of dirt was frozen solid. It was like chipping concrete, but Jake was nothing if not persistent, and he kept at it until he broke through the top layer and into the warmer soil below.

Four hours later, he'd buried the Russian and covered the freshly turned earth with pine needles, sticks, branches, and shovelfuls of white snow. It wouldn't survive a close inspection for a few weeks, but the farm wouldn't be used much for at least a couple of months.

Jake mounted the ATV and continued away from the house, making a giant loop around the property so there wouldn't be any out-and-back tracks in the snow. He had some cleaning to do before the sun came up. Just in case the cop returned.

Like Jake, Rooney didn't seem the type to let something go once he'd sunk his teeth into it.

Jake vacuumed the interior of the Russian's SUV, then rinsed the cargo area with a hose and sprayed an industrial-strength cleaner over everything to destroy any remaining hairs, fibers, or skin cells before wiping down the interior to remove any fingerprints. He next stripped off his clothes, combined them with the dead man's clothes, and put them all in the washing machine for a long cycle in scalding-hot water—with a double dose of detergent and half a gallon of chlorine bleach. The combination would destroy the fabrics but would also destroy any traces of DNA. Jake tossed the wet clothes in a garbage bag and left it by the front door. The only thing left to clean was himself, so he scrubbed his body with a soapy washcloth under the hottest shower he could stand.

SUNRISE WAS STILL an hour away when Jake drove the Suburban back to the same Manassas, Virginia, shopping mall. He tossed the clothes in a dumpster and reinstalled the fuses for the GPS and cellular transceivers. Within seconds, the rental car popped back onto the grid exactly where it had left off—leaving no electronic trail of the overnight detour to the farm.

Wearing leather gloves, a reversible jacket with the collar pulled up high, a wool hat pulled down low, and a pair of sunglasses, Jake set off for Dulles International Airport. He stopped at a busy gas station on the way and disposed of the dead man's gun when he placed a small bag of untraceable household garbage in a trash bin. Jake continued on to the airport and anonymously dropped off the SUV in the rental company's return line before slinging his backpack over his shoulder and taking a Metrobus into Washington, DC. He got off the bus at a local hotel, reversed his jacket and took off the hat in the men's room, then caught a taxi to another hotel before finally catching a second taxi home.

The falling snow had changed over to rain by the time he shut off the alarm and entered the carriage house. Jake glanced at the clock, realized he'd been up for twenty-eight hours straight, and smiled.

It felt good to finally be on offense.

THIRTY-SIX

NEED FIVE MINUTES," Jake said into the phone. He was sitting in a silver Chevy Tahoe he'd rented.

"*I can't get away today,*" said Clements. "*I'm heading overseas with Director Feinman in two hours.*"

"I'm in the parking lot."

Clements put him on hold.

"*The Bubble is empty,*" said Clements. "*I'll be there in twenty minutes.*"

The two men entered the enormous headquarters auditorium within a minute of each other. It was a calculated risk. Seemingly coincidental meetings in the Agency's cafeteria or the library were impossible in a campus full of people trained to spot them. It was better to play the odds that anyone wandering into the Bubble was unlikely to recognize Jake and would undoubtedly leave as soon as the associate director fixed them with a stare.

Clements checked his watch and sat down. "Clock is ticking."

"Russia is killing our paramilitary officers."

"Tell me what you know."

Jake filled his former boss in on the intel he'd gleaned on Syria, the Central African Republic, Russian cooperation with Iran at the time of Jake's detention there, and the most recent attempts on his life.

"The man who ran me off the road was definitely Russian."

"Is he talking?"

Jake shook his head.

"What about physical evidence?"

"Just his dental work."

Clements raised an eyebrow, but knew better than to pursue it.

"Russia has someone inside the Agency," said Jake, "most likely inside the Special Activities Center."

"That's a bold indictment."

"The operational intelligence behind the attacks is too good to be coming from anywhere else. They know routines and travel plans."

"It could just be good surveillance."

"I know how to spot surveillance. These people are one step ahead."

Clements tented his hands under his chin and stared at Jake.

"How did you find out about the Central African Republic and Syria?"

"MI5 and DGSE."

Clements's eyes narrowed. "Are these sources official or unofficial?"

"Unofficial."

Clements knew of Geneviève, and while he didn't consider her an explicit security risk, a romantic interest inside a foreign intelligence service was never encouraged. After his "death," Jake had been instructed to never contact her again.

"Then they're unusable from my perspective and most definitely from yours."

"You could make official inquiries to our liaison officers."

"I could," said Clements, "but I've reached a position where everything I do attracts a great deal of scrutiny. There are policies and procedures, watchdogs and oversight committees. I'd have to take it to the director and he'd have to loop in the inspector general."

"Isn't that what we want?"

"That's the last thing you want," said Clements. "Aside from alerting any mole, a formal investigation will expose your sources, destroy their careers, and maybe land them in jail."

Jake shook his head. He couldn't burn Ian like that, and dragging Geneviève into a formal inquiry was just about the only way their relationship could get any worse.

"We don't need them," said Jake. "We have the dead paramilitary officers."

"And yet you don't have a shred of evidence. None of the other divisions are reporting anything like this and Director Feinman spent twenty years as a U.S. attorney. He isn't going to start a confidence-eroding, morale-destroying, scrutiny-attracting mole hunt based on one man's hunch."

Clements glanced at his watch again and walked out.

JAKE MADE HIS way to the parking lot amid a light rain. He climbed into the Tahoe. It was a perfectly nice truck, but he missed the Gladiator. Aside from being one of the few ties to his past, the old Jeep—with its lethargic engine and recalcitrant brakes—had forced him to slow down and helped him decompress on his rotations home. After assuming his new identity and severing all ties with his family and friends at twenty-eight years of age, Jake had found it difficult to adjust his body and his brain to life stateside. The isolation just made it worse, but he didn't have time to feel sad about a wrecked truck when people were dying.

Jake was more disappointed with Clements. The associate director's entire career had been built on deciphering shades of gray, and now he was insisting that Jake provide him with black-and-white evidence of something specifically designed to avoid it. It just wasn't realistic. Jake was used to dealing with setbacks—every mission he undertook seemed to start with him on his back foot—but that was in the field against his adversaries. He'd expected more support from his own team.

Jake switched on his cell phone and saw a text message from Jeff. The Delta Force troop sergeant major was back from Fort Bragg. The two men met for lunch at a Peruvian restaurant in Arlington.

Jeff was just walking in when Jake pulled up in the Tahoe.

"Finally," Jeff said.

"I'm five minutes early," Jake protested.

"I meant you finally got rid of that shitty pickup."

Jake explained over lunch that Russian intel had been responsible for the death of the CIA operative in Syria.

"Not surprising," said Jeff. "We were running into them or their private military contractors at least once a week."

"Russia also targeted a paramilitary officer in the Central African Republic, and the Russians outed me to the Iranians in an operation I did a couple of years ago."

"That doesn't mean cause and effect. They're everywhere you want to be."

"Isn't that from a credit card ad?" Jake said.

"Maybe," Jeff conceded, "but we're always stepping on each other's dicks. That's the nature of geopolitics."

"This isn't politics. These are targeted killings of Agency officers. The reason I don't have the pickup anymore is because a Russian national ran me off the road yesterday."

"I'd like to buy him a beer."

"That's not possible."

"So how do you know he was Russian?"

"Dental work."

Jeff nodded. "Cops involved?"

"The situation didn't lend itself to police involvement."

"Careful, bro. This ain't Yemen."

Jake leaned in close. "That's my point. Operating in the West is riskier for them too. They've taken the fight out of the conflict zones and brought it to the U.S. They're getting desperate."

"Are you working something with a Russia angle?"

"I'm on leave. I'm not working anything."

Jeff picked at the food on his plate. "I think you're reading too much into a string of bad luck. This stuff goes in cycles. Russia has just been lucky lately."

"It's not luck. Someone at CIA is feeding them detailed operational intelligence: names, photos, movements."

"That's quite an accusation," said Jeff. "I mean, who would have that kind of information?"

THIRTY-SEVEN

'M HERE TO see Ted Graves."

"He's running late," said his assistant. She was new, Jake noted without surprise. Graves's previous assistant, a personable guy in his late twenties with a master's degree in electrical engineering, had lasted only a few months, but that was par for the course. "Patient" was not a word that came readily to mind when describing Ted Graves.

Jake poked his head into Kirby's office but she was out, so he took a chair in the hall and waited. Several people entered and departed Graves's office. Jake heard him on the phone with his door open, talking about who was favored to win the upcoming Super Bowl. After thirty minutes, Jake approached Graves's assistant a second time.

"Tell him I stopped by," Jake said.

He was almost to the exit when he heard Graves's raspy voice behind him.

"Keller. My office. Now."

Graves motioned to a chair and closed the door.

"I don't have a lot of time, so let's get right to it," he said. "Where—"

"A lot of paramilitary officers are dying."

"It's a dangerous job."

"It's gotten more dangerous since you took over as chief of Special Activities."

Graves leaned forward and placed his thick forearms on the desk.

"I expect a lot from my people. I expect them to perform at one hundred percent. I expect them to execute the strategic objective and not just the tactical one. I expect them to follow orders."

"And what happens when they don't?"

"People die."

The two men stared at each other for a minute that felt like an hour.

"You missed your last check-in," Graves said.

"Was that an order?"

"Everything that comes out of this office is an order."

"And I almost died."

Graves leaned back in his chair and crossed his arms.

"We operate as a team, and when members of the team don't run the plays that were called, people get hurt."

Jake shrugged.

"Where is your head at?" said Graves.

"We've lost too many men for it to be a coincidence."

"Are you talking about the plane crash?"

"That's one data point."

"I know we don't always see eye to eye, Jake. Part of that is on me, but part of it is on you. Have you thought any more about your career here?" Graves said.

"It's all I think about."

"And what have you decided?"

Jake shrugged. He still wasn't sure whom he could trust at the Agency. If he had to bet, whoever was betraying his fellow paramilitary officers was sitting somewhere in the same building.

Possibly on the same floor.

Maybe in the same office.

THIRTY-EIGHT

JAKE ROLLED DOWN the Tahoe's passenger window as he pulled up to the curb.

"Get in," he said.

"You got rid of the pickup?" Clap was grinning like a child.

"Get in, or I'll leave you out in the rain."

"This could be the start of a whole new life for you," Clap said as he climbed into the warm SUV, turned on the seat heater, and put his coffee in one of the eighteen cupholders around the interior. "I mean, we're talking chicks, friends . . . no more arrests for vagrancy."

Jake pulled into traffic. "We need to talk about Russia."

"I've heard of it."

"It was Russian mercenaries who ambushed your team in Bangui."

Clap arched an eyebrow. "Reliable source?"

"British SAS."

Clap nodded. "They were in the north."

"You don't sound surprised," Jake added.

"Russia is our evil twin. There's going to be friction."

"There's more than friction. There's a pattern. I've looked at three incidents so far and Russia's fingerprints have been on each one. I was compromised in Iran, another officer was executed in Syria, and then your team leader was killed in the Central African Republic. They're targeting specific officers."

Clap stared out the windshield before making a halfhearted protest, "It wasn't just our team leader; we lost our 'terp too."

"How did it go down?" said Jake.

Clap took another long sip of his coffee.

"We were driving to M'Poko airport, rolling up the Avenue of the Martyrs in two old SUVs and a minivan. It was low-visibility, but you know Africa, somebody is always watching. We were about two clicks out from the airport when we came upon an accident, so we detoured off the avenue onto the city streets. The next block in, we ran into a broken-down car, then some kids playing soccer on the side street, then a delivery truck blocking the road . . ."

"You were funneled?"

"Masterfully. We came around a corner and a bunch of guys wearing balaclavas were waiting for us with AK-47s and mounted machine guns, signaling for us to get out of our vehicles. We tried to back out but a second truck had pulled in behind us and blocked the road, so we dismounted and started maneuvering toward cover. We'd made it maybe five yards when the opposing force opened up with a SAW and pushed us back to our vehicles. Our 'terp took a few rounds in the back and our team leader took one in the forehead. By the time we started laying down effective fire, the enemy had popped smoke and were gone."

Clap was silent for several seconds. A deep ridge had formed across his brow as the memories of his teammates lying dead on the road of some third-world country came rushing back. "I'd always assumed it was an ambush."

"It was an assassination."

Clap was unconvinced. "What about the interpreter?"

"Local guy?"

Clap nodded.

Jake continued. "So only one paramilitary officer was killed in the whole ambush, and he took a single round to the forehead, and the only other casualty was the one local in the group, and he got chewed up by a SAW. That difference doesn't strike you as important? A sniper killed the PMOO. Killing the 'terp was just cover."

"How'd they know which guy was the 'terp?"

"You ever seen a 'terp maneuver under fire?" Jake asked.

Clap nodded. Everyone else on the team had spent at least a decade in combat. The interpreter's lack of training and experience probably identified him the second he stepped out of his vehicle.

"The Russians were after a specific paramilitary officer."

"Why would they care about one man?"

"Did your team leader have any issues with headquarters?"

"Who doesn't have issues with headquarters?"

"There's another force at work here besides the Russians," said Jake, "possibly someone inside the Agency."

"That's quite a leap."

"I haven't connected all the dots yet. I need more information."

"Look, brother. I think you're chasing shadows, but I'll help if I can. I have another dot for you."

Jake glanced over.

"Another paramilitary officer disappeared last year."

"Suspicious circumstances?" Jake asked.

"Do people disappear under any other circumstances?"

Jake shot him a dirty look.

"But this guy didn't get a star on the wall," said Clap.

"I get that. The Seventh Floor doesn't want to declare him dead in case he turns up alive and well a few months later."

"That's what everyone assumed . . . at first. This guy was working solo in Libya, so we figured maybe he was taken prisoner or dead— or maybe both given the mission profile—but what's messed up is that his disappearance was never discussed, even within Special Activities. One day, he was one of us. The next day, it was as if he never existed. There was no investigation, no rescue mission, no ceremony, not even drinks after work. It was like he was actively forgotten."

"Tell me about him," Jake said.

"His name was Mike Walker. I didn't know him well, but he had a hall rep as a stone-cold killer. He joined the Agency from the SEAL teams, spent a couple of years on a secret-squirrel task force, and then about two years ago—right after Graves took over as chief of Special Activities—Walker started doing low-vis solo ops, the same shit you do, skulking around sketchy areas with no support. Supposedly he was wired supertight: competent and smart, but real aggressive. Knives, guns, hand-to-hand . . . he liked the wet stuff. He didn't seem the type to just punch out."

Jake stared out the window. He'd only known Clap a few months, but the two men had gone through hell together in Somalia and Jake knew in his heart that he could trust him.

"Between us," Jake said. "I sometimes wonder if I draw those high-risk solo ops precisely because they're high risk."

"Like, you're expendable?"

"Not just expendable. Somebody has had rock-solid intel on my movements over the past few weeks. It's crossed my mind that there is someone inside the building who wants me dead."

Clap shifted in his seat, as if he didn't want to ask the next question, but had to.

"Who would have that kind of intel while you're on leave?"

Jake shrugged.

Clap grimaced.

The windshield wipers sounded like a ticking clock as Jake stopped the Tahoe on the side of the road.

Clap opened his door.

"You may have found the only way to make this job more dangerous than it already is."

THIRTY-NINE

I T WAS DARK by the time Jake returned to the farm. He was about to turn into the carriage house when he spotted the glint of a flashlight inside the barn.

Jake killed his headlights and pulled out of sight. He shut off the Tahoe's interior lights and exited the SUV with his pistol drawn. He held the weapon low in both hands and crouched in the woods next to the gravel driveway.

The light flashed across the barn window again. Someone was searching the interior. Jake walked a hundred yards over the muddy ground, using darkness and the rain to mask his approach, until he was next to the barn. He approached along the sidewall, raised his weapon, and peeked around the front.

The sliding doors were still closed.

Jake crossed in front of the barn. On the far side was a vehicle idling with its parking lights on—a white Ford Explorer. The man with the flashlight was standing outside the barn, searching the interior through a window.

Jake holstered his weapon under his jacket and turned the corner with his hands in plain sight. The flashlight locked onto him almost immediately.

"Evening, Mr. Keller."

"Help you find something, Officer?"

"It's 'Detective.' I was just checking to see if you were home."

"I don't live in the barn."

The cop kept the flashlight in Jake's face for a few more seconds.

"So why are you here?" said the detective.

"I saw the light and thought it might be a burglar."

CIA and most of the other three-letter agencies operating in the area maintained friendly relations with local law enforcement. Extensive operations and covert training in and around the nation's capital were bound to cause issues from time to time—especially in the era of "see something, say something"—but a discreet phone call from the right person was usually enough to make the problem go away.

But not this time.

Jake had a dead Russian buried in his yard.

"I think we got off on the wrong foot," said Jake. "Why don't we sit down and talk?"

Rooney nodded. "Any chance we can get out of the rain?"

They walked along the gravel driveway as they headed for the carriage house.

Jake kicked off his muddy boots at the door.

"Would you like some hot tea?" he said.

"You got any coffee?"

Jake grimaced.

Rooney followed him into the kitchen and stood against the wall. He eyed the custom millwork, the six-burner gas stove, and the thick granite countertops.

"Nice place," said the cop. "You must do pretty well for a guy your age."

"I'm renting. The owners furnished it like the main house in case they ever want to use it as a guesthouse."

"The wife and I did the same with our toolshed."

"Look. I didn't mean to be standoffish the other night," said Jake. "I was sore. I was tired. I just wanted to go for a walk."

"So why'd you gun up after the crash?"

"Coyotes," Jake said.

"Right. You carrying now?"

"I am."

Jake kept his hands in plain view as he heated the water for the tea.

"So where were you tonight?"

"Visiting a friend," Jake said.

"Drinking?"

"No."

"Were you drinking the night you crashed the truck?"

Jake smiled as he poured two cups of tea.

"I already answered that," he said.

"Remind me," said Rooney.

"No."

"So what do you do for a living, Mr. Keller?"

"I'm a consultant."

"In DC?"

"I travel quite a bit."

"How did you see my flashlight?"

"Come again?" Jake said.

"Earlier tonight. You couldn't have seen my flashlight from the carriage house. I was on the far side of the barn."

"I saw it shining through the windows on the other side. It was poor light discipline."

The men were quiet for a few seconds. Jake noticed the detective's elbow brush against his handgun. It was a classic cop tell. He was subconsciously locating the weapon in case he needed it in a hurry. Something, or a lot of somethings, was agitating him.

Jake laid his hands flat on the table.

"You said you're a contractor?" said Detective Rooney.

"Consultant." Jake smiled at the cop. "Contractors do work. Consultants create work."

"I served with a few guys in the Marines who ended up as private military contractors. Guys who got out of the Corps but missed the action or liked the money. You ever serve?"

"No. I started this job right out of college."

"But you know about 'light discipline.' Seems more like a contractor term than a consultant term."

The cop hadn't touched his tea. His hands were tented in front of him with his fingertips touching, but not interlaced. It was called "the interview position" and it was the fastest stance from which to draw and fire his gun. Jake could do it in a little over a second. Rooney probably wasn't far behind.

And something clearly had him on edge. Maybe it was knowing Jake was armed, maybe it was Jake's cold eyes, or maybe the cop didn't know what it was—but his instincts were good, because something was definitely afoot. Unfortunately, the detective had no way of knowing that he and Jake were on the same side of the fight between good and evil.

Jake, in turn, found the aggressive line of questioning unsettling. Though he'd spent his professional career keeping secrets—and half of it operating undercover in hostile environments—he'd spent his entire life thinking of the police as the good guys, and now he was under suspicion and lying to them, just as his faith in CIA was faltering.

"What was the name of the person who picked you up after the crash?" the cop asked.

"I don't remember."

"Male or female?"

"Male," said Jake.

"How old?"

"Fifty, maybe fifty-five."

"What kind of car?"

"An SUV, I think. It was dark out and I was pretty banged up."

"You don't remember much, do you?"

"I have a little post-traumatic amnesia. That whole night is a blur."

"Did you see a doctor?"

"No."

"How do you know you have post-traumatic amnesia? That sounds like a pretty specific diagnosis."

"I've had it before."

"Being a consultant sounds like a rough job."

Jake shrugged.

"I won't take up any more of your time," said the detective. He held out one of his business cards. "In case you remember anything else."

"I still have the first card you gave me."

The cop smiled.

"Well, how about that? Your memory is coming back already."

FORTY

THOUGH IT HAD been bitterly cold overnight, Nikolai Kozlov had been born and raised in Moscow. Something as trifling as subzero temperatures wasn't going to keep him from his customary predawn ascent of the mountain. The rest of the guests were still asleep when he and Misha set off from the chalet. While relations were still strained between the two men because of Jake Keller's persistent good health, Kozlov wanted a bodyguard on the mountain and the Triplets always slowed him down.

The strong winds that had ushered the biting cold into the valley had also pushed the clouds up and over the mountain peaks, where the dry, high-altitude air further robbed them of heat and their ability to hold moisture. The resulting snowfall had left the valleys covered in several inches of light powder. The large, brittle crystals stuck to nothing, including one another, and in the silence of the early morning, they sounded like tiny shards of broken glass as the alpine touring skis sliced through them. The two men used red-tinted headlamps to light their paths until they climbed above the tree line, where they continued on under nothing but starlight and a quarter moon.

"Didn't you tell me this kind of snow causes avalanches?" said Misha, still wary of the enormous wind-driven cornice atop the mountain.

Kozlov didn't break stride.

"It contributes to avalanches, but it does not cause them. This snow is ninety-five percent air. I could dump a truckload of it on you and it would feel like you were being kissed by a flock of butterflies. The danger comes if heavy, wet snow should fall on top of it. The two layers will not bind. The new snow will simply sit there until its weight exceeds the lighter snow's ability to support it."

"What about a loud noise? Could that trigger an avalanche?"

Kozlov stopped climbing and leaned on his poles. Both men were breathing heavily from trying to simultaneously talk and ski uphill in the thin mountain air.

"Maybe," said the oligarch. "A gunshot is loud but sharp. It would not cause an avalanche, but an explosion causes low frequency sound waves that could cause the heavy snow to shear away, like ice sliding off a roof."

Kozlov tried to take a drink, but the water inside his bottle had frozen solid.

"Are you coming to lunch today, Misha? We're going to La Folie Douce afterward."

Misha tried not to roll his eyes. He knew he should go to the slope-side nightclub to work his way back into Kozlov's good graces, but he'd honestly rather have his fingernails torn out. The last time he'd been there he'd had to arrange ground transportation back to Courchevel for several of Kozlov's friends who'd been too drunk to ski home.

And Misha was a killer, not a goddamned babysitter.

"Take Ilya. I'm heading back to the chalet and taking a steam."

FORTY-ONE

MISHA STOOD OUTSIDE the steam room and hung his robe on a peg.

He loved the ski house when it was empty; when there was no electronic dance music pumping through the audio system, no Russian mobsters suckling at the oligarch's teet, and none of the brain damage that routinely came with Kozlov's wealth and connections. There was just bare wood, soft light, and solitude. The only sound was the soft hiss of the steam from inside the frosted-glass door.

"I thought you were at lunch."

Misha turned and saw Mrs. Kozlov standing behind him, her own robe tied loosely around her waist.

Very loosely.

"And I thought you were at lunch," he said.

She made a dismissive face.

"Nikolai can stay in Méribel with that little whore of his . . . Nadia, isn't it?" She smiled. "I can always find something to do here."

She leaned against the wall and her robe opened completely, pulled apart by the relentless force of her silicone-infused breasts.

"You forgot your bathing suit," observed Misha.

She ran a fingertip from his lips, over his chest, down his wash-board abs, and hooked it inside his bathing suit. She pulled him closer and inhaled deeply as the smell of lavender oil seeped out of the steam room.

"It's warm and wet inside," she said.

"And it smells funny," said Misha. "I was just leaving."

He reached past her to retrieve his robe when he noticed someone standing in the darkened hallway.

Grigory.

Mrs. Kozlov followed Misha's gaze. The Triplet was grinning as if he'd just found a winning lottery ticket. She cinched her robe and walked barefoot to the elevator.

"Nikolai won't protect you when he finds out you're fucking his girlfriend *and* his wife," said Grigory.

Misha snapped his body to the left and launched an elbow strike at the goon's head, stopping it an inch from his temple just as the big Russian flinched. The area around his nose was still black-and-blue from the last time Misha had hit him.

"I don't need anyone to protect me," said Misha.

He turned his back, kicked off his cashmere slippers, and walked into the steam room.

MISHA WAS IN his bedroom, a hundred pages into a book on Russian military history, when someone knocked on the door.

It was Kozlov.

Misha concealed his surprise. The oligarch always used the intercom to summon people within the chalet. If the incident with Mrs. Kozlov outside the steam room was going to be an issue, this would be Kozlov's manner of resolving it—direct and immediate—

but Misha didn't notice one of the Triplets standing beside their boss with a gun in his hands.

"How was La Folie Douce?" Misha asked.

The oligarch entered the room and closed the door.

"Has your room been swept recently?" Kozlov said. He was asking about surveillance, not housekeeping.

"Just yesterday. Something wrong with your office?"

"It's being used."

Misha nodded. Kozlov usually kicked Nadia out as soon as he'd finished with her. Perhaps he was treating her better now that he had competition for her affection.

Kozlov sat at a small table in one corner of the room. "Tell me the plan."

Though Misha genuinely believed that keeping Kozlov out of the details was better for everyone concerned, now was not the time to further piss off his boss. Misha sketched a diagram of the route and where he would be set up; he discussed the live intel he'd have on the president's motorcade and where he was planning to take the shot.

"The president's limousine is heavily armored, is it not?" said Kozlov.

"And we're using that against them. The cannon round will penetrate the armor and explode inside the passenger compartment, where the armor will contain the blast. It'll be like detonating a stick of dynamite inside a safe. The pressure will be astronomical."

"Will it be lethal?"

"Lethal? They'll be cleaning him out of there with a mop."

Misha spent the next half an hour reviewing infil and exfil routes, timing, locations, sight lines, communications and surveillance, go-mission triggers, and abort scenarios. The oligarch asked a dozen questions and Misha answered each one systematically and comprehensively.

"The president's security can't defend against something they've never thought of. That's the whole idea behind the cannon. It is going to work."

"I am impressed, Misha. Perhaps I underestimated you."

"It's hard not to."

Kozlov stood to leave.

"Have you heard from Boris?" asked Misha. As far as he knew, the Triplet hadn't checked in since arriving in America.

The oligarch shook his head.

"You're throwing amateurs up against a professional. I was one of these guys. Let me handle Keller."

Kozlov pointed a finger at him. "You stay focused on London."

FORTY-TWO

NEED YOU TO pull a personnel file," Jake said. He and Jeff were having lunch in Arlington again.

"I think you have me confused with someone else," said Jeff. "I'm a sergeant major on temporary duty at the Pentagon, not chairman of the Joint Chiefs of Staff."

"I thought you Delta guys were sneaky."

"Not as sneaky as you Agency guys. Who's the subject?"

"Mike Walker, a former SEAL who joined Special Activities. He disappeared last year."

"Forget it," Jeff said. "I can't access it, and even if I could, there will be fifty flags on that file. SOCOM, JSOC, FBI, DIA, CIA, and probably the White House would know the minute I pulled it."

"He might still be alive."

"Then I'd think the Agency would be all over it."

"Just the opposite. It's as if he never existed."

"Maybe your organization knows more than they're letting on."

"That's a given," Jake said, "but even the hall chatter is nonexistent."

"What did this guy do?"

"Paramilitary ops officer. A singleton mostly—low-vis stuff in denied environments."

"Sounds like you."

"Not only that," Jake said. "He disappeared in Libya."

Jeff nodded soberly. The two men had met in Libya when Jake had accompanied Jeff's Delta Force troop on a raid. They'd both narrowly escaped with their lives while searching for two rogue politicians who'd nearly started a war between China and the United States. Jeff had brought an AK-47 round home as a souvenir—in his thigh.

"You looking for something specific?" he asked.

"A Russia connection."

Jeff pushed back from the table. "You and I have been through a lot together, and you know I respect you, but seriously, dial this shit back before it turns into an obsession. You're going to make yourself crazy."

The two men made idle chitchat while they finished their lunch, and Jake dropped Jeff back at the Pentagon. The encounter left Jake feeling very isolated. Effectively reborn two years earlier with no friends and no family, he'd immediately stepped into a challenging career he couldn't discuss with anyone. It had left him with a very small circle of confidants—all experienced intelligence and military types, none of whom shared his conviction that there was Russian, and potentially CIA, involvement in the deaths of his fellow paramilitary officers.

Jake stopped at a red light and pulled out his mobile phone. Hoping he could find out more about the missing paramilitary officer from open-source information, Jake did a quick internet search for "Michael Walker." There were eight thousand hits before the light turned green—and that was just in the United States. If Walker was still alive and had gone AWOL, the likelihood that the former SEAL/CIA operative was living in the U.S. under his given name was approximately zero.

Open-source information wasn't going to get Jake what he needed.

He dialed Peter Clements.

"I need help."

FORTY-THREE

HELP ME THINK through this thing," Jake said. He'd picked up Clements in downtown Bethesda and they were having a rolling meeting in Jake's rented SUV.

"What thing?"

"Russia."

Clements groaned.

"And the mole," added Jake.

Clements groaned again, louder than the first time.

"Pull over," he said. "I need something for the pain."

He came back a minute later with two double espressos.

"You know I don't drink that stuff," Jake said.

"The second one is also for me. Has it ever occurred to you that maybe the Russians uncovered the only man in the worldwide intelligence community who doesn't drink coffee? Zac disappeared. Then Jake appeared a few months later. Neither one drinks coffee . . . Mystery solved. Let me off up at the corner."

"A lot of people don't drink coffee."

"A lot of unproductive sloths. Can we please get this over with?"

"The plane crash in France," Jake said. "It's the only event that occurred in a vacuum."

"Explain."

"My detention in Iran and the deaths in Syria and the Central African Republic had direct links to Agency operations to advance U.S. interests, but not the plane crash."

"Maybe the crash was an accident."

"What is our investigation saying?"

"There is no investigation. You were the only American on the plane and you weren't on Company business. If we started making inquiries, French intelligence would wonder why. Given your history there, we didn't think that was in your best interests."

"Do you think it was an accident?" Jake said.

"I don't have enough facts to have an opinion. What do you remember?"

As he'd done a hundred times since the crash, Jake racked his brain for something tangible, but for the first time, he made a little progress.

"There was something in the snow," said Jake. "I can't remember what it was but I know it somehow proves the crash wasn't an accident."

Clements looked out the window as Jake turned south on Wisconsin Avenue.

"What do you know about Michael Walker?" said Jake.

"The name means nothing to me. Did he use an alias?"

"He also went by Mike."

Clements shot him a dirty look.

"He was a paramilitary officer. He disappeared last year during a solo op in Libya."

"A singleton in Libya? It's not hard to figure out how that story ended."

"So now you're willing to speculate? What happened to your obsession with facts?"

"The fact is that an officer working alone in Libya comes with a high probability of a negative outcome."

"Why didn't the Agency put his star on the wall?"

"It's unusual, but not unheard of," said Clements. "Is Walker part of your Russia quest?"

"Maybe. Right now I'm just wondering why everyone in the building seems to have actively forgotten about him. It's like someone erased his memory."

Clements peeled the lid off his second cup of espresso.

"Can you look into it?" Jake said.

"His disappearance?"

Jake nodded.

"People are going to wonder why."

"I know you don't see the connection yet, but you knew when I worked for you as an analyst that I saw relationships before other people—even when I couldn't explain them."

"Yes. You kept grinding away until you convinced everyone around you."

"That's where I am now. There's a pattern to the deaths and too much operational intelligence for it to happen without someone inside the Agency feeding them details."

"Assuming, hypothetically, you are correct and Russia has someone inside the Special Activities Center, a few dead paramilitary officers could be just the tip of the iceberg," said Clements.

"And the numbers bear that out. There's been a spike in deaths over the past two years."

"So expand your investigation."

"I can't. I've already exhausted the circle of people I can trust.

That's why I need to figure out what happened to Walker. He's my last lead."

"I'd have to pull his file. How bad do you want it?"

"I wouldn't waste your time, Peter."

"It's not my time that I'm worried about. It's Newton's Third Law: For every action there is an equal and opposite reaction. If I pull Walker's file, alarms are going to go off in every department from human resources to Special Activities."

"So what? You're associate director."

"Which is why I can access the file, but I rarely meet paramilitary officers and I'd never heard of Mike Walker until now, and Ted Graves will know that. Given that Ted is one of the handful of people at CIA who knows of my relationship with you, it will take him somewhere between one and two seconds to figure out that I pulled the file for you."

Jake frowned as he steered through traffic.

Clements continued. "Are relations still strained between you and Mr. Graves?"

"That would be an understatement."

"Then the question you have to ask yourself is, Do I care if Ted knows I'm looking into it?"

Jake didn't hesitate. "Skip the file."

"I think that's the right call," said Clements. "Crossing Ted Graves has never been good for anyone's career."

"Or their health."

FORTY-FOUR

JAKE LEFT HIS meeting with Clements more certain than ever that something dangerous was going on inside CIA. Because of his senior role at the Agency, Clements normally would have been briefed on the death or disappearance of any employee in the field. The fact that he'd never even heard of Mike Walker meant that somebody was intentionally keeping him in the dark.

Jake had to find a different way to connect the dots.

He replayed the series of events in his head, searching for the anomaly, the elusive thread that would help him put it all together.

He focused on the plane crash.

As he'd said to Clements, it was the only event that had occurred in a vacuum. No one could claim that it was just an operational hazard as they had with the dead paramilitary officers in Syria and the Central African Republic.

Someone was clearly trying to kill Jake, but why him and why now? Who stood to gain?

To be sure, he had made his share of enemies in the field, but he was an abstraction to all of them: often in disguise, never operating under his own name—a faceless agent of some opposing force. Here one day, gone the next. The odds were long that a warlord in Somalia or a terrorist cell in Yemen could identify him by name, much less find, fix, and finish him.

So Jake did what he always did when he hit a roadblock; he reframed the question to examine the problem from a different angle.

Why the flight to Courchevel?

Taking down an airplane in the post-9/11 world was extremely challenging, but having it pass for an accident would be almost impossible for anyone but the most highly skilled operatives with extensive resources. Crash investigations were carried out by large teams of highly skilled investigators, aviation experts, and aerospace engineers. The people Jake was up against were not run-of-the-mill criminals or homegrown terrorists. They had assumed a great deal of risk to prevent him from reaching Courchevel, which meant they were trying to protect someone or something of even greater value in the alpine village.

Who or what it was Jake didn't know, but in a moment of clarity he realized that the only way he would ever find out was to go back.

FORTY-FIVE

JAKE FLEW OUT the next morning, but not to Courchevel. While he didn't always respect the line between being aggressive and being reckless, whoever was trying to kill him had already demonstrated that the resources and intelligence network at their disposal demanded respect. Jake didn't need to make their job any easier by attempting to fly into the already-dangerous mountainside Altiport a second time. Instead, he took a red-eye flight to Amsterdam and connected on a budget carrier, using a different passport, to Paris.

It was eleven a.m. by the time he arrived at Orly Airport and rented an all-wheel-drive Audi station wagon for the trip to the alpine village.

He texted Geneviève.

Jake couldn't undo the damage he'd done in the past two years, but he couldn't let his last memory of her, and her last memory of him, be of the night when she'd stormed out of his hotel room after thinking he'd been with another woman.

I'm in Paris, he wrote. *Meet for lunch?*

Busy day, came the reply.

Jake stared at the disposable Bic Phone he'd needlessly carried back and forth across the Atlantic in a radio-frequency-shielded bag with the battery removed.

I'm sorry about everything, he sent back. *Good-bye.*

Jake dropped the phone on the seat next to him and loaded the route for the seven-hour drive into the car's navigation system.

The phone pinged.

I'm stopping at a patisserie on my way home. 22 rue des martyrs, 9th arr. 18:00 hours.

THE WALLS OF the brightly lit bakery were lined with glass cases filled with pastries and cakes, most of which had been brought to life around a core of fruit or chocolate. The aroma inside the shop was tantalizing but Jake meandered around the store without buying anything while he waited for Geneviève. Soon, she was five minutes late, but five quickly became ten and ten became twenty. The shop-keeper was cleaning countertops and removing trays from the display cases.

"We close in five minutes if you're planning on buying anything," he said in French without looking up.

Ah, the charm of the French shopkeeper, Jake thought. He resisted the urge to throw the man through the plate-glass window and glanced at his phone instead.

No messages.

"We're closed now," said the shopkeeper. Somewhere in his mid-forties, with greasy hair and an ugly mustache, his stained apron rode high over his large belly. He waddled around the counter and opened the door for Jake to leave.

"I'm waiting for someone," Jake said in French.

"They're not here," observed the shopkeeper.

"No . . . they're not."

There was no disputing that. Jake had put one foot out the door when Geneviève's Porsche stopped out front.

"Mademoiselle Marchand!" gushed the shopkeeper. He bowed as if Charles de Gaulle had just risen from the dead to purchase a chocolate croissant.

"Bonjour, Louis," said Geneviève. She stared at Jake as if she still couldn't match the face to her memory.

The shopkeeper sneered at Jake as he followed Geneviève back inside, but Jake met the man's gaze and stared him down. Lots of people acted tough until their actions had repercussions.

Geneviève quickly filled two boxes with an assortment of desserts and paid for them in cash. She looked at Jake again. Neither one had said a word to the other since she'd arrived. They walked outside, where a damp mist softened the city lights.

The shopkeeper locked the door behind them.

Geneviève started walking along the sidewalk, away from her car. Jake fell in beside her and they walked in silence to the end of the block.

She turned and looked at him.

"Why are you here?"

"I'm going to Courchevel tomorrow."

"That's not what I meant, but we can keep this professional if that's what you want. Did you find your Russia connection?"

"Why do you say that?"

"Because a quarter of Courchevel is owned by Russians."

Jake hadn't known that.

"Organized crime?" he said.

"They pay for everything in cash and bring a lot of security."

They turned at the end of the street and walked back toward the bakery. The lights on Geneviève's SUV flashed as she unlocked the doors.

"I'm sorry," Jake said, "for everything I've put you through. After I crossed the Channel, after I changed my identity, before I returned to France—I should have called you. I was serious when I told you that the oath I swore is important to me, but I've also been selfish. I've been living a dangerous existence for the past two years and I felt better knowing I wasn't putting you at risk."

"I can make those decisions myself."

Jake nodded.

She scrutinized his face again, like she was trying to solve a puzzle.

"Are you involved with someone?" she asked.

"No," Jake said. "The other night in my hotel . . . I ordered a lot of food and room service set two place settings while I was in the shower. It was too depressing to ask them to come back and take the other one away."

Geneviève frowned.

"You deserve better," Jake said.

"Yes, I do."

She climbed into the driver's seat and closed the door, and Jake watched the taillights fade into the mist.

FORTY-SIX

AS JAKE HAD done so many times, he boxed up the hurt and the loss and put it out of his mind. How long he could keep it boxed up was anyone's guess. It would all come out eventually, and hopefully not catastrophically.

Maybe he was never meant to lead a normal life.

After waiting all day for Geneviève, it was too late to leave for Courchevel. The front desk at his hotel would be closed long before he arrived. Jake checked back into the Nolinski in Paris, ordered room service for one, and slept restlessly.

He awoke before dawn and spent an hour swimming laps in the hotel pool. He was back in his room and about to get on the road when he glanced at his phone and saw a text message waiting.

Call me.

Only one person had the number.

Jake stood at the foot of his unmade bed, wearing the hotel robe and the stupid little sandals that came with it, and stared at the screen, wondering what he'd done now to raise her ire. He certainly wasn't over Geneviève, but she'd made it abundantly clear that she had moved on. He tossed the phone on the bed and took a long shower to wash the chlorine from his skin.

The phone was flashing again when he'd finished.

Missed Call

Jake redialed the number.

"Hey," he said without enthusiasm. Though Geneviève spoke excellent English, up till now they'd always spoken French when they were together. It just didn't seem right anymore.

"I'm coming to Courchevel," she said.

Jake stared at the phone.

"Jake?"

"Yeah, sorry. I'm still in Paris."

"Even better," she added. *"We can drive down together. A man traveling by himself will attract attention."*

Jake hesitated. "That's why you're coming?"

There was silence on the phone for several seconds.

"I haven't been fair to you," she added. *"I was focused on how hard this has been for me. You gave up everything."*

"The trip may be dangerous."

"I can take care of myself. Besides, it will be less dangerous having a native along—you didn't even know about the Russians in Courchevel."

"I don't need your charity."

"Stop being so damn independent. Let me help you."

"What does your boyfriend think?"

Geneviève hesitated. *"We're taking a break."*

"I'll be ready in five seconds."

Geneviève giggled. *"I need to get some things from my office. I'll pick you up at 13:00."*

JAKE WAS STANDING on Avenue de l'Opéra as Geneviève slotted the Porsche into a space in front of the hotel. He climbed into the passenger seat and tossed his duffel bag in the back. Jake leaned over to kiss her cheek but she pulled away immediately to get ahead of a busload of tourists.

"You said the trip might be dangerous?" she said in French.

"Someone took down my plane the last time I tried to go to Courchevel."

"Was this a month ago?"

"A little less."

"I read about the crash. I was surprised anyone lived."

Jake forced a smile. More than once he'd felt guilt about being the only survivor when he'd been the target of the attack.

"I think the aviation safety bureau is leaning toward declaring it a mechanical malfunction," she added.

"I don't recall much about the crash, but I do remember seeing something in the snow that convinced me it wasn't an accident."

"That changes things," said Geneviève. She cut across three lanes of traffic and turned north.

"Isn't Courchevel south?" Jake said.

"Later," she said.

THEY MADE TWO stops and were at Geneviève's parking garage in half an hour. She changed the license plates on her car to a phony set she'd taken from DGSE and led him upstairs. She had to make a phone call, so Jake meandered around the apartment, looking at photographs, opening closets and wardrobes, and checking out the master bathroom.

Geneviève finished her call and met Jake in the kitchen. She told him to strip to the waist and sit in front of the sink while she ran warm tap water through her fingers. Jake arched his back and spread his arms along the kitchen countertop as she eased his head back into the sink, poured warm water over his forehead, and massaged shampoo into his hair. He exhaled deeply and consciously relaxed the muscles in his face, his neck, and all the way out to his fingertips and his toes. The tension seeped from his body.

"When did you get these?" she said, running a soapy fingertip over two bullet-sized scars on his left shoulder.

"After I crossed the Channel."

It had been two years ago when he and Geneviève had said good-bye at a marina in France. Moments later, he'd set off across the English Channel into an approaching gale, alone in a small boat, at night. Jake had promised to call her the moment he was safe but never had. Despite the oath of secrecy he'd sworn to CIA, a part of him wondered if he'd never called because he'd never felt completely safe again. While he didn't fear death in the abstract, he of course preferred to live. Jake had learned to control fear, to use it as a driving force instead of a paralyzing one.

Geneviève rinsed the shampoo from his hair.

"What are we looking for in Courchevel?" she said.

"I didn't know until you told me about all the Russians there," said Jake, "but now I'm convinced it's someone high up, probably GRU or a private military contractor, someone with the resources to take down a commercial aircraft and make it look like an accident."

"What were you working on when your plane went down?"

"That's the strange part. I wasn't working on anything. I'd just gotten back from a difficult deployment and wanted to do some skiing."

Geneviève winced. He'd been going to France but she hadn't been part of his plans.

"I didn't call you then because I had to clear my head. As hard as this reunion has been, I was in much worse shape then. I needed some time alone."

"You can't do everything yourself."

Jake heard Celia's voice echoing the same rebuke.

"Why are you smiling?" Geneviève asked.

"I'm in love with another woman."

Geneviève's nails dug into his scalp. "You said room service—"

"She's about eighty years old," Jake continued, "half drill sergeant and half grandmother, and she told me the same thing."

Geneviève retracted her claws. "I like her."

"She's also the one who told me I needed to make things right with you."

Geneviève started massaging his scalp again. "I like her even more."

Geneviève donned a pair of latex gloves and squirted a thick paste into her hands. She worked it through Jake's hair.

"Once we reach Courchevel I want to hit all the Russian hangouts," he said. "We're going to have to do a lot of reconnaissance and a lot of research on everyone who seems like a player."

Geneviève smiled again. "I picked up a gadget from the office that might help."

"Let's hope so, because someone wants me dead. I've had a couple of 'accidents' since the plane crash, and I have a feeling that they'll find us if we don't find them first."

Geneviève looked pensive.

Jake put his hand gently on her hip. "We'll be fine."

Geneviève leaned over. "Close your mouth," she said softly.

Jake did. He closed his eyes too.

She smeared his lips with a thick coating of petroleum jelly.

"That's disgusting," he said. "What the—"

"Stop talking," she said as she brushed some paste into the three-day growth on his face.

A few minutes later she wiped away the petroleum jelly, rinsed his hair and face, and gently dried his hair with a towel. She led him to a mirror.

His beard and his hair were blond.

He'd dyed it before. Naturally dark brown, he'd colored it black when working in the Middle East—but he'd never made it lighter. It was closer to dirty blond than platinum, but the transformation, especially with the matching beard, was shocking.

And not just to him.

He reached out for Geneviève's hand but she pulled away.

"I'm sorry," she said, "but this is all too much for me to process . . . the new face, the new name, now the hair." She walked to her bedroom. "The guest room is made up. Good night."

FORTY-SEVEN

THEY WERE ON the road by 07:00 the next morning.

"So why are you and the boyfriend taking a break?"

"He got upset when I asked him about Syria," said Geneviève. "He's arrogant and stubborn."

"But he gave you the information?"

"It was meant to be an olive branch, but it was too late. The relationship wasn't going anywhere anyway. It's over."

Jake nodded.

"Does that complete your reconnaissance?" she said.

Jake feigned surprise.

"I saw you inspecting my apartment. We weren't living together if that's what you were looking for."

Jake grimaced.

"You're disappointed?" said Geneviève.

"Not at all. It's just that you've foiled my spy skills twice already. First, you found my hotel because it had a pool, then you caught me tossing your apartment. You'd make a formidable adversary."

"Or a valuable ally . . . Stop thinking it's you against the world."

Jake nodded, but it was easier said than done. He'd been acting that way since he was fourteen.

"I spent some time with our domestic security liaison," Geneviève continued. "I wanted to compile a list of Russian military and intelligence officials with homes in Courchevel, but she said that most high-government figures don't directly own property outside the country because of the sanctions risk."

"So we're looking for someone with connections, but not control."

"Several oligarchs own chalets in town. About half of them are involved with what we would call organized crime, but the line between the state and organized crime has blurred in modern Russia."

"That profile makes sense," Jake said. "A cutout between the government and whoever is killing our officers would give Moscow plausible deniability. They used mercenaries in the Central African Republic for the same reason."

"But it doesn't explain why they're after you."

"Someone thought I was getting too close."

"Too close to what?"

Jake shook his head. "I have no idea."

THE PORSCHE'S TIRES bit into the snow as Geneviève scaled the winding alpine road into Courchevel. The pavement was lined with towering snowbanks where plows had carved a path just wide enough for two lanes of traffic. As they reached the town's lower elevations, après-skiers and shoppers emerged on the wide sidewalks, joyfully navigating their way between mounds of freshly fallen snow and trees decorated with Christmas lights. Off in the distance, a soft pink glow bathed snowcapped mountain peaks under a purple sky.

For most visitors, it was magical place, portending incomparable food, incredible views, and the largest skiable terrain in the world, but Jake wasn't most visitors. His head was on a swivel, watching everyone and everything for any clue that would pull it all together.

"The hotel is up here on the left," he said.

Geneviève smiled politely and drove past the modestly priced establishment.

"I'm sure it's lovely, but the people we're looking for wouldn't set foot inside. I made a reservation for us at Le Chabichou."

"'The shabby shoe'?" said Jake.

"It's a type of cheese."

"Shoe cheese . . . sounds great."

Le Chabichou was anything but cheesy. Geneviève had barely stopped the SUV when valets and bellmen swarmed it like a pit crew. In a matter of seconds, the luggage was unloaded and the Porsche was gone. Jake and Geneviève were whisked inside and up to their room, a one-bedroom suite with a sitting area.

"Fancy," he said.

"It was the only room available, with a two-night minimum, and I had to call in a favor to get it."

"Thanks for doing that. At least let me pay for everything while we're here."

"OK," Geneviève said without a hint of protest.

Jake took in the exposed wood beams, the heated floors, and the mink throw across the foot of the hand-carved four-poster bed.

"Just out of curiosity . . . how much is it?" he asked as he opened a bottle of water.

"The room? Two thousand . . ."

Jake nearly choked.

"Euros," she added.

He sat down.

"Per night," said Geneviève. "That bottle of water was probably twenty euros."

"You're buying dinner," he said.

THEY ATE IN the hotel that night, a Michelin two-star restaurant where the food looked like art. The only thing that looked better was Geneviève. Tall and elegant, she walked to their table wearing a formfitting cashmere sweater and her dark hair pulled up in a high ponytail.

Every head turned.

Which had been the plan all along.

She pulled out her phone and set it on the table.

"Any luck?" Jake said.

Though the hair clip she was wearing looked like a collection of lacquered black beads, it was actually a multilensed camera—much like an insect's eye—that took in 360 degrees of the room at once. She'd retrieved it from her office before picking Jake up at his hotel, and it fed the take via Bluetooth to her phone, which transmitted it to DGSE headquarters. The images were analyzed for biometric data such as facial geometry, ear shape, and the subject's gait against everyone who'd ever crossed the spy agency's radar.

Geneviève read the results from her phone.

"One hit at your eight o'clock—the man with thick eyebrows seated at the corner table in back. It says he built an empire of car dealerships on a pile of bodies after Yeltsin left office, but no activities outside Mother Russia—strictly domestic *mafiya*. Probably not our subject."

Jake smiled at her. "You look stunning tonight."

Geneviève wasn't sure if he was acting out their cover or speaking from the heart. They were traveling as a couple very much in love, chatting in French, gazing at each other and holding hands across the table.

The rest of the dinner passed uneventfully until the bill arrived.

"What was the damage?" Jake asked.

"I didn't look," she said. "I just charged it to the room."

Jake went pale.

"What's next?" he said as they exited the restaurant. After years as a CIA singleton, it was nice to let someone else lead for a change, and he had complete confidence in Geneviève.

"We're going clubbing," she said.

"I'd rather be waterboarded."

The pink, purple, and green lights at Les Caves flashed in time with the techno music while machine-generated fog and pulsing lasers filled the air. The sides of the club were lined with dozens of booths, where magnums of Dom Pérignon and double magnums of Cristal rested inside lighted plastic champagne buckets. High-end cognacs and vodkas, some costing five thousand euros a bottle, lay strewn about like beer cans at a fraternity party. It was a competition to see who could spend the most money, in the most conspicuous way, without appearing to care.

Jake and Geneviève took two stools at the bar. Maybe three hundred people were packed onto the dance floor. At least 80 percent of them were women—each more beautiful than the next—and all were clad in silks and cashmeres from the world's top fashion houses. The conversations shouted over the music were occasionally in French or English, but mostly in Russian. Jake spotted a lot of muscle under the balloons and disco balls. Bouncers and bodyguards—indistinguishable except for the earpieces worn by the club employees—were everywhere. They weren't dancing and they weren't drinking. They were watching.

"Your phone must be blowing up," Jake said.

Geneviève glanced at it and frowned. There was only one hit, and like before, the subject didn't fit their target profile.

"The players must be in the booths," she said. "Let's take a walk."

Jake followed a few steps behind as she picked her way through the crowd. Expensively dressed men, some in dinner jackets and some in T-shirts, were packed shoulder to shoulder, and occasionally closer, to young women whose plunging necklines and slit skirts belied the fact that they were at a ski resort.

A man in his thirties stepped out of a booth and approached Geneviève with a bottle of champagne in one hand and two glasses in the other, but he promptly retreated when she reached back and clasped Jake's hand, which she held for the rest of their lap around the club.

Geneviève glanced at her phone when they'd returned to their seats. They'd scored two more hits—a professional soccer player from England and a German media executive.

"Any luck?" Jake shouted.

"Not unless they're trying to fix the World Cup," she yelled back.

"What?" The deafening music made conversation impossible.

"We should go."

Jake dropped a hundred-euro note on the bar and waited for his change. The bartender looked back. "It's one hundred twenty for the two drinks."

They returned to their hotel suite with their ears ringing and none the wiser for the expenditure of time and money. Geneviève said good night and closed the door to the bedroom.

With Jake on the other side.

FORTY-EIGHT

JAKE WAS FALLING.

It began slowly, just the faintest hint of weightlessness—an overwhelmingly pleasant sensation, as if all the obstacles and worries in his life had been lifted from his shoulders. It was like a state of euphoria.

But it didn't last long.

Something clawed at his hips. He looked down and saw a seat belt. It squeezed harder, unyielding, like a boa constrictor wrapped around his thighs. The blissful sensation of weightlessness gave way to a panicked loss of control. He tumbled forward and began falling in earnest, accelerating face-first toward mountains and rocks and trees and snow. In the fraction of a second before he smashed into the ground, Jake awoke with a start, lying on the floor next to the sofa where he'd slept.

He cursed under his breath.

While he and Geneviève were speaking again, not much else about the trip to Courchevel was going to plan. They'd found a few

Russians, but none who held any promise. Though Jake had come to France not knowing what he was looking for, he'd expected to know it when he saw it—but the alpine village wasn't giving up its secrets so readily.

Jake knocked softly on the bedroom door and checked on Geneviève. She was sleeping peacefully, so he wrote her a short note and had one of the hotel's courtesy shuttles take him to the local aquatics center. He needed to loosen up his body after tossing and turning all night on the damned sofa.

With his blond hair mostly tucked into his swim cap and his goggles strapped on tight, he swam sets for an hour. There was another American in the lane next to him and the two men slowly fell into an undeclared competition. It had been almost a month since the plane crash and, despite the altitude, Jake was feeling stronger every day. He was making a fast pace, but the other American was in excellent shape, and there was no clear winner.

Geneviève was standing in the lobby when Jake returned to the hotel.

"We need to rent some skis," she said.

Though they'd come to a ski resort, neither had planned on actually skiing. Jake gave her a quizzical look.

"New intel," she said. "Apparently, the richest and most powerful Russians have discotheques inside their chalets. They don't go out for dinner. They don't go out at night. They invite hundreds of people into their homes and have private chefs cater the parties."

"How do we get invited?"

"We don't. The chalets are like fortresses with heavy security and they only invite people they know. My source said there are too many illicit activities going on for them to invite strangers."

"So why are we going skiing?"

"Because there's a slope-side restaurant two valleys over where the same Russians eat and party during the day. We need to leave soon to make our one o'clock reservation."

Jake was impressed. She'd pushed the mission forward while he'd been splashing around in the pool with his little friend.

"That's great work," Jake said as they walked toward the hotel's ski room. "Who's your source?"

Geneviève waved at the concierge as they passed by.

"I brought her a chocolate croissant and an espresso and asked her where we had to go to avoid the Russians, so she told me exactly where they were. I made the lunch reservation myself."

Jake smiled and took her arm.

"I need to keep an eye on you," he said.

"You'd better keep them both on me."

LA FRUITIÈRE WASN'T what Jake expected. Rustic and bright, it looked more like a farmhouse than a nightclub. Its thirty tables were just beginning to fill up when he and Geneviève arrived. Skiers were peeling off jackets and helmets, unbuckling ski boots, and generally trying not to fall on the slick wood floors. Jake and Geneviève were seated in the sunroom, overlooking the slopes and the village of Méribel below.

Geneviève shook out her long dark hair and pulled it into a ponytail on top of her head, using the covert bug-eye camera to hold it in place. As before, she put her phone on the table next to her.

The next table was occupied by a Russian family. Jake watched enviously as the three preteen children devoured a fresh-baked loaf of bread and a quarter pound of butter.

"Are you sure this is the right place?" he said to Geneviève.

"The club is next door," she said, gesturing down the slope to a massive deck attached to the building. A hundred people in ski clothes were already standing around the outdoor tables, drinking, listening to dance music, and watching half a dozen professional dancers gyrate atop the elevated platforms that were spaced throughout the club.

"The concierge said there's a shortcut from the restaurant into the club," Geneviève added.

Jake watched as a fit man in his fifties skidded to a stop outside the restaurant. His ski instructor arrived a few moments later and the men entered without speaking. They sat separately, each at a table for twelve. Fifteen minutes later, both tables were filled with more Russian men, and more French ski instructors, plus a third table with a dozen women who'd arrived wearing Chanel leather jackets and Manolo Blahnik glitter pumps. Bottles of champagne and bowls of caviar were spaced evenly across the three tables, but it was clear from the body language of the others, and the positioning of the muscle-bound goon who was acting as security, that the fit man was the center of attention.

"Anything?" Jake asked.

Geneviève glanced at her phone and shook her head, but Jake's predatory instinct was stirring.

"This guy in the white sweater is hosting lunch for thirty-six people with champagne, caviar, and a bodyguard. There are no toasts, no celebrations. This is just an everyday ten-thousand-dollar lunch on the mountain, and from the way the women are dressed, I'm guessing they're all going to continue the party down at the club."

"Is he facing this way?" Geneviève asked.

"No," Jake said. "I can only see the side of his head."

"I think I need to powder my nose," she said with a mischievous smile.

Geneviève rose from the table and walked past the Russians'

tables, attracting looks from most of the women and all of the men—including the man in the white sweater.

She returned a few minutes later, but her flirtatious grin was gone. Her jaw was set, her eyes focused.

"His name is Nikolai Kozlov," she said as she covered her mouth with her napkin. "He owns half the steel mills in Russia, is personal friends with the Russian president, and is former GRU."

"Well, you got his attention," said Jake. "He's staring right at me."

Kozlov had watched Geneviève return to the table but quickly shifted his attention to Jake. The Russian was speaking quietly to his security man, a muscle-bound goon dressed entirely in black. The goon looked at Jake for a few seconds, then rubbed a few strands of his hair between his fingertips and shook his head.

"I think we've found our man," Jake said.

"Kiss me," said Geneviève.

"What?!"

She leaned across the table and kissed Jake on the mouth. It lasted several seconds and no one in the restaurant thought it was faked.

Including Kozlov.

He turned away and resumed speaking with his guests.

"What did I do to deserve that?" Jake said. "I'd like to know so I can do it again."

"I wanted to show Mr. Kozlov that we're just a couple in love and you're not the man he's been trying to kill for the past month."

Jake glanced at Kozlov. The Russian was facing the other direction, having a relaxed discussion with a few of the other men.

"He's staring right at me," Jake said. "I don't think he believed the kiss . . . You and I should go back to the hotel and practice our cover story . . ."

Geneviève smirked. She knew what Jake was up to.

"How much practice do we need?" she said playfully.

"A lot and in depth."

She paid the bill in cash and they walked outside to their skis. Down the hill, the music at the club was thumping, the dancers swirling, and the guests smiling.

Watching through a window from inside the restaurant, Kozlov's goon grimaced as Jake and Geneviève skied away.

AROUSED BY THE hunt, Geneviève shoved Jake up against the wall of their hotel room and kissed him again before the door was shut. A minute later they were pulling off each other's clothes. Geneviève was down to a skintight top that looked like a cross between a spandex T-shirt and an exercise bra. Jake started to tug it over her head but she shoved him away.

He took a step back, breathing heavily, and watched as she drew a small semiautomatic pistol from the top and placed it on the dresser.

Jake smiled at her. "I thought I was supposed to bring the protection."

An indeterminate period of time later, Jake was lying in bed, at peace. While the mystery of who was trying to kill him and his fellow paramilitary officers was far from solved, for the first time in weeks, it wasn't front and center in his mind. Geneviève was wrapped in his arms and both were slowly drifting off to sleep.

Jake sat up in bed. "The plane crash," he said. "I remember what happened."

FORTY-NINE

GENEVIÈVE LEANED AGAINST the headboard and pulled Jake gently to her. His heart was pounding.

"Tell me what happened," she said.

"It was late in the day. The sky was incredibly clear, like you could reach out the window and touch the mountains. We were descending into a valley, everything was normal, and then there was an explosion—a small one, more like a pop than a boom—on the right side of the aircraft, but I've heard enough explosions to know what it was. A couple of seconds later, everything started shaking and the right wing dropped. We just started falling. I felt my seat belt pulling me down and the engine started whining as we picked up speed. A woman a few rows in front of me was screaming. The plane was oscillating from side to side. I guess the pilots were wrestling with the controls to keep us airborne but we just kept accelerating toward the ground. The mountain kept getting bigger in the windows until it was just a blur of snow and rocks and trees. We were going down hard, practically nose first. I was sure I was going to die, but just before we hit, the pilots leveled off for a couple of seconds and we plowed into the snow. My seat was in the back of the plane, which I guess was lucky, because when the violence was over, everyone in front of me was dead."

Jake was breathing hard and soaked in sweat, but his eyes were hyperfocused, as if he were living through the crash a second time.

"There was another helicopter," he continued. "It came before the rescue helo. The pilots came in nap-of-the-earth, maybe a hundred feet off the snow, and flew directly to the crash site. They didn't search. They didn't fly a couple of high orbits. They knew exactly where we would be. It hovered overhead, two men fast-roped down to the wreckage, and it was gone. They'd been expecting the crash . . . waiting for it."

"Did they see you?"

"No. I was pretty banged up, but my survival instinct drove me into the trees as soon as I heard the first helicopter."

"Did they track you?"

"They did, but the crazy part is, I don't think I was their primary objective. I know it sounds ridiculous, but they were using a tight, expanding-box search pattern from the center of the crash site. I've trained for mountain rescues and that's not how you do it. These guys were scouring every foot of the wreckage. They were looking for something else."

"And you think they were professionals?"

"Definitely. They fast-roped down from the helo with snowshoes and weapons. It wasn't their first time in the mountains."

"So what were they looking for?"

"Do you remember when I said I knew the crash wasn't an accident but I didn't know why? There was something man-made sticking out of the snow. It had three coaxial antennas, like a cellular device. Even then I knew it was connected to the crash, maybe part of the bomb trigger. I didn't have time to grab it before I ran into the woods and it was gone when I came back."

"The men took it?" asked Geneviève.

"They must have. Then they tracked me into the woods. They would have found me except the PGHM rescue helo showed up a few minutes later."

Jake and Geneviève sat silently on the bed as his breathing and heart rate returned to normal.

"I think we need to be very careful around Mr. Kozlov," Geneviève said eventually.

"Thank you for believing in me. You're the only person who never doubted me."

She kissed the back of his head. "Always, but we should return to Paris, where it's safer."

Jake turned and kissed her on the mouth.

"Not just yet," he said, as his breathing, his heart rate, and everything else, went right back up.

EVERY SPY AGENCY in the world taught its operatives that bribing hotel staff was a simple and inexpensive way to keep tabs on surveillance targets, so when Jake called the front desk and ordered a wake-up call for eight a.m., he did so with no intention of ever answering the phone.

He and Geneviève were on the road by five a.m.

Jake drove while she worked on her laptop.

"Kozlov is a serious player," she said, reading from her screen. "'Maintains close ties with the Russian president and former colleagues at GRU. Willing to kill to advance his interests. Suspected in the murders of at least a dozen rivals—'"

"But never convicted?" Jake said.

"Not even arrested. He keeps his hands clean."

"What about a connection to CIA?"

Geneviève read the rest of the DGSE dossier, including a list of the oligarch's known associates.

"Nothing," she said.

"Does he own a helicopter?"

Geneviève paged through several pages of records.

"No, at least not in his name. I'll do more research once I'm back at my desk. I can't access *très secret* files on my laptop."

Jake cursed as he stopped outside the international departures area at Charles de Gaulle Airport. There was no question in his mind that Kozlov was the one he was looking for, but Jake was heading back to the States without the proof Clements and the others would demand before taking action.

"Don't worry," Geneviève said as if reading his mind. "We'll get him."

Jake kissed her good-bye, leaving unsaid what he was thinking.

As long as he doesn't get us first.

FIFTY

ILYA EXITED THE terminal at Dulles International Airport wearing black jeans and a black leather jacket. Though Kozlov had sent him to America to retrace Boris's tracks and find out what happened to his fellow Triplet, there had been a change of plans while Ilya was forty thousand feet over the Atlantic.

The Russian rented a blue Ford pickup. Though he often mocked America, he'd always longed to experience the freedom of driving a pickup truck around the open roads of the United States. And while Kozlov couldn't have cared less about Ilya's escapist fantasy, he allowed the big goon to rent the F-150 because it was one of the most popular cars in America and would seamlessly blend into the landscape—especially in Virginia farm country.

Though Misha's and Kozlov's anxiety about Jake Keller had initially come from Shadow, their own experience with the CIA paramilitary officer had made them increasingly wary. Despite repeated attempts to kill him, they'd been unable to do so, and instead of retreating, Keller had continued to attack. He still hadn't raised the alarm within CIA about the plan to assassinate the president, but every day the operative remained alive put all their hard work and planning in greater jeopardy. Kozlov wanted the American taken care of.

Now.

Hence Ilya's change of plans while flying to the United States. He spent two hours driving around the capital region behind the wheel of the pickup. He made cover stops at a gas station, a convenience store, and a coffee shop before entering a crowded deli. A table opened up just as he approached, and he quickly devoured the chicken parm sandwich he'd ordered.

The burly Russian returned to the pickup with the small backpack that had been left under the table. He drove another twenty minutes before pulling into a busy highway rest stop and examining its contents. It was first-rate equipment—equal or superior to what he'd used when he was in the Russian military. He holstered the suppressed pistol but left the rest of the gear safely in the pack.

It was just after seven p.m. when he turned onto a dirt road in northern Virginia. The small commercial farm would probably be busy in the summer, but it was deserted in late January. Ilya killed the truck's headlights and drove half a mile over the rutted track until he reached a set of GPS coordinates that had been left on a note in the backpack. He parked the truck, donned a black watch cap and winter gloves, and after a forty-minute walk through the woods, peered through a compact night vision scope.

All was quiet inside the carriage house.

Ilya advanced to within a hundred yards and waited. The ground was damp underfoot and the air smelled of earth and pine, much like the farm he'd grown up on outside Rostov Veliky. Ilya slowed his breathing, relaxed his body, and waited. Patience had never been his forte, but he remained still for nearly an hour. At one point a deer approached within twenty yards of his position and Ilya slowly drew his pistol. He pointed it at the deer, tempted to test his skill, but was interrupted by a phone vibrating in his pocket. Ilya holstered the weapon and answered the call.

"He's not here," he said in Russian.

"He will be," said Kozlov. *"I sent Grigory to Le Chabichou this morning with three Bratva, but Keller and the girl slipped away."*

"You still want me to look for Boris?"

"Take care of Keller first. Do you have what you need?"

"Oh, yes. I will leave a very nice present for him."

Ilya ended the call, picked up the backpack, and set out for the carriage house.

FIFTY-ONE

JAKE'S TRIP TO France had been a resounding success, both personally and professionally, but knowing Kozlov's name still wasn't enough to take him down. Jake needed to understand why the oligarch was killing paramilitary officers. Was he calling the shots, or were his orders coming from his friend the Russian president? Most importantly, Jake needed to root out the mole inside the Agency.

Jake needed something to tie all of the unknowns together.

"I need to see Mike Walker's file," he said into the phone.

"Ted will know," Clements reminded him.

"Ted already knows more than he's letting on."

"All right," said Clements, *"but you'll have to read it in my office."*

Though the two men kept their friendship a secret, some risks needed to be taken.

SO MANY OF CIA's senior executives sat on the seventh floor of the old headquarters building at Langley that the "Seventh Floor" had

---

become synonymous with the Agency's leadership. The entire floor was a secure compartmentalized information facility, colloquially known as a SCIF, which meant Jake had to leave his phone and other electronics with the security officers at the entrance. Several pairs of eyes watched his unfamiliar face as he walked the long hallway to Clements's office.

The whole place gave Jake the creeps.

He entered Clements's inner office and closed the door. The associate director's assistant looked at her boss's schedule and noted that the intense-looking young man in the blue jeans wasn't on the calendar, but the assistant had worked at CIA long enough to know that if she didn't know, it was because she didn't need to know.

"Just give me a minute," Clements said to Jake as he finished typing an email.

Jake sighed.

"I'm sorry," said Clements, still typing and staring at his computer screen. "Is national security interfering with your unsanctioned witch hunt?"

"I'm on leave."

"And yet here you are on the Seventh Floor, with your hair dyed blond, using my time and Agency resources."

Clements sent the message and smiled at Jake.

"Now, what can I do for you?"

"Michael Walker, likely MIA or KIA last year."

"Ah, yes. The paramilitary officer who went to Libya by himself."

"On Agency business, just like I did."

"Maybe Ted was trying to get rid of both of you," Clements joked.

But Jake wasn't laughing.

"Pull up a chair," Clements said as he started typing again.

Jake slid behind the desk and looked at Walker's photo.

"I've met this guy somewhere."

"You overlapped in the Special Activities Center."

Jake shook his head.

"Maybe it will come to you when you read the file."

Walker had enlisted in the navy at eighteen and tried out for the SEAL teams the following year. He'd been injured during training but was rolled back through BUD/S and graduated with the following class. After qualification training and assignment to his team, he'd attended sniper school, SERE school, and advanced close-quarters-combat school.

Walker had served three deployments to Iraq and four deployments to Afghanistan before trying out for, and being accepted to, SEAL Team Six. He served two years on the black side, doing advance force operations work before joining the Agency.

Walker had initially come to CIA as a contractor based in the National Capital Region and had been assigned to a group that handled renditions—and not just routine renditions, if there was such a thing, but the blackest of black renditions: politically connected persons, foreign agents with diplomatic immunity, American citizens fighting overseas against their countrymen.

Walker was viewed as an immediate asset to the team: highly skilled, very aggressive, and willing to take exceptional risks to accomplish the mission. One former team leader said the former SEAL seemed to thrive on the action, getting better with each mission. After two years, he was given his last assignment based in London, where he worked as a singleton, doing sensitive solo operations in denied areas. It didn't state it specifically in the file, but Jake knew how to read between the lines—Walker was a killing machine.

"Shit," Jake said. "Now I know why Ted flagged the file."

Clements raised his eyebrows.

Jake pointed to a paragraph onscreen: *Three years ago, the Office of the Inspector General of the Intelligence Community opened an investigation into allegations that Walker had conducted three murders-for-hire while still a contractor at CIA.*

"Shit indeed," said Clements. He leaned back in his chair and looked at the ceiling.

"It gets better," Jake said as he continued reading. "All three victims were Russian."

"What were the results of the investigation?"

"'Inconclusive,'" Jake said. "Walker disappeared two weeks after it was opened."

"Think he skipped town?"

"Or the Russians had him killed," said Jake. "By the way, I went back to France. There was definitely a bomb on the plane, and I think I know who planted it."

"Let me guess . . . A Russian?"

"Nikolai Kozlov, currently of London, England. Ex-GRU, billionaire, friend of the Russian president." Jake looked at Clements's keyboard. "Do you mind if I—"

"Sorry, Jake. Only one top secret security violation per visit. Besides, Kozlov's file is probably flagged too. If you're right about Russia, and if you're right about a mole inside the Agency, then you don't want them to know what you know. It's too early in the game."

Jake nodded. He was still staring at Walker's file. "So Walker killed three of Kozlov's goons and Kozlov retaliated by killing Walker."

"And if Kozlov believed his men were killed on orders from the Agency, then Kozlov might have started assassinating CIA officers as payback."

"Exactly," said Jake.

"That would require someone inside the Agency to feed Kozlov names and operational details."

"Which is what I've been saying all along."

"Yes, but it sounds more credible when I say it."

Jake smirked.

"Your paranoia may be less acute than I'd initially feared," concluded Clements. "The problem is, you still don't have any proof, just a lot of suppositions. Let me tell you how this is going to go down. Thirty seconds or so after I close Walker's file, Ted will get an email letting him know I accessed it. Don't be surprised if you're 'randomly selected' to go on the box in the next few days. You should be prepared for Walker's name to come up."

Jake nodded. Like all operations officers, he'd been trained to beat a lie detector, but the Agency's polygraph examiners were the ones who'd taught him how. They'd know all his tricks.

It was with that distinctly unpleasant experience on his mind that Jake retrieved his cell phone and left the building. It was close to eight p.m., a light rain was falling, and he was parked about as far from the original headquarters building as was physically possible.

"Hey!" a woman's voice called out.

He turned to see Christine Kirby jogging toward him from the new headquarters building.

"What a coincidence," Jake said, not for an instant believing that it was.

"What are you doing here?" she said with a smile.

"Just had to drop something off in the production office. How about you?"

"East Asia briefing."

Kirby opened an umbrella and nudged up against Jake so they could both fit underneath.

"You were going to call me," she said.

"I didn't think you were serious."

"You have no idea how serious I am."

Jake considered telling her that he was madly in love with some-one else, but the less anyone at the Agency knew about Geneviève, the better.

"I've been out of town," he said.

Kirby opened the door to her car.

"You're not out of town now. How about dinner?"

Jake smiled at her.

"Come on," she said. "You can fill me in."

FIFTY-TWO

THEY ATE AT Aracosia in McLean. It was an Afghan restaurant close to CIA headquarters, and though the Agency employees who dined there prided themselves on being objective, most secretly believed that at least half the waiters were not only feeding their customers but feeding the Taliban scraps of Agency gossip as well.

But national security be damned, the food was just too good to pass up.

Jake and Kirby were seated by a window in the back of the elegant dining room. She let her strawberry blond hair down.

"Did you dye your hair?" she said.

"It's from the chlorine," Jake lied. "I've been swimming a lot since the crash to get my body back in shape."

"Mission accomplished," she said as she gave him a once over. "What else are you doing on your 'leave of absence'?"

"I had some unfinished business to take care of."

"Personal or professional?"

"Personal, but it's finished now."

Kirby's mischievous smile reappeared and they spent the next hour eating and catching up on people they knew in common. They had worked together in London and Kirby was one of the few people in the Agency who'd known Jake when he was still Zac Miller. Their conversation was interrupted a few times by her incoming emails but that was nothing unusual for people in their line of work. They'd just finished their main courses when Christine finally gave him the opening he'd been waiting for.

"How are you feeling after your latest brush with death?" she asked.

"Luckier than most," said Jake. "We've lost a lot of officers in the past two years."

Kirby reached across the table and took his hand firmly in her own, but for once she wasn't flirting and she wasn't being suggestive; she was just being compassionate.

"It's a hard job. You have to do distasteful things to prevent much worse things. I know it takes a toll—and it's cost you more than most. You're the best paramilitary officer I've ever seen and you've made a huge impact, but there's no shame in walking away. If this isn't what you want, you can leave now and still have a normal life."

She squeezed his hand and let it go.

"Thanks, Christine. Did you know any of the officers who died last year—"

Her phone vibrated on the table.

"Sorry," she said. She glanced at an Afghan busboy hovering nearby and walked outside to take the call.

As Graves's deputy, she would have visibility into operations, relationships, and personnel issues like few others. She could be a valuable ally if Jake could get her to open up, but he was walking a tightrope. Christine was fiercely loyal to Ted Graves. He'd brought her with him from when he was running operations in London to his current role as chief of the Special Activities Center.

She was back two minutes later, but she didn't sit down.

"There's a situation," she said. "I have to go back to headquarters."

"Any excuse to stick me with the check," Jake said with a smile.

She smiled back. "You can stick it to me next time."

THE TIMING OF Christine's call to return to headquarters had sabotaged Jake's effort to ask her about Mike Walker and the other dead PMOOs, and Jake drove home wondering if maybe someone at the Agency had been eavesdropping on their conversation. It wouldn't have taken more than a few seconds to activate the microphone on her work phone.

Jake killed the Tahoe's headlights and turned slowly onto the farm's driveway. He slow-rolled across the gravel with his windows open, scanning the fields on either side and listening for anything out of the ordinary. It was his first time back to the carriage house since identifying Kozlov in Courchevel, and the vast resources at the billionaire's disposal and his demonstrated willingness to use them to end Jake's life left no doubt about the seriousness of the threat posed by the Russian oligarch. The fact that someone inside the Agency was helping him only made the danger more real.

Jake had always taken his security seriously while abroad because it was essential to completing the mission. The logic was simple: If he was captured or killed, the bad guys won. But now, for the first time in years, Jake had something to live for besides the mission or—more precisely—someone to live for. Love was a powerful force and Jake hadn't realized how severely its absence had affected him.

He parked inside the barn, drew his HK VP9 pistol from its holster, and ducked into the woods to approach the carriage house on foot. He crouched around the perimeter, examined the locks, and verified that the alarm was still on. Everything was as he'd left it.

Jake entered through a back door, punched his code into the alarm panel, and went straight to the gun safe in his bedroom.

He wasn't there to stay.

Jake removed a bug-out bag. He'd preloaded the heavy nylon duffel with weapons, cash, body armor, false identities, drop phones, and other essentials. He filled a second bag with clothes and hauled them both into the kitchen.

His laptop was charging on the counter.

Though modern intelligence work relied heavily upon technology, Jake had learned never to rely on a single piece of hardware. More than once he'd been stripped of everything he possessed—usually while naked, bloodied, and given up for dead. Now he was caught in a mess involving Russia and CIA, and he needed to upload his data to the cloud, where he could access it from anywhere, just as if he were going into the field.

Jake opened the laptop and pressed the power button. He'd owned the computer for a couple of years, and there was always a delay of a second or two before the screen lit up. It was something to do with something he knew nothing about, but in that second or two, he noticed a tiny stainless steel machine screw, no more than an eighth of an inch across and an eighth of an inch deep, lying on the counter next to the computer.

It was a tiny little thing, and if the overhead recessed lights hadn't been on, he probably wouldn't have seen it at all, but the owners of the farm had installed a dozen of the high-output lights—along with the thick granite countertops and the six-burner gas stove—when they'd redone the kitchen.

Jake dove for the floor.

FIFTY-THREE

THE EXPLOSION was deafening.

Debris rained down across the kitchen: broken wall-board, splintered wood, fragments of glass and pottery. Bare electrical wires and mangled pipes hung from the damaged walls and ceiling. Somewhere, in another part of the carriage house, a smoke alarm wailed.

Jake rose up on one elbow, coughing and covered in dust. He felt as if someone had dropped a piano on his chest.

A few of the recessed lights had survived the blast. They lit the room through a thick cloud of pulverized drywall that hovered in the air like early-morning fog.

Jake put a hand on the countertop and pulled himself upright. The ringing in his ears was affecting not only his hearing but also his balance.

He looked around. Shards of glass and bits of ceramics tumbled from shelves. Cabinet doors hung from their hinges at odd angles. The air smelled of burnt plastic, charred wood, and crushed wall-board. The countertops were blanketed in rubble.

The countertops, Jake thought.

The thick granite had saved his life, directing the blast up and out—and over his head. Jake had spent a great deal of time studying improvised explosive devices and was well-acquainted with the concept of a laptop computer bomb. Just a few months earlier, he'd been in Somalia and seen the ten-foot hole a similar device had blown through the side of a commercial airliner. The bomber had meant it as an act of terror, seeking to take down the plane and indiscriminately kill everyone on board, but that wasn't the case here. The device that had nearly killed Jake was known as a victim-operated IED.

It was meant to kill the user.

Jake had become an expert in the design, assembly, and deployment of similar devices during his time in the Horn of Africa. It had been a difficult mission, filled with treachery, darkness, and danger, but without the experience he'd gained there, a loose screw on the countertop wouldn't have meant much to him.

Granite countertops just made the must-have list for his next home.

Jake dusted himself off and looked at the two go bags. They were covered in fragments of everything, but intact. He lifted one in each hand and headed for the barn, eager to put some distance between himself and the house in case Kozlov's goons returned to confirm his death.

He'd just loaded both bags into the back of the silver Tahoe when he heard the sirens.

Lots of sirens.

The alarm system . . . He'd barely noticed it through the ringing in his ears.

Two large fire engines turned down the driveway, their red-and-white emergency lights lighting up the property in every direction.

Jake walked to the driveway and flagged down the lead truck. A lieutenant riding shotgun jumped down, wearing his thick turnout coat and helmet. Jake stood there in the light rain and explained that he'd been broiling a steak in the oven with the music blasting and hadn't heard the smoke detector that was hardwired to the alarm system. He apologized for the callout on the wet January night, but the firefighters had been through false alarms before and were glad that no one was injured and no damage had occurred. They turned their engines around at the barn and had just turned onto the county road when a white Ford Explorer turned down the driveway and stopped in front of Jake.

"Mr. Keller," said Detective Rooney, "why am I not surprised?"

"False alarm," said Jake.

The cop switched on his vehicle's high-intensity spotlight and aimed it at the house.

"You always leave the windows open in the rain?"

"Just airing the place out," said Jake.

Rooney radioed his status back to the county dispatcher and stepped out of the truck. Even in his mid-forties, the detective looked fit and every inch a former Marine.

"How about we take a look?" he said, removing a flashlight from his belt.

Jake started walking.

The beam of Rooney's light washed over the house and it soon became evident that the windows were not open. Half a dozen of them had been blown clear out of the frames.

Jake looked at Rooney. The cop's jacket was open, his hand resting on his gun. Though Jake knew at least a dozen ways to disarm and disable a man, striking a cop was a line Jake would never cross. His mission was to protect American citizens—the same as Rooney's—even if the detective didn't know it.

"You've got nothing to fear from me, Detective," Jake said.

Something registered in the detective's mind as he stared at Jake. Whether he recognized a kindred spirit or his instincts told him that Jake was a man he could trust, Rooney seemed to relax a little. He took his hand off his gun, but left his jacket open.

"I'll show you around," Jake said.

The detective followed him into the house, past the blown-out windows, over the debris field in the hallway, and into the kitchen. He looked around for a few seconds.

"So what happened here?" asked Rooney. "Gas leak?"

It was a test. The veteran officer had spotted the epicenter of the blast the second he'd walked in. The starburst pattern on the countertop was hard to miss and looked nothing like the damage one would expect from a gas leak.

Jake shook his head.

"Any theories?" Rooney said.

Jake shrugged.

"Is your hair blond?" the cop asked.

"My girlfriend did it," said Jake.

Rooney spent a few minutes walking through the house, shining his flashlight in every room. He returned to the kitchen holding a framed eight-by-ten-inch photograph of a dramatic mountain range. The glass had cracked when it had been knocked off the wall.

"You take this?"

Jake nodded. "About a year and a half ago."

Rooney pulled out one of the dust-covered chairs and sat down. He gestured for Jake to do the same.

"Beautiful photo," said the cop. "Reminds me of a place I visited a long time ago when I was a newly minted Marine E-5. I was in 1st Fleet Anti-Terrorism Security Team. We called ourselves 'First FAST Company.' We trained in hostage rescue, critical installation defense—stuff like that. We were ready to go, anywhere, anytime, at the drop of a hat."

Jake didn't want to hear the story. He was worried that whoever had planted the bomb might return to finish the job, but he didn't want to upset the cop because Rooney could make Jake's life distinctly unpleasant—especially if he ever found the dead Russian Jake had buried on the property.

Jake pulled out a debris-covered chair and sat down diagonally from the detective, hoping Rooney could cover one half of the house if it became necessary.

"October of 2000," the detective continued, "the hat drops. We get the call. *'Chambers Field, two hours, bring your desert gear.'* We load into two C-17s and we're gone: eighteen hours in the air, lying on the cargo floor or sitting in webbed seats hanging from the walls with no sound insulation and nothing to eat but MREs—and it was downhill from there. We got our mission brief over the Atlantic: Some jackasses in a speedboat filled with homemade explosives detonated it alongside a U.S. destroyer, blowing a fifty-foot hole in the side of the ship."

Rooney ran his finger through the drywall dust that had settled on the table.

"Do you know the first thing I saw after eighteen hours in the air, wondering what sort of mess we were about to step into? It was the volcanic rim around the city. I'm thinking we're going into the desert to fight al-Qaeda—you know, sand dunes and camels—and then the ramp drops on that flying warehouse and here are these red and gold and gray mountains behind the city."

"Beautiful," Jake said.

"Memorable," Rooney corrected. He pointed to Jake's photo. It was the same mountain range. "Not a lot of tourists in Aden, Yemen, these days, what with the civil war and all."

"It was a work trip."

"Right," said the cop. "'Consulting.' So I figure you're either in some black-side military unit or Other Government Agency, but all the photos like this that I have are of groups of guys. Military units work as teams, value the team, so I'm going with Other Government Agency, probably CIA, because you're all alone."

"No comment," Jake said.

"A bullshitter would have said yes."

Jake shrugged.

"Let's try this again," said Rooney. "What happened here?"

Jake smiled. "My laptop overheated."

The cop chuckled as he took in the devastation. "That's like saying Chernobyl overheated."

"It's related to my work," Jake said.

"And your pickup in the ditch?"

"Also related."

"Two attempted homicides in Prince William County are my responsibility. I can't look the other way."

"I wouldn't expect you to . . ."

"But?"

Jake smiled. "I would ask that you keep my name out of the press. Otherwise, my operation, my career, and probably my life are over."

The cop nodded. "Media blackouts I can do. They're no friend to the police."

"And maybe keep it off the radio?"

"They're encrypted," said Rooney.

"Might not matter in this case," said Jake. GRU or the Agency could crack almost anything.

The police officer didn't try to hide his surprise. Cracking encrypted communications implied a level of sophistication the county police did not usually encounter. It implied a nation-state was involved.

"Maybe we should call the FBI," said Rooney. "Attempted murder of a federal agent is a federal crime."

"But I'm not a federal agent . . ."

"Right . . ."

"Be careful, Detective."

"Is that a threat?"

"It's the exact opposite. It's a friendly warning. You are wading into very dangerous waters."

"I'm getting that sense."

Jake walked Rooney to his vehicle. The cop took a hard look around the expansive property.

"I'm guessing someone didn't just walk in and plant that thing. They were probably observing you for a while from the fields or the woods. I'll get a K-9 search team out here to search the property and see if they find any traces of human presence . . ."

"That's really not necessary," Jake said.

"Yes, it is," said Rooney. "And I don't care who it is. If someone commits a felony in my county, they're going down."

FIFTY-FOUR

JAKE WAS LONG gone before the K-9 team arrived. There was nothing for him to do at the farm except hope that he'd buried the dead Russian far enough away and deep enough underground that the dogs would never pick up the scent; but hope was not a strategy, and every instinct Jake possessed told him that the clock was ticking on something big. Kozlov was getting more desperate and going to more extreme measures. Jake still didn't know why the Russian was trying to kill him, but he would as soon as he uncovered the link between Kozlov and the Agency.

Jake checked in to a Manassas, Virginia, hotel room using a fake identity. It wasn't one of his CIA covers either—it was one he'd created on his own after learning the tricks of the trade. He hauled his bags to his room and a crippling wave of exhaustion hit him as the adrenaline left his bloodstream and his blood sugar level crashed. But Jake did not sleep. There was simply too much to do. He took a long shower, dyed his hair back to its normal dark brown, and sat down on his bed with a sandwich, a six-pack of Red Bull, and a new laptop computer.

Something about Mike Walker wasn't adding up.

Jake had been operating under the assumption that Walker had begun freelancing while still at CIA, was at some point hired to kill three of Kozlov's goons, and was then killed by Kozlov once the oligarch identified Walker as the shooter.

But walking through his theory step by step led Jake to a gaping hole: If Kozlov killed Walker, then started killing Agency paramilitary officers as revenge for what the oligarch assumed was a CIA mission, how did Kozlov get the detailed operational intel that had enabled the assassinations in Syria and the Central African Republic, and the multiple attempts on Jake's life?

There was no link to CIA.

Jake had memorized the names of the dead Russian gangsters in Clements's office when they'd read Walker's file, and he began searching open-source media on the internet for anything he could about the brazen hits—though *mafiya* murders were routine, precision sniper shots were not. Jake was two hours into his research when his secure cell phone rang.

It was Geneviève.

He'd called her after the explosion but had gotten her voice mail. He explained about the blast at the carriage house and, after confirming several times that he was unharmed, told her he loved her.

He could feel her smile through the phone.

"I love you too," she said. "I also have some news for you."

"Good news?"

"Of sorts. You were right about the object you saw in the snow after the plane crash."

"It was a cellular receiver?" Jake said.

"Yes, which is clever, because no one would use a cellular trigger to take down an aircraft since they only work a few thousand feet from the ground."

"Unless the cell towers are located on the mountain peaks—"

"And you're flying in the valley below them," added Geneviève.

Jake smiled. They were already finishing each other's sentences.

Geneviève continued. "The aviation safety bureau's preliminary report says the black box showed the plane behaving erratically at 16:02:25, so that was probably the time of the explosion."

"Were there any cellular calls made in the area at 16:02?"

"One hundred twelve," said Geneviève.

Jake cursed, but she talked right over him. "One hundred eleven of the calls lasted between thirty seconds and two hours. The remaining call lasted two seconds and the receiving number was located roughly four kilometers east of Moûtiers, in the middle of a valley."

"Or the middle of the sky," Jake said. "What about the number that initiated the call?"

"A disposable phone, unfortunately, but the call was made from a mountaintop to the south. They probably had someone there with a telescope and a cell phone who triggered the bomb when they saw your plane's tail number."

"Thanks, Geneviève, and thanks for believing in me. Everyone else thought I was paranoid when I told them the crash wasn't an accident."

"You're not paranoid," she said, "and I've always believed in you."

"I need to go, babe," Jake said. He had an appointment with Clements in a few minutes.

"Wait!" she said. "There's one more thing. It took me forever to dig through the paperwork, but one of Kozlov's shell companies owns a black Airbus Helicopter H-135 like the one you described."

"Then that seals it."

JAKE AND CLEMENTS were walking through Bluemont Park in Arlington.

"I was wrong about Walker," said Jake.

"How so?"

"The men he killed weren't part of Kozlov's crew. They were members of the Chechen mob—Kozlov's main rival."

"So why did Kozlov kill Walker if it wasn't for revenge?"

"Kozlov didn't kill Walker," Jake said.

Clements looked expectantly at his protégé.

Jake continued. "After Walker left the SEALs, he finished his Agency training and started doing renditions. Two years later, he transferred to London to work as a singleton. A year after that, the first Chechen mobster was killed. A month after that, the second one went down. Two weeks later, the third man was killed—all from long-range rifle shots."

"And Walker was a trained sniper . . ."

"Walker was working for Kozlov, not against him."

"How did no one at the Agency figure this out?"

"Someone did figure it out."

"It wasn't in the report."

"Whoever discovered it held it back to blackmail Walker into doing their dirty work."

"You're saying someone inside the Agency discovered what Walker was up to, but instead of turning him in, they used him to kill Agency paramilitary officers?"

"Yes. Someone inside CIA is not only feeding the Russians information but calling the shots as well."

"That's a bold accusation."

"It gets worse. GRU lives for situations like this. If they're running this operation and someone inside the Agency is directing the killings of CIA officers, then the Russians are probably using it to blackmail the Agency employee. There is a very real possibility that the Russians now have a direct line of sight into all of our paramilitary operations."

"If you're right," said Clements, "and I'm still not convinced . . . why would someone inside the Agency be trying to kill you? The other paramilitary officers were all deployed when they died."

"The Agency mole knew I was going to Courchevel, knew Kozlov was there, and thought I was onto them."

The two men walked across the park's rolling hills. Clements listened intently as Jake explained Geneviève's revelations about the bomb on the plane and Kozlov's black helicopter.

"What I still can't get my head around," said Clements, "is who inside the Agency would be so furious with specific paramilitary officers that he'd want them dead?"

Jake's phone started ringing. He pulled it from his pocket and looked at the caller ID.

It was Ted Graves.

FIFTY-FIVE

T AKE A SEAT," said Graves. He closed his office door behind him. "You missed your check-in, again."

"I saw Christine yesterday."

"Remind me who the chief of center is?"

"You, Ted."

"That's right," said Graves. "I thought we covered this last time. You're supposed to check in with me, and you've done a piss-poor job of it."

"Well, now you're up to speed."

"Am I?" said Graves. "Then why did I get a call an hour ago from the Prince William County Police Department?"

Jake's gut tightened.

"It was a detective," said Graves. "He asked if I knew how to get in touch with you. He said he wanted to ask you some questions . . . Of course, I could neither confirm nor deny that you work here."

"Of course."

"So, given that Agency regulations specifically prohibit disclosing that you work here, how the fuck does he know what you do, who I am, and why is he calling?"

"There was an incident."

"Did you tell him you worked for CIA?"

"Absolutely not."

"Did you insinuate? Did you hint? Don't play word games with me, Keller."

"He's a detective," said Jake. "On my wall was a picture from Yemen. He'd deployed there as a Marine and put two and two together."

"I should've hired this guy instead of you. He knows what's going on and keeps me in the loop."

"Are we finished?" Jake asked.

"Not even close. Tell me about the 'incident.'"

"My laptop overheated. It set off the smoke detector and the cop showed up with the fire department."

"Right," said Graves, "so this detective—this highly competent investigator who deduced in no time at all that you work in covert operations for the nation's lead intelligence-gathering agency—decided to call CIA headquarters and locate the chief of the Special Activities Center because your laptop overheated?"

"Overheated-slash-exploded."

Graves leaned forward in his chair. "Do you think it's related to the plane crash?"

"Do you?"

"I might, if I knew why you were flying all over Europe."

"Who says I am?"

"Don't insult me, Keller. It's my job to know where every one of my officers is at every moment."

The two men studied each other before Graves spoke again.

"Keep the local police out of this. I'll assign a couple of protective agents to you."

"I'm perfectly capable of protecting myself."

"Do you know who's behind it?"

"I've got some ideas."

"I'm going to take a personal interest in this."

"I feel safer already."

The two men walked to the lobby and waited in silence until the elevator arrived.

"Speaking of traipsing across Europe," said Graves, "how is Peter Clements these days?"

The elevator door opened and Jake stepped inside without saying a word.

Graves's eyes bored into Jake. "Send him my regards."

FIFTY-SIX

TED SENDS his regards."

"*I feel warm all over,*" said Clements. "*He and I haven't spoken since he maneuvered behind my back to force me out as London chief of station.*"

"You landed on your feet," Jake said. He'd called his mentor the moment he'd left Graves's office.

"*Thanks to you,*" said Clements.

Jake had restored Clements's reputation in short order by salvaging a mission gone bad. The two men had had each other's backs ever since.

Clements continued. "*By the way, I pulled Nikolai Kozlov's file after our last call. Mike Walker filed a contact report on him after they met at a diplomatic party.*"

"When?"

"*In London, six months before the first killing.*"

"Why would Walker file a contact report tying him to Kozlov?"

"*Maybe it was their first meeting, before Walker turned.*"

"But it wasn't in Walker's file," Jake said, "which means it was deleted by someone who had access to Walker's file, but not Kozlov's—maybe someone inside Special Activities."

"Many people would have access to one and not the other, not just those inside the Special Activities Center. I have to go now, the director is calling me."

"Thanks, Peter."

Jake was deep in thought as he drove back to his hotel. Clements was right: The contact report had probably been from an early meeting between Walker and Kozlov, before their relationship had taken a sinister turn. The two men had undoubtedly met again while Walker was still at CIA, but Clements hadn't mentioned any other contact reports in Kozlov's file.

But that was just CIA. Every intelligence agency in the world filed contact reports.

Jake used his secure phone to dial another number.

"Hunter," said the man.

"Ian, it's Jake Keller, Sir James's friend—"

"Oh, I won't forget you, mate. You made quite a grand exit, you did, blasting that gun around Sloane Square like you'd just landed at Normandy. You still wading through that giant bog of shit?"

"Neck-deep," said Jake. "I was wondering if you could do me another favor."

"Sir James's credit never runs out with me. What's your pleasure?"

It took Jake two minutes to explain what he needed and another minute for Hunter to catch his breath.

"Maybe you'd like a date with the queen while you're at it? Sir James will have to call in a few favors for this one."

"Thanks, Ian."

Hunter called back eight hours later.

"I got what you need."

"And?" said Jake.

"Not over the phone—not this."

JAKE CAUGHT THE last red-eye flight to London and was at the Security Service's headquarters by eleven the next morning. Hunter escorted him into Thames House through the back entrance on Thorney Street and into a glass-walled conference room on the fourth floor. The MI5 officer pressed a button on the table and the glass walls turned opaque.

He sat opposite Jake at the long wood table.

"Your Mr. Kozlov gets around," said Hunter. "We got twenty-eight contact reports on that bugger, including three I think you're going to care about. Eighteen months ago, Lithuanian embassy, Nikolai Kozlov, Michael Walker, and a man who introduced himself as a USAID official with the U.S. embassy."

"An intelligence officer, most likely."

"You think?" Hunter deadpanned. "Second report, Walker and Kozlov were spotted again in London but contact was not made by our agent due to circumstances outside his control. Third report, eight months after the last one. Another one of our chaps ran into Kozlov at a fancy restaurant. He was eating dinner with a few other Russian expats. One of the guests introduced himself as 'Mikhail' but our guy thought he recognized him. He assigned a fifty percent probability that it was your boy Walker. The file said that this was communicated to MI6, who communicated it to CIA."

"Does it say who at CIA?"

"It does not."

Jake take took a deep breath and exhaled loudly.

"Bad news?" said Hunter.

"It's better that I know, but it would have been better if it had never happened."

"Like finding your wife in bed with the plumber," said Hunter. "Bloody wench."

"It means someone inside the Agency is manipulating contact reports."

"So you got a former agent working for a Russian crime boss and a mole inside the Agency . . . A fucking disaster, that is."

Jake nodded. "Any luck with the CCTV?"

"Unless Mr. Walker has an identical twin, he is very much alive and back in London."

Hunter pushed another button and a flat-screen monitor lowered from the ceiling. A dozen images of Walker appeared on the screen—all with date stamps from the past six months.

"Can you map the locations?" Jake asked.

"Brilliant," said Hunter. "Never would have thought of that."

The next slide was a map of London with red flags where Walker had been sighted. There was a single flag at Heathrow, but the rest were in central London.

"What's that area?" Jake gestured to the largest cluster of flags.

"Oh, that?" Hunter grimaced. "That's Buckingham Palace."

FIFTY-SEVEN

KOZLOV WAS IN the chalet's living room, playing solo chess. The set had been handcrafted in 1897 by Carl Fabergé for Czar Nicholas II, and the oligarch wiped his fingertips on a linen cloth before moving each piece.

"Someone at CIA accessed our files," said Walker. "Shadow thinks Keller was behind it."

"Are you concerned?"

"Not in the slightest."

Walker plopped down on the sofa across from Kozlov and picked up the opposing king. He hefted it in his palm, noting the weight of the gold-and-jeweled piece.

"Why do you have such a hard-on for the president anyway?" Walker continued. "Do you really need more money?"

Kozlov took the chess piece, spent two minutes meticulously cleaning it with the linen cloth, and placed it back on the board exactly where it had been.

"Do you like sports, Misha?" said the oligarch.

"I'm a man, aren't I?"

"Do you like to lose?"

"A famous American football coach once said, 'Show me a good loser and I'll show you a loser.'"

"Tell me, how does one determine the winner of a sporting contest?"

"It depends on the sport, but it's usually whoever has the highest score."

"Exactly. I want for nothing, but for men such as myself, money is not for things. It is how we keep score. The yachts, the jets, the balances in the offshore bank accounts. They are my trophies."

The oligarch stood and walked to the window. The midday sun shone brilliantly on the snow-covered Alps.

"Did I tell you I'm supposed to have dinner with the president that night?" said Kozlov. "I've been invited to the state dinner at Buckingham Palace."

"Don't pack your tux. The guest of honor is going to be dead."

Kozlov smirked. Walker was capable but cocky. Sometimes Kozlov wondered if he'd put too much faith in the former SEAL's abilities. Misha would rather die trying than admit he couldn't handle something on his own.

"When do you leave for London?"

"Two hours," said Walker.

Kozlov nodded, then picked up the phone and paged Grigory over the chalet's intercom system.

"Grigory is going with you."

"No, he's not," said Walker.

"Excuse me?"

"Those idiots screw up everything they touch. My entire escape plan is built around melting into the population after the shooting.

How am I going to do that with that ape in tow? I'll tell you what: You handle strategy, let me handle tactics."

"Might your ego be clouding your judgment? You once told me that every sniper has someone to pull security."

Grigory emerged from the elevator wearing black shorts and a sleeveless black shirt that was soaked through with sweat. Veins bulged from his thick arms from lifting weights in the gym. Though the bandage was gone, his face was still bruised from when Walker had shattered his nose in the disco.

"You're going with Misha for a few days," said Kozlov.

"He's a thick-skulled brawler who barely speaks English," said Walker, gesturing dismissively at the larger man.

"Go fucking yourself!" yelled Grigory.

"You see what I mean?"

Kozlov inserted himself between the two men. "The time for subtlety is over. I don't care if you have to kill Keller in his bed—"

"He doesn't have a bed," said Walker. "He's staying in a hotel because these Neanderthals blew it up."

"Enough!" Kozlov shouted. His eyes hardened. His voice lowered. "Grigory is going to London, Misha. The only question is, are you?"

"You can't do this without me, Nikolai."

"You also told me to always have a backup plan, did you not?"

"Fine. I'll bring the ape."

"And you will be paid once Keller and Shadow are both dead."

"That wasn't our deal."

"It's what's necessary. I do not like loose ends."

"Killing Shadow is a bad idea. Sources take precautions."

"Losing your nerve, Misha? I am feeling even better about my decision to have Grigory accompany you—in case you should have a debilitating pang of conscience at the last minute."

"The only thing I'm worried about is blowback, but it's your call. Consider it done. The President, Keller, and Shadow, all dead."

Walker left the room and headed downstairs. Nadia was sitting on the steps one level down. She didn't look up. She was anxious, wringing her hands and tapping her foot on the step. She'd heard the men yelling at one another.

"It's OK," said Walker.

"I don't like conflict." Her voice trembled as she spoke. "My parents were both heavy drinkers and they would fight about anything. They would scream and smash things in our little apartment. I used to turn up my radio and hide under my pillows, but I heard every word."

"It was just a disagreement."

"About killing someone?"

"The less you know, the better."

"You told me once that you needed Nikolai's protection because of your past."

"Yeah . . . well . . . there are a lot of moving parts right now."

Nadia rose to her feet and looked Walker in the eyes. He gently brushed the hair from her face. She clasped his face with both hands and pulled him toward her. They kissed gently at first, then passionately, then greedily, as if they both recognized that nothing would ever be the same, but were unwilling to let the moment slip by yet again.

Kozlov's voice boomed over the intercom.

"The helicopter will be at the Altiport in twenty minutes."

Neither one flinched. When they finally took a breath, Nadia was grinning like a girl who'd just kissed her first boy. Walker leaned in and kissed her again.

"Come find me when you're back," she said.

Walker nodded. "Just stay away from Grigory until we leave."

———

THE BIG RUSSIAN sneered as Walker cinched his seat belt and slid the helicopter's side door closed. They were seated facing each other in the passenger compartment. Both were wearing noise-canceling headsets that were jacked into the intercom system.

"Chambéry in twenty minutes," the former Russian air force pilot said. The helo climbed from the Altiport as the mountain dropped away below, and they were soon cruising through a cloudless blue sky two thousand feet above the jagged mountain peaks.

Walker unscrewed the lid on a bottle of celery-and-ginger juice the chef had made for him and took a sip.

Grigory looked contemptuously at the green liquid.

"Don't drink too much of that," he said over the intercom. *"You might wet your panties."*

Grigory laughed at his juvenile joke as the helicopter flew through some light turbulence. The warmer air on the sunlit side of the mountain was mixing with the cooler air on the shaded side, and it caused Walker to spill a few drops of the green juice on the helicopter's custom-designed Hermès leather interior.

"Nikolai will have your ass for that," said Grigory, grinning from ear to ear.

Walker looked down at the juice bottle. There was half a liter left.

He threw it in Grigory's face.

"You f—"

The Russian's exclamation of displeasure was drowned out by the whine of the engines and the thrum of the rotors as Walker slid open the side door. Wind whipped through the cabin like a tornado.

Walker hurled a punch into the Russian's already broken nose. Blood and tears mixed on his face as the big man yelled in pain. Walker reached across the cabin with both hands, grabbed Grigory by his stupid black jacket, and yanked him toward the open door. The big Russian might not have been a chess grand master, but he had nearly made the country's Olympic wrestling team. If he knew anything, it was how to break a hold. Grigory swept his arm up over Walker's, rolled forward, and used his fifty-pound weight advantage to break the American's grip on his favorite leather jacket.

But the former Navy SEAL and CIA paramilitary officer had not just expected the move, he'd invited it. He pulled the Russian forward and used the larger man's inertia—and a carefully placed leg—to roll him out the door.

Secured comfortably by his seat belt, Walker leaned out of the helicopter and smiled as he watched Grigory flail helplessly against the force of gravity. The big Russian was probably making 120 miles per hour when he plunged into the snow half a mile from where Keller's plane had crashed a month ago. The body wouldn't be found till spring.

Walker slid the door closed and settled back into the cabin.

The pilot was staring at him.

Walker smiled. "You're missing a headset."

FIFTY-EIGHT

THE REMAINDER OF the trip passed uneventfully.

Walker shook the rain from his brown Barbour jacket, disabled the high-security alarm system, and stepped into the office. Every time he was in London, he wore a hat and gloves, but it wasn't the English weather he was guarding against, it was the ever-present CCTV cameras and the risk that he might leave a stray fingerprint behind. He threw the hat and jacket on a chair, but kept the gloves on as he entered the code that caused the two hydraulic rams to open the hidden door to the "secretary's office" behind the fish tank. Walker climbed onto the casket-sized platform made from four thousand pounds of concrete, lay on his stomach behind the cannon, and snugged his shoulder against the stock.

The president would arrive tomorrow.

Walker pressed a button on the platform and cool winter air rushed in as a pair of electric motors opened the window in front of the cannon. Though the window would be open for only a few seconds before and after the shot, firing through the glass would decrease the accuracy of the round and draw the world's attention as the glass shattered and fragments rained down upon the street below. The retractable pane would give Walker irreplaceable minutes to escape while the authorities searched more obvious locations for the shooter's position.

He looked through the cannon's scope, down Marlborough Road, toward the red-tinted Mall. Stands of plane trees lined both sides of the road, limiting the width of the kill box. Walker would have to acquire the moving limousine on the left side of the intersection and pull the trigger before it reached the right side.

He could do it in his sleep.

WALKER CLOSED the glass.

He opened a foam-lined case containing the cannon shells. Each of the high-explosive armor-piercing 30mm rounds was nearly eight inches long and weighed three-quarters of a pound. He inspected each shell visually, turning it in his gloved hand. Though duds were rare in modern ammunition, he couldn't afford a patch of rust or a loose crimp to jeopardize the entire mission. He needed every component, from the electric primer to the shaped copper penetrator, to perform flawlessly.

He pulled the cannon's bolt rearward to expose the weapon's breech and inserted a shell with his right hand. He pushed the bolt forward and locked it into place.

Walker looked through the scope, panned smoothly across the intersection as if he were tracking the president's limousine, and imagined pulling the trigger.

Even with the fish-tank silencers, the roar would be thunderous.

His hand shot forward, opened the heavy bolt, and ejected the live cannon round as if it had been fired. Walker grabbed a second round with his left hand, reached over the top of the weapon to insert it into the breech, and rammed the bolt home.

Too slow.

He did it again.

He did it with the cannon moving left and he did it with the cannon moving right. He lubricated the bolt and did it twice more. Though Walker never missed, he'd also never gone into the field without a backup plan, so even if the unexpected happened, he could reload the weapon with a second shell, fire at the limousine, and still complete the mission.

By the time he finished practicing, the motion was fluid and his hand was nothing but a blur. He could eject a spent shell, reload a live one, and be back on target in a little over a second and a half. Walker stepped down off the concrete platform and laid three shells—one for the kill and two for insurance—alongside the cannon. The sniper's hide was ready.

It was time to head down to street level and see what the president's advance team was up to.

PUBLISHED ITINERARIES FOR visiting heads of state were intentionally left vague until the last minute, and diplomatic protocols often weren't finalized until the incoming flight touched down. Armies of assistants spent countless hours negotiating over which dignitary would stand where or who would take the first question at a joint press conference. Every detail was covered, from who rode which elevator to what refreshments would be served. No one wanted an ass chewing from the chief of staff because the boss felt slighted.

Security protocols shifted just as fast. New intelligence, logistical developments, and updated threat assessments all had to be incorporated the moment they became available. Advance teams, plane teams, and jump teams all had to be coordinated. Every site had to be cleared by intelligence services, protective details, and local law enforcement, then locked down for the duration of the visit.

Walker spotted a knot of men in gray uniforms, balaclavas, and Kevlar helmets. The UK Counter Terrorist Specialist Firearms Officers were armed with submachine guns, fully automatic carbines, and countersniper rifles. They were considered one of Great Britain's most elite police units.

Walker smirked.

They didn't have a clue.

He strolled through St. James's Park and down to the Thames embankment, where two matte-black police boats patrolled the river. Walker kept moving. Everywhere he looked he spotted uniformed and undercover security personnel, bomb-sniffing dogs, and welders securing manhole covers into place.

Walker had to stay ahead of all of them—plus that walking hemorrhoid Jake Keller—but the assassin's main concern had been with the motorcade's route. Fortunately, the Brits had a well-established protocol for calling on their queen. The visiting head of state always drove along the half-mile-long Mall from Admiralty Arch to Buckingham Palace. While security details loathed being so predictable, no world leader wanted the world to think he was frightened of a little parade.

But that would change after tomorrow.

FIFTY-NINE

"GOOD AFTERNOON, SIR," said the man at the door. It appeared to be a greeting, but was in fact a challenge.

"I'm here to see James Houghton," said Jake.

"Very good. Sir James and his guest are in the Coffee Room—through the hall, up the grand staircase, last room on your left. Welcome to Grey's."

Located in the heart of Mayfair, Grey's was one of the most exclusive clubs in London. It had opened in the late 1600s as a chocolate house—the height of decadence at the time—but the long line of princes, dukes, earls, barons, and knights who drank and gambled in its upstairs rooms soon turned the building into a private club.

Jake walked under the vaulted ceilings and up the enormous staircase past a pair of blue-blooded Oxbridgers in three-piece suits who, like a pair of ventriloquists, were having a conversation though neither man's lips seemed to be moving.

As promised, James and Celia were in the last room on the left, seated by the window. Jake smiled warmly at the two Brits as he sat down, suddenly realizing that they were the closest thing he'd had to parents since he'd lost his own.

But that didn't stop him from having a little fun with them.

"I seem to have forgotten my ascot," he said.

"Not to worry," said James. "They always keep a few behind the bar."

"I do believe he's pulling your leg, James," said Celia.

"Ah, yes. Subtle wit from an American. Fancy that."

Celia scowled at her old friend.

"So, Jake," said James, "have you found your Russian connection yet?"

"Please, James," said Celia. "I'd like to hear about his trip to France."

"What's in France?" said James.

"A woman," Celia said.

"And the answer to both of your questions," said Jake.

"I think I'm going to like this one," James said.

A waiter set three cups of coffee on the table.

"I thought it was called 'tea time,'" said Jake.

"Indeed," Sir James said with a grand smile, "but we know Americans prefer coffee, so we ordered this in your honor."

Jake smiled politely.

"Now, tell us about this Russian girl," said James. "Did you sleep with her?"

"Oh, James, do shut up," Celia said. "The girl is French. He broke her heart when she thought he was dead. Now he's trying to get back together."

"Celia 'helping' with your love life, is she?" said James. "May God have mercy on your soul."

Jake quietly explained the saga of his reconciliation with Geneviève and the discovery of the Russian oligarch and the former CIA officer who were trying to kill him.

"Can't your employer protect you?" said Celia.

"Unfortunately, someone in Jake's firm may be complicit," said James.

Celia frowned. "Do you know who?"

"Not yet." Jake shook his head. "But I'm close."

Jake's cell phone vibrated. He'd received a text message from Hunter.

Walker sighted two minutes ago heading west through Admiralty Arch.

Jake's demeanor changed instantly.

"News?" said Sir James.

"Ian has been running real-time facial recognition on the London CCTV network. He spotted the man I'm after two minutes ago at Admiralty Arch. Is it far?"

"Less than a mile," said Celia.

"I'm sorry," Jake said, "but I have to go."

"Left out the door, down Marlborough Road, then left on the Mall," said James. He handed Jake a small package. "You left this in my car—in case you need it again."

Jake shook James's hand, kissed Celia on the cheek, and stuffed the 9mm handgun in his jacket pocket.

He glanced at the table one last time before heading for the door.

No one had touched their coffee.

SIXTY

J AKE CALLED HUNTER as soon as he was outside.

"I'm heading south on St. James's Street."

"Go straight till you reach Marlborough Road. I ran Walker's picture through the immigration database. He flew in from France on a private jet, using a French passport. You want me with you?"

"I need you where you are," said Jake. "What's he wearing?"

"Blue jeans, tweed cap, brown Barbour jacket. There are a lot of cameras on the Mall. We've spotted him there before."

"Call me if you get another hit." Jake disconnected the call.

Fifty feet down Marlborough Road, five heavily armed men in gray uniforms with "CTSFO" stenciled on their vests stood next to a steel barrier blocking vehicle entrance to the Mall, but they were still letting foot traffic through. Jake's eyes scanned distant pedestrians for Walker's cap and jacket before evaluating the faces of those closer by. He spotted more police and more of the gray-clad men.

His phone rang. It was Hunter again.

"Got another hit. He's on the Mall, headed west toward Buckingham Palace. Where are you now?"

"Marlborough Road, halfway to the Mall."

"Get moving."

A minute later Jake reached the Mall. There were more cops and more gray-uniformed men on the corner. He looked left and right down the red-tinted road leading to the palace, methodically scanning the crowd and analyzing each person in case Walker had changed his appearance.

Jake paused on a man in a brown jacket standing on the far side of the wide promenade. The sun was low in the sky, casting long shadows over the ground and muddling his appearance. After a few seconds, he walked out of the shadows and looked up Marlborough Road.

The afternoon sun shone brightly on his face.

It was Walker.

Sonofabitch, Jake thought. He knew they'd met before. Walker was the American Jake had swum against in the Courchevel aquatics center—before Jake had seen his photo or known he was working for the Russians.

"I've got eyes on," Jake said into his phone.

"I'll have the Security Service detain him."

"No," Jake said. "Then I'll never find the mole inside the Agency."

"That man tried to kill you."

"A lot of people have tried. I need to let this play out. Thanks, Ian."

Jake hung up, gripped the pistol in his jacket pocket, and followed Walker down a tree-lined footpath into St. James's Park. Walker paused often to admire the scenery, made several turns, and discreetly checked for surveillance, but Jake kept his distance as the path wound its way back to the Mall and the sun set behind the London skyline.

The encroaching darkness forced Jake to tighten up coverage. It was a warm evening for late January and dozens of tourists were strolling along the wide promenade. Walker dissolved into the crowd, moving no slower and no faster than the people around him. Half the men in the park seemed to be wearing some variation of his barn jacket and blue jeans, and keeping track of him became more difficult by the second.

The crowd eventually separated and Jake spotted the traitor standing alone in the light of an old-fashioned pole lamp, once again looking up Marlborough Road. Jake followed his gaze, but could not discern what had caught Walker's eye. Walker paced nonchalantly from one side of the intersection to the other, casually glancing up Marlborough Road at each corner, before looping around and doing it again, moving from light to darkness to light again as he passed under the old-fashioned pole lamps.

And then he was gone.

Walker had stepped into the darkness and never emerged. Jake searched a few minutes more, but St. James's Park was enormous. Jake had lost him.

Jake headed back up Marlborough Road to see if he could deduce what Walker had been staring at, but there wasn't much there except for a limestone-covered seven-story building that overlooked the park. When Jake reached the vehicle barrier, he approached the nearest cop, a compact woman with sergeant's stripes on her sleeve.

"What's with all the security?" He motioned to the men in the gray uniforms.

"Counterterror police," she said. "Just a precaution for tomorrow."

"What's tomorrow?"

The sergeant looked at him as if he'd been living in outer space.

"The presidential visit," she said.

Jake started to walk away, but turned back to the police officer.

"Which president?" he asked.

"Why, the Russian president, love."

SIXTY-ONE

IT WAS TWO A.M. when Jake approached the seven-story building overlooking the park. He'd broken into his share of buildings over the years—usually with a hard kick and a weapon in hand—but surreptitious entry was not his forte. Military special mission units, law enforcement, and intelligence agencies all had specialists for black bag jobs and Jake wasn't one of them.

But Ian Hunter was.

The MI5 officer placed an RFID transceiver against the heavy-duty electronic lock securing the rear door, but like any system, the lock was only as good as its brain, and this one was operating at a third-grade level. The transceiver tricked the lock into revealing the last code used to open it, then transmitted the same code back to the lock. The door was open in less than a second.

"Leg it," said Hunter. "The curtain twitchers will be up soon."

Wearing hats, glasses, and makeup that subtly altered the appearance of their faces by creating shadows where none existed, the two men hustled inside and entered the freight elevator. Earlier that night, Hunter had queried the Security Service's extensive databases and discovered that a new tenant had signed a lease in the building just three months earlier—at roughly the same time planning would have begun for the Russian president's visit.

Jake and Hunter made their way to the sixth-floor suite, where the Englishman retrieved another gadget from the small knapsack he was wearing: an ultra-wideband scanner that could detect the motion and frequency of a human's breathing. He aimed it inside the office and the search came back negative—there was no one inside.

The third piece of equipment in Hunter's bag of tricks was a restricted-access item available only to government and military buyers. It assessed the extremely faint electromagnetic and acoustic signals emitted by the alarm system's microprocessor and compared them to a database of known manufacturers. The system defending the suite was more formidable than the simple lock guarding the lobby and had been installed by someone who took his security seriously. There were multiple layers of protection, with a total of fourteen sensors covering two distinct zones.

Hunter flipped another switch on the device. "This may take a while."

Much like the attack on the exterior door, the second device used the signals it had gathered and began hacking the alarm system, not with a conventional software attack, but by overpowering the processor with the recorded signals from each of the alarm sensors, effectively fooling the system into thinking each sensor was still operating normally—even when a sensor was breached. The device's display showed the number of working sensors decrease swiftly from fourteen to ten, then slowly to four, where it held.

"What does that mean?" Jake said.

"Four live sensors? No problem if they're on the windows, but if they're motion detectors, pressure pads, or there's a switch on the door we're about to walk through, we're bollixed. I can talk to the police if the alarm goes off, but they are going to want to know why we're here, which could get a bit sticky, as we're not precisely on official business."

"Will they make it official?"

"In about three seconds. Nobody is going to stick his neck out with Comrade President arriving in the morning."

"If we don't get inside, I'll be looking over my shoulder for Walker for the rest of my life."

Hunter moved the gadget in random arcs along the exterior wall of the suite.

"Now what are you doing?" Jake asked.

"Security systems are like women, mate. Some open up right away but most of them need a little massage before you go in."

A green LED lit up on the gadget as the live-sensor count went to zero. Hunter used the RFID transceiver to defeat the door lock and smiled as he opened the door.

The two men used dim flashlights to search the suite. While they didn't care about preserving their night vision, the lights wouldn't be visible to anyone outside the building. They examined the desks, the walls, and, most of all, the windows overlooking the Mall.

"They're sealed permanently," said Jake. "Not good for a sniper."

"The timing of the lease fits, but we don't know if Walker is the one who leased it. Maybe we've got the wrong building."

"No. He was staring at this building when he paced off the square."

"Maybe he's studying architecture."

Jake scowled as he looked around the office. "How big was the suite that was leased?"

"Two hundred square meters."

"What's that in real numbers?"

"Do I look like a bleeding calculator?" said Hunter. "I don't know, maybe twenty-one hundred square feet?"

The two men looked around.

"There's another office," they said at the same time.

They returned to the hallway and found a second door down the hall on the same side of the building. Hunter reset the electromagnetic-acoustic transceiver and located a second alarm system—identical to the first.

"Fourteen live sensors," he said as he massaged the system through the exterior wall. The jammer had learned from the prior system and quickly overpowered the second system's main processor.

They were inside in under a minute.

The suite was laid out and furnished identically to the first, including a fish tank against the shared wall.

"Sorry, mate," said Hunter. "I think this one's a bust."

Jake paced off the room and did some math in his head.

"We're missing something," he said.

"Yeah, like any sign Walker was here, may one day come here, or anything indicating a crime might, at some future date—"

"That's not what I meant," said Jake, "and just for future reference, two hundred square meters is not twenty-one hundred square feet. It's twenty-one fifty square feet. Even if you combine the area of the two suites, we're still missing fifty square feet."

Hunter looked around. "Now that you mention it, both security systems were configured for two zones, but they're each just one big room."

The two men searched along the shared wall between the two offices. Hunter checked the cabinet under the fish tank.

"Have a look at this," he said. "You see those pipes? That's precipitation-hardened stainless steel."

Jake stared at him blankly.

"It's what they use in nuclear reactors," said Hunter. "It's overkill for a bunch of fish."

"And the pipes lead into the wall. There's no pump."

Hunter ran the RFID transceiver over the wall from top to bottom, left to right, until the wall began to open on two hydraulic rams.

Jake shined his light inside. "You're going to want to see this."

Hunter looked at the cannon.

"Bloody hell."

Jake climbed onto the platform and looked through the scope. It was aimed at the intersection of Marlborough Road and the Mall, exactly where Walker had been standing earlier that evening.

"Have you seen the route for the president's motorcade?" Jake asked.

Hunter nodded.

"Will it pass through that intersection?"

"After World War II, the Mall was tinted so it would look like a red carpet in front of Buckingham Palace. Every visiting head of state drives up it right to the palace gates."

"Is that a yes?"

"Easy there, smarty pants. You know what they say about those who don't learn from history."

"I saw Walker pacing off that intersection this afternoon," Jake said. "It's about twenty meters wide, which will give him around two seconds to acquire the target and fire."

"He could do it in less than half that," said Hunter. "I need to call this in."

"Ian, if you call this in, I'll never find Walker and I'll never find the mole."

Hunter stared at him for a moment.

"Hey, mate, you seem like an all-right chap, and I literally owe my life to Sir James, but I'm a Brit and I'm a cop. I can't have a dead Red on the queen's doorstep."

Jake looked through the cannon's scope and put his shoulder against the stock.

"Don't worry, Ian. Nobody is going to die until I say so."

SIXTY-TWO

NO ONE DID pomp and circumstance quite like the British.

As the sun rose through a cloudless blue sky above London, towering flagpoles along both sides of the Mall were alternately draped with the Russian tricolor and the British Union Jack. From Trafalgar Square to Buckingham Palace, a thousand Coldstream Guards stood at attention in their iconic red tunics, white belts, and black bearskin helmets. Waiting in the wings were dozens of horse-drawn carriages, brass bands, and ceremonial flag bearers.

The crowd assembled early. While the Russian president might not have been the most popular person in the world, he was undeniably fascinating. Part myth, part man, his carefully engineered public persona brought equal parts scorn and admiration, and watching his motorcade arrive at the queen's door was sure to entertain both camps. Every tourist in London wanted to see the state visit of such a notorious rogue.

It was a few minutes past ten in the morning when his plane landed at Heathrow. The twin-engine Tupolev-214 taxied to a closed-off high-security area of the airport where the Russian Federation's ambassador, the media, and a host of local and national dignitaries were assembled. The president nodded once to the crowd and descended the stairs with his wife two steps behind him. After shaking half a dozen hands, he was escorted to the fifteen-vehicle motorcade.

Forward-deployed two days earlier and guarded round the clock by the Russian Federal Protective Service, the president's Aurus limousine was the first domestically built car to carry a head of state in fifty years. Long, sleek, and powerful, it looked like a Russian Rolls-Royce. Its armor could stop any rifle in the world, and its self-contained air system could keep its occupants alive for hours during a chemical, biological, or radiological attack. The president was immensely proud of it.

High in the sky were a Metropolitan Police helicopter on overwatch duty and a BBC News helicopter intent on providing live coverage to the network's viewers. The president stepped into his limousine, the door was secured, and the entire fifteen-vehicle motorcade moved as one out of Heathrow Airport.

It was 10:20.

MIKE WALKER LOOKED away from the BBC livestream on his laptop and started the countdown timer on his watch.

It was set for thirty minutes.

Wearing a suit and tie, he'd entered the sixth-floor suite overlooking Marlborough Road and the Mall an hour before sunrise. While he wasn't expecting any difficulties, there was always a remote chance that an unconnected event or new piece of intelligence might cause the Metropolitan Police to expand the security cordon. Walker wasn't carrying anything incriminating—they could give him a body cavity search and discover nothing of his plans—but the one thing he couldn't get back was time. He didn't want to be entering the building just as the motorcade was arriving at Buckingham Palace.

Besides, he'd needed some time to clean the office.

Walker wanted to enjoy the twenty-five million dollars he was getting from Kozlov, not worry about the Russian security services discovering who'd assassinated their president. They wouldn't kill him, at least not right away. They'd make him suffer mentally and physically until he spent every conscious moment wishing they would kill him. When he was about to cross the threshold, they would nurse him back to life so they could torture him again. And so on—indefinitely. Walker had heard many stories over the years from Kozlov and from others, and spending a few hours cleaning the suite seemed like a small price to pay for peace of mind.

Wearing gloves and a hat, Walker filled a two-gallon sprayer with a powerful disinfectant and coated every surface from the walls to the floors to the desks and the doorknobs. By the time he was finished, there wasn't a fingerprint or a usable piece of DNA from the building's entrance to the cannon room. There would be no time to clean it all again after he pulled the trigger.

And while the Russian security apparatus presented the greatest long-term risk to Walker's health, the biggest short-term risk continued to be from that asshole Keller. But aside from his fellow American's stubborn refusal to die, Walker was confident that he'd stayed ahead of his former Agency coworker at every turn. The odds that Keller had learned anything actionable about the upcoming festivities were slim to none. Walker's operational security had simply been too good.

The assassin sat cross-legged on a desk and meditated. It was a calming technique he'd developed in the SEAL teams to use during helicopter insertions. Everyone had dealt differently with the anticipation and the stress of impending missions. Some guys checked and rechecked their gear, some watched the countryside pass by with their legs dangling out of the helo, some visualized the assault plan in their heads, and some slept. Mike Walker focused on a point of infinite stillness deep inside his mind. He slowed his breathing, lowered his heart rate, and relaxed his muscles. Whether he did it for two minutes or for twenty, his body and his brain emerged sharper and more capable than ever.

He was six minutes into his meditation when the disposable cell phone in his pocket pinged. Walker opened his eyes and checked the screen. The waiting text message showed only a single number.

1

Walker glanced at his watch. Eighteen minutes to go. He entered the cannon room and placed his open laptop and his phone on the concrete platform. The assassin cracked his neck, loosened his tie, and lay down on the yoga mat atop the concrete. While he wasn't worried about comfort, he didn't want to ruin his suit. It was a critical part of his escape plan. An average cop's eyes tended to skim right over clean-cut men in two-thousand-dollar suits because they didn't commit many street crimes. It was urban camouflage. The plan was for him to exit the building's rear door seconds after he pulled the trigger and disappear into a series of pedestrian walkways. In less than two minutes, he'd be three blocks from the building where a hired car was already waiting, its driver believing Walker to be in a business meeting. It would drop him across town at a posh hotel where a second car would take him to the airport. He would be back on Kozlov's jet and out of the country ninety minutes after he pulled the trigger.

And then he'd deal with Keller.

Walker nestled his cheek against the cannon's stock and looked through the Schmidt & Bender scope. Today, rapid acquisition of the moving target would be more important than pinpoint accuracy, so he zoomed out to see the full width of the intersection. Walker tracked an imaginary vehicle moving across his field of view, from the trees on the left to the trees on the right.

He glanced at his laptop and checked the motorcade's progress on the BBC. He estimated it would be moving at twenty to twenty-five miles per hour as it rolled down the Mall. The cannon round would take a quarter of a second to reach its target. It didn't sound like much, but it meant that he would have to lead his desired point of impact by about eight feet, which could be difficult to estimate on an unfamiliar vehicle. Fortunately, much had been written about the Aurus Senat limousine and Walker knew that it was twenty-three feet long, which meant he'd have to aim at the driver in the front seat if he wanted to hit the president in the back seat.

Plus, he had a wide margin for error.

The beauty of using the cannon was not only its armor-piercing capability that was far superior to any rifle, but that Walker didn't actually have to hit the president to kill him. The round would penetrate the vehicle's armor before exploding, at which point the armor would contain the blast, concentrating the explosive power and gelatinizing everything inside the passenger compartment.

Pretty sweet, thought Walker.

He scanned the assembled members of the Metropolitan Police, the counterterrorism officers, and the Coldstream Guards. The Coldstream Guards were facing inward, like an honor guard for the Russian president, which Walker found ironic, as they were all fully trained active-duty army infantry, and many had probably seen combat against Russian proxy forces around the world. Very few would mourn his death.

Walker's cell phone pinged again.

2

He glanced at his watch.

Five minutes.

Three hundred seconds until he could pull the trigger. He could almost feel the twenty-five million dollars. Of course, Kozlov had also guaranteed a ten-million-dollar payout to Shadow, and now Shadow was on the target list. It was always possible that Kozlov would try the same with Walker, to tie off loose ends and save himself some money, but Walker had spent the last two years studying the oligarch's operations and he made sure Kozlov knew it. Walker did worry that Shadow had taken the same precautions, but there was nothing he could do about it now.

Four minutes.

Walker watched the BBC broadcast. The motorcade was just passing the British Museum. He opened the weapon, inserted a round into the chamber, and closed the bolt. The cannon was ready to fire. There was no safety. Though Walker had fired tens of thousands of rounds and killed dozens of men, he didn't want to blow the most important shot of his life by forgetting to disengage a safety.

Three minutes.

The BBC helicopter showed the motorcade passing the Hippodrome on Charing Cross Road. Though the broadcast said "LIVE," Walker knew that security agencies occasionally delayed such footage to make what he was about to do more difficult. He snugged his cheek against the stock and looked through the scope. The motorcade would approach through Admiralty Arch, by Trafalgar Square, before driving down the perfectly straight Mall to the palace.

The crowd would notice. Some people would point. Others would crane their necks. The building excitement would precede the imminent arrival of the target.

Two minutes.

It was two thousand feet from the Arch to the kill box. It would take a full minute for the motorcade to cover the distance. Walker slewed the cannon left a few degrees, to the very edge of the intersection, and put one of the Coldstream Guard's fur hats in the crosshairs.

One minute.

The crowd began to come alive. Some people pointed. Others craned their necks. A police sergeant turned toward the Arch and spoke into her radio.

Walker slammed his hand against a large red button next to the cannon and the two electric motors slid the exterior window open six inches. The sniper's senses went into overdrive as cool air and the sound of a brass marching band flowed into the room. Walker eased his finger inside the trigger guard and prepared to fire.

A Metropolitan Police SUV acting as the route leader came into view. Its flashing blue lights and fluorescent paint made it impossible to miss. Walker tracked the driver for two full seconds across the intersection, just for practice.

Piece of cake.

He reset his point of aim to the left side of the intersection and waited. A dozen motorcycles went by in a vanguard, chirping their sirens, flashing their lights, and sweeping stragglers from the pavement. According to the live feed on BBC, the next vehicles would be the electronic countermeasures van—bristling with antennas to jam any radio-controlled explosives that might be in the area—an SUV with the president's security detail, and the limo.

The ECM van passed by. So did the SUV with the security team.

Walker spotted the limousine, remembering that to compensate for the vehicle's speed, he'd have to aim at the driver in the front seat to hit the president in the back seat. He exhaled. A Russian flag flying from the car's right front fender passed in front of his crosshairs.

Walker began to pace the limo, slowly drifting his point of aim back from the flag, across the car's hood, and settling on the driver's head.

He held his fire.

The first limousine was a decoy. The Federal Protective Service repeatedly rotated the position of the president's car to make an attack more difficult, but one of the many people on Kozlov's payroll was a part of the presidential detail. He'd spent four years guarding the president, taking his abuse, absorbing his threats, and developing a distinct hatred for the man. For two million euros, he'd agreed to text which limousine the bastard was riding in. The 1s and 2s Walker had been receiving on his phone for the past half hour were the current position of the president's limo in the motorcade.

Walker swung the cannon to the left side of the intersection and took the slack out of the trigger so it would break cleanly when he was ready to fire. The second limousine came into view. Walker saw the Russian flag flying from the car's right front fender and once again shifted his aim slowly backward from the flag, across the car's hood, to the driver's head.

This time he pulled the trigger.

SIXTY-THREE

THE CANNON WAS rock steady as the 30-millimeter round leapt from the barrel and flew through the open window. Walker kept his cheek pressed tight against the stock, still tracking the limousine through the big Schmidt & Bender scope as the shell arced down to street level.

The armor-piercing round was halfway to the target when Walker realized there was a problem. The shell had been in the air only an eighth of a second, but the former SEAL Team Six sniper had fired tens of thousands of rounds over the years and his keen eyes observed the shock wave around the supersonic projectile diverge from its expected path.

Ten feet behind the limousine, the cannon round smashed into the road and exploded, destroying nothing but a small section of pavement.

Walker's hand shot forward while the president's car was barely halfway through the intersection. As he'd practiced so many times before, Walker pushed the bolt forward and shoved another round into the breech. He yanked the bolt home and prepared to fire, but the limousine had already passed through the far side of the intersection and out of sight.

Walker held his aim on the intersection: furious, paralyzed, mystified. All the time and planning—all the risk and danger—all for a motherfucking pothole.

Panic ensued down on the Mall. Still glaring through the scope, Walker saw the counterterror police scanning nearby rooftops. The Metropolitan police and the Coldstream Guards were herding spectators away from the site of the blast. Walker was about to close the sliding glass panel and execute his escape plan when he saw a lone man walk to the middle of the road and stand in the pothole. Clad only in street clothes, the man looked directly up at Walker's position and raise his middle finger.

Walker zoomed in.

It was Keller.

Walker pulled the trigger.

A second round flew through the window, as fast and as menacing as the first, but fury rose in Walker's soul as the shell followed the same flawed path. It impacted the road fifteen feet to the left of where Keller was standing.

Still centered in Walker's crosshairs, Keller shrugged.

Walker screamed. One shot off by fifteen feet could have been an anomaly—maybe a bad round of ammunition or maybe a freak gust of wind—but two shots off by the exact same distance told the veteran sniper only one thing.

Someone had fucked with the scope's zero.

And there really wasn't any question about who it was.

Walker ejected the spent casing, loaded the third round he'd place alongside the cannon, and rammed the bolt home. He aimed exactly fifteen feet to the right and put his finger on the trigger.

But Keller was gone.

SIXTY-FOUR

B UT THE RUSSIAN president made Kozlov a billionaire," said
Clements. "Why would Kozlov want to assassinate him?"
Jake was back in the States with a pistol on his hip, a
knife strapped to his ankle, and his short-barreled rifle tucked between the seats of his truck. He and Clements were having a rolling
meeting through the Virginia countryside.

"Because Kozlov would have doubled his income overnight," said
Jake. "The president became the richest man in the world by siphon-
ing the earnings of men like Kozlov. He steers inflated government
contracts to Kozlov's steel mills and supports his organized-criminal
activities in exchange for half the profits."

Clements regarded his protégé dubiously.

"What you did was reckless. What if Walker had succeeded?"

"First off, what I did was the exact opposite of reckless. I knew
exactly where that round was going to hit. Second, if by some miracle Walker had killed the president, then there would be one less
politician mortgaging his country's future to keep himself in office.
I don't see the downside."

Clements took a sip of his coffee.

"You think Walker recognized you?"

"I made sure of it," Jake said.

"Why?"

"Now it's personal. The plot to kill the president drove the events of the past month. Walker has been trying to kill me to prevent me from interfering with their plans. Now that I've won and he's lost, he's going to be furious."

"You think he comes here?"

"His psyche profile indicates that he's volatile and violent. He'll want to finish this thing in person, and when he does, we'll track him to his source inside the Agency."

"Any thoughts on who the mole might be?"

"My contact in MI5 said they spotted Walker and Kozlov in London last year with a suspected U.S. intelligence operative who claimed to be a USAID program officer."

Clements sighed and looked out the window. It was a dark, blustery day in the capital region.

"A USAID program officer?" he said.

"That's right. I was right about Kozlov. I was right about Walker, and I'm right about this."

"I'm sorry, Jake, but Director Feinman will argue that you've got nothing but hunches, supposition, and a few widely scattered data points, plus you'll be forced to disclose that you knew about an imminent assassination attempt on a foreign head of state and didn't escalate it. Taking this up the chain won't accomplish anything except end my career and land you in prison."

Jake respected Clements, but Peter was a senior CIA executive who stood a very real chance of becoming the next director of Central Intelligence. The scrutiny surrounding his every action necessitated he do everything by the book. Meanwhile, Jake couldn't get any further off the books. He'd just let a man take a shot at the Russian president, and he had another Russian buried in his yard. Clements's guidance and support had been invaluable, but he wasn't the right person for the next phase of the operation. It wasn't fair to ask him to risk everything he'd worked so hard for.

"I'm sorry, Jake, but officially, there's nothing I can do."

"I understand."

"But unofficially," continued Clements, "that sonofabitch got my officers killed. I can't stand by and do nothing. Just tell me what you need."

"Thanks, Peter, but I have to warn you that Walker isn't going to go peacefully. I suspect that when he and I next meet, only one of us is going to walk away. Then I'm going to take whoever has been feeding him information from inside the Agency and wring them out until they've got nothing left."

"I have no problem with that conceptually, but from a practical standpoint, it may be more difficult than you think. You see, when we were in London, Ted Graves was covered as a USAID program officer."

SIXTY-FIVE

GENEVIÈVE HAD BEEN the first.

Then Celia and James, then Hunter, and now Clements.

Jake was building a coalition.

No longer committed to bearing the weight of the world solely upon his shoulders, he'd leaned on his allies to gather the intel, analyze the data, and identify the perpetrators. Now, as he prepared to neutralize the men who'd been killing his fellow paramilitary officers and trying to kill him, Jake needed operators—men of action.

Jeff and Clap were with him in his Manassas, Virginia, hotel room, eating steaks from room service at a small table. Jake spent an hour explaining how he'd found Kozlov in France, discovered how the oligarch had recruited Walker, then foiled the plot to kill the Russian president. There was no question in Jake's mind that Walker was coming for him next—and that Jake needed their help.

The men ate in silence for a few minutes until Jeff spoke up.

"How is he going to find you?"

"He has a source inside the Agency."

"Any idea who?" said Clap.

"I have my suspicions, but I don't want to bias you. I'm just going to let Walker lead me to him."

Jeff picked at his food. "You should be talking to the FBI."

Jake shook his head. "There's no evidence tying Kozlov or Walker to anything. I'm guessing the police won't find any in London either. Walker may be a traitor, but he's a pro. This is going to go down in the next forty-eight hours and the FBI isn't going to mobilize on what I've got. They'll want to build a criminal case that can hold up in court."

"Speaking of court . . . If we grab this guy and you're wrong, we're all going to prison," said Jeff.

"It could be worse if you're right, depending on who his contact is at the Agency," added Clap. "Didn't you say Walker specialized in renditions? What if he's a step ahead of us and leads us into a trap? We could end up in some black site for the rest of our lives."

"There's a lot of personal risk here," Jeff added.

Jake placed his napkin on the table. Barely two months earlier, half of Clap's Ground Branch team had been wounded or killed while attempting to rescue Jake in Somalia. A year before that, Jake and Jeff had been shoulder to shoulder during a joint operation Jake had led in Libya. The Delta Force operator had taken a bullet in his thigh while clearing a room and nearly bled out as they'd fought their way back to their helicopter—together.

He owed these men a lot, and they each had a lot to lose. In addition to putting their careers at risk, both men were married, and Jeff had two kids and a third on the way.

"OK," Jake said. "I hear you."

Jeff and Clap shared a look.

"Cool," said Clap. "I just want to make sure we're all going into this with our eyes open."

"Works for me," said Jeff. He licked steak sauce from both sides of his knife. "How are we going to take these fuckers down?"

Jake squinted across the table. "What happened to all the bitching and moaning about getting killed and going to prison?"

Clap laughed. "I may not understand the whole picture, but I don't doubt that you do."

"There's no way in hell I'd let you do this alone," added Jeff.

Jake strapped his knife to his ankle, holstered his pistol, and smiled at his friends.

"Here's what I have in mind."

SIXTY-SIX

"*W*ALKER'S ON HIS WAY,*"* said Hunter. As part of the international Five Eyes security alliance, the UK Security Service had access to the flight records of the five largest English-speaking countries in the world.

"How?" said Jake. They spoke over a secure comms network that even NSA couldn't break in real time.

"Air France into Philadelphia, arrives 16:20 local time."

"Any connecting flight?"

"Lots of options, but no reservation—at least not in the same name."

"Thanks, Ian."

"I'm here for you."

Jake hung up.

"He lands in Philly in four hours. It's a go mission."

Clements, Clap, and Jeff were there with Jake, seated around his Manassas, Virginia, hotel room. The team had spent the last several hours making plans, checking gear, and waiting for Hunter's call. Without further discussion, they each donned the encrypted in-ear communication sets that Jeff had "borrowed" from his Delta gear locker, did a final comms check, and staggered their exits from the building. They left in separate cars: different models, different colors, different rental agencies. They departed in different directions and drove different surveillance-detection routes before converging on I-95 north toward Philadelphia.

Everyone except for Jake.

Jake stayed behind, working at the hotel room's desk with his laptop and assorted communications equipment, to act as the mission's tactical operations center and the team's last line of defense in case Walker took a connecting flight into DC or Baltimore.

The only member of the team Walker hadn't met and couldn't recognize was Jeff, so when the team reached Philadelphia International Airport, it was Jeff who blended into the scenery inside the crowded international-arrivals area. Wearing sunglasses and a black suit jacket, the troop sergeant major held a limo company sign for a passenger who didn't exist.

Walker's flight arrived ninety minutes later. The former SEAL emerged from customs, pulling a medium-sized rolling suitcase, walking calmly, and looking none the worse for wear after the nine-hour flight.

"*Target in sight,*" Jeff said over the radio.

Clements was parked outside in the airport's cell phone lot. His vehicle, like all the vehicles, was equipped with an IMSI catcher, a hot piece of technology that could not only intercept nearby cell phone communications, but track their locations and also act as a secure data network for the team. Clap had acquired the devices "for testing" from a friend in the Agency's Directorate of Support.

"*Roger,*" Jake said.

Walker stopped in the men's room and Jeff casually removed his hat, glasses, and jacket and stuffed them into a backpack that had been at his feet. By the time Walker emerged, Jeff was wearing a blue fleece jacket and a winter hat and looked completely different from the limo driver Walker had passed just moments ago.

Walker exited the terminal with Jeff fifty feet behind him.

"Target is heading toward the car rental agencies. I'm also ninety percent sure he switched bags in the bathroom. It's the same kind of bag, but the one he arrived with was scuffed from the flight. The one he's carrying now looks brand-new."

"That means he's got support in-country," Jake said. *"I'd like to see who comes out with the other bag, but we don't have the manpower."*

"What if it's the mole?" said Clements.

Jake cursed. *"Jeff, how long was Walker in the men's room?"*

"Less than sixty seconds."

"That's not enough time for the mole. They have too much to talk about," said Jake. *"Jeff, stay with Walker and keep your eyes open for countersurveillance."*

"And a weapon," said Clap. *"That bag swap wasn't for a change of clothes."*

Everyone on Jake's team was armed, but tonight they were going up against one of their own. The advantages they normally had in skill and training would be negated—if they didn't act as a team.

As expected, Walker entered a car rental agency. Jeff was two places behind him in line and staring at his phone when Walker approached the rental counter. The reservation agent was a pleasantly plump woman in her early thirties with a big smile and lime green highlights in her hair.

Walker slid a credit card and a California driver's license across the counter.

"I've always wanted to see San Diego," the agent said as she entered the details into her computer.

"Great. I need a midsized sedan."

"Would you like GPS?"

"No."

"Collision insurance?"

"No."

"Prepaid fuel?"

"No."

"Car seat?"

"No."

"Ski rack?"

"No."

"Extended roadside assistance?"

"No."

"Liability insurance?"

"No."

"Additional liability insurance?"

"Why would I want additional liability insurance when I didn't take the regular liability insurance?"

"I'm supposed to ask."

"No."

"Emergency sickness plan?"

"No."

"Satellite radio?"

"No."

"Are you a member of our rewards club?"

"No."

"Would you like to join—"

"No."

She frowned at him, raised a key to eye level, and dropped it on the counter.

"White Nissan . . . F62."

Two spaces back in line, Jeff sent a text message.

Hertz, white Nissan sedan, space F62, repeat, fox six-two.

Walker stepped out of the rental office and looked for row F, space 62. The car was barely inside the airport grounds.

Clap was there in twenty seconds.

"It's a white Altima," he said over the radio. *"Pennsylvania tags, juliet-alpha-romeo, one-one-six-one-nine."*

The veteran CIA officer untied the laces on his running shoe and put one foot on the car's bumper as if to tie them. He reached into his pocket, pulled out an object an inch around and half an inch thick, and affixed it inside the car's plastic bumper with super-adhesive tape.

Walker might not have wanted GPS on his car, but he was getting it anyway.

"RESERVATION FOR DIRK Ryan," Jeff said when he reached the counter.

"I'm sorry . . . ," said the rental agent. "I'm not seeing a reservation in that name."

Jeff looked at the thirty-foot-wide black-and-yellow Hertz logo behind the counter as if he'd just noticed it.

"My bad," he said. "I thought this was Avis."

"TRACKING ALL," JAKE said.

Walker's GPS beacon showed up as a red diamond on Jake's screen while the team's positions were displayed as green circles. Jake was watching on his laptop, but the other team members could see the same data on the phone-based Android Tactical Assault Kits in their vehicles.

"Target is on the move," Jake said. *"He's approaching the airport access road."*

"*Roger, in position,*" said Clements. He was idling half a mile away on I-95 south, prepared to intercept Walker once he turned onto the highway.

Clap and Jeff were walking back to their own vehicles.

"*We just lost the target's position fix,*" Jake said.

Clap and Jeff started running.

"*Did it fall off?*" said Clements.

"*Negative,*" said Jake. "*It would still be transmitting. He's jamming the signal.*"

"*I'm at my car,*" said Clap.

"*So am I,*" Jeff said.

The rest of the team heard doors slamming and engines starting.

"*Peter, head south four miles and hold position just past the Prospect Park cloverleaf in case he takes surface roads,*" said Jake. "*Clap, make your next left onto the access road, then right onto the ramp for I-95 north. Jeff, follow Clap up the ramp, but turn right toward long-term parking in case Walker doubles back through the airport.*"

It didn't take long for the small size of Jake's team and Walker's years of training to put Murphy's Law into effect. Everyone felt the tension as darkness fell and the team scrambled to adapt.

"*I have a visual on the target,*" said Jeff. "*He's heading toward long-term parking.*"

"*Give him space,*" said Jake. "*The access road is one way. He's not going anywhere.*"

Walker pulled into the long-term lot and made a U-turn just before the gate. Jeff passed by without raising suspicion.

"*Clap, turn west on 291 and wait at the Bartram Avenue intersection.*"

"*Target is heading back through the airport,*" said Jeff. He'd spotted Walker in the rearview mirror.

"*In position to acquire,*" said Clap.

"Clap, cross the intersection now. Jeff, break off coverage."

"I've got eyes-on," said Clap. *"He's a hundred yards behind me heading toward I-95."*

Jake was staring at his computer screen, providing new instructions every few seconds to the men in the field. Walker was making highly thought out but seemingly random turns designed to reveal a tail and it required enormous coordination to avoid being spotted.

"He's taking the ramp onto the highway," said Clap.

"Peter, he'll be behind you in thirty seconds. Kill your brake lights and stay in front of him."

Before leaving the hotel, the men had performed some basic and easily reversed modifications to the rental cars. Aside from the tail-light kill switches—used so Walker wouldn't see the car in front of him constantly braking to match his speed—they could disable one headlight or adjust the patterns of the marker lights to change the cars' appearance at night.

Jake's heart was pounding. He'd fought hand-to-hand battles with terrorists and been in gunfights with African warlords, but running surveillance at night without being made was as nerve-racking as any life-or-death experience he'd had. If Walker spotted the team and broke contact, they would never find the mole and Jake might never see the former SEAL Team Six sniper again until it was too late.

"Peter, point your antenna to the rear. Jeff and Clap, aim yours forward. I'm going to try to isolate his signal."

Each IMSI catcher was acquiring every cellular phone signal within a half-mile radius—up to eight hundred phones per minute. The volume of data was overwhelming Jake and his laptop, but the team could eliminate most of the extraneous signals by using directional antennas.

"Clap, accelerate to seventy-five miles per hour and keep your antenna trained on the Nissan."

With Peter in front, Jeff in the rear, and Clap passing Walker's car on the highway, Jake was able to block out every signal that didn't hit all three antennas.

"Got him," Jake said. He locked onto the unique identity number coming from Walker's mobile phone, and it immediately appeared as a yellow diamond on the team's displays with location and speed data next to it. The team would also be able to intercept any transmissions to or from the targeted device.

"He's up to sixty-seven miles per hour," Jake said. *"Expand the box and give yourselves some room to breathe. Clap, take lead position half a mile in front. Jeff, you're backup one mile behind in case he gets cute and pulls over or hops off at an exit at the last minute, and Peter, you can slow down to sixty-two. Let him pass and you take up trail position half a mile behind. Great work."*

Jake periodically ordered additional adjustments to speed and distance to account for variations in cell coverage and traffic density, but Walker drove normally and appeared confident that he was clean of surveillance. Jake rotated each of the cars at random intervals so Walker wouldn't notice the same vehicle near him for too long. The lead car would usually pull into a rest stop or off an exit, let Walker pass, then head right back onto the highway as the new backup car. The trail car would pass Walker and take up position as the new lead car, and the backup car would move up into the trail position behind Walker. The target was driving steadily, the team had settled into a rhythm, and the miles were passing by uneventfully. It was a straight shot to the capital region.

"Crickets," Jake said. He'd taken to checking in every few minutes even when there was nothing to report, but that changed as the team approached Baltimore and everyone saw Walker send a text message.

On time

A response came a few seconds later.

OK

Walker shut off his phone.

Jake cursed as Walker's signal disappeared from their screens along with his position.

"He just exited onto Monrovia Road," said Jeff. *"I'm on him."*

The abrupt maneuver isolated Clements, who had been lead, and left him far out of position. Walker proceeded to drive through a 720-degree collection of one-lane underpasses and overchanges around O'Donnell Street that quickly forced Jeff to break coverage to avoid being spotted.

Clap switched off one of his headlights as he followed Walker into the 1.4-mile-long Harbor Tunnel. He was the only one with eyes on the target. The tunnel's double yellow line should have bought the team some breathing room but Walker crossed it twice to pass slower-moving vehicles, forcing Clap to also break contact or expose himself.

Sixteen excruciating minutes passed by with Walker completely out of sight until Jake directed the others onto the Baltimore–Washington Parkway where they were able to reestablish visual contact.

"This is only going to get worse as he nears the Beltway," said Jake. *"There are just too many options for three cars to cover. I'm going mobile."*

"Uh, Jake," Jeff said calmly, *"who's going run tac ops with you behind the wheel? You're kind of the nerve center of this whole thing."*

The question was answered a moment later when a woman's voice came over the comms net.

"Good evening, gentlemen."

"Team, meet Geneviève," Jake said. *"She's running tactical operations from now on."*

The radio was silent for several seconds as the group processed the abrupt and unexpected change.

"*Jake, you're like a brother to me,*" said Jeff, "*but are you sure this is a good idea?*"

"*The accent is sexy as hell,*" added Clap, "*but I don't think—*"

"*Clap,*" said Geneviève, "*tighten coverage two-tenths of a mile in case Walker takes the next exit. His last evasive maneuver was on the half hour and we're approaching 19:30. Peter, reduce speed by five miles per hour. Walker has slowed since he exited the tunnel and you're going to outpace him. Since he isn't using his phone, I'm pinging his vehicle now with an RRC reconfiguration command to see if I can trick the rental company's vehicle tracking device into transmitting its GPS data to the IMSI catchers.*"

"*Disregard my prior transmission,*" said Jeff.

"*Apologies, ma'am,*" said Clap. "*Tightening coverage now.*"

Jake raced north to meet the oncoming crew as Walker drove south along I-95, then west along the Beltway—the enormous ring road surrounding the heart of the National Capital Region. Jake's silver Tahoe joined the others just as Walker crossed into Virginia.

The team was quiet as Walker approached CIA Headquarters in McLean. Everyone expected him to make a move, but the traitor drove past his old office and turned west toward Manassas—and Jake's hotel.

Clap was in the lead car a quarter mile ahead of Walker when the target's headlights veered away.

"*I think he just turned right on Yorkshire,*" said Clap.

"*That's affirmative,*" said Jeff from the trail car.

"*Clap,*" said Geneviève, "*turn right on Rugby Road. You can get ahead of him if you move.*"

"*Walker's slowing down,*" Jeff interrupted. "*I'm breaking off.*"

"*Turn right on Old Centreville and then left on Parkland,*" Geneviève said. "*You'll be in position to intercept him if he heads north.*"

"*Roger wilco,*" said Jeff.

"*Peter, you're in trail position,*" said Geneviève.

"I do not have eyes on Walker," said Clements. *"Repeat, no eyes on target."*

Walker had turned into a quiet residential neighborhood. On each side of the road were one- and two-story homes with basketball hoops in the driveways and cars parked on both sides of the street. Short blocks and lots of intersections made it a guessing game where he would emerge.

"Got him," said Jake. *"He just turned west on Manassas Drive."*

"That puts Clap out of position," said Geneviève. *"Jake, you're the only car on Walker right now."*

"Roger that, but it's like a maze here," said Jake. *"I'm not sure how long I can do this without being spotted."*

Geneviève rattled off new instructions to everyone, then spoke to Jake.

"I'm vectoring everyone around you. Peter is closest, but he's five minutes away."

Jake cursed as he crested a hill. *"Target lost. I'm approaching Lomond."*

"Turn left on Victoria," Geneviève said. *"You might be able to get in front of him if you move."*

Jake gunned the rental car through the quiet neighborhood, silently praying that no one would be walking their dog down the middle of the street on the cold winter night. Geneviève twice updated her directions to the others, but at this point, she was only playing the probabilities. Walker was gone.

"SHIT!" Jake yelled into the radio. Screeching tires and a car horn punctuated his transmission.

"Give me a SITREP," said Geneviève, using the acronym for a "situation report."

"I missed a stop sign and almost wrecked," Jake said.

A moment later he chuckled as the other car pulled through the intersection.

"It was Walker . . . Target is heading east on Liberia."

"OK," said Geneviève. *"You're on your own."*

Jake smiled. For the first time in years, she couldn't have been more wrong. He was part of a team again and working with the woman he loved.

"He just pulled into the strip mall on Mathis Avenue," said Jake. *"Where is everyone?"*

"Jeff is three to five minutes out. Peter and Clap are five to seven," said Geneviève.

"Walker is out of his vehicle and heading toward the mall on foot," Jake said. *"Does this place have a rear entrance?"*

Geneviève searched the online satellite map she'd been using to direct the team.

"Yes. The parking lot wraps around both sides."

"I'm going in."

"Jake, wait," said Clements. *"It could be a trap."*

"Or he could be meeting the mole or planning to slip out the back door into another vehicle," Jake said. *"We can't take that chance."*

Jake parked his car, adjusted the pistol holstered on his belt, and headed for the strip mall. He was halfway to the door when he spoke into the radio.

"I should've known it would end like this . . ."

The dread in his voice was plain for all to hear.

"It's Walker," Jake continued. *"He's in a goddamned coffee shop."*

SIXTY-SEVEN

JAKE STEPPED THROUGH the doorway and skulked along the back wall. The coffee shop was large and surprisingly crowded for the late hour. There was a cluster of small tables in the center of the room plus a few booths around the walls. A hallway on the right led to the back entrance.

Walker was at the counter, standing between a heavyset man in a flannel shirt and a woman with dark hair and a diaper bag. Jake quickly scanned the other patrons' faces, but recognized no one.

"Target in sight," Jake whispered over the comms net. *"No sign of his contact."*

"Jeff is four minutes out," said Geneviève. She didn't tell him to be patient or careful, but Jake could hear it in her tone.

"Holding tight," he said.

Jake pulled down the lid of his baseball cap and turned up the collar on his canvas work coat. He made his way to a corner booth far from the counter and took a seat. The crowded café would be an easy place for someone with Walker's tradecraft to make contact with his coconspirator.

Jake couldn't let him out of his sight, even for a second.

Patrons came and went, through the front door and the rear, while Walker waited in line. The man in the flannel shirt was still at the counter, still waiting for his coffee. Whether they were brewing it, grinding it, or growing it, Jake could not have cared less, but he was grateful for the delay as it kept Walker waiting while Jake's reinforcements closed in.

The man in the flannel shirt finally got his coffee.

He blew on the tall paper cup as he squeezed between another customer and the frosted glass divider that separated the front of the shop from the restrooms and the rear exit. Jake watched Walker speak with the young man working behind the counter, but there was nothing overtly suspicious about the interaction.

Walker paid cash for his coffee and glanced around the café as if looking for a place to sit, but he and Jake had been trained by the same organization, and Jake had anticipated Walker's casual scrutiny of the crowd. Jake kept his head down for several seconds. When he looked up, he glimpsed Walker disappear around the frosted glass partition that led to the back door.

"He's going out the back," Jake said over the radio. *"I'm pursuing on foot."*

Jake garnered a few unpleasant looks as he pushed through the crowd but no one said a word once they'd seen the look in his eyes. He was halfway to the back door when the men's room door opened five feet in front of him.

And Walker stepped out.

He'd executed a quick cover stop in the bathroom and come right back out to see if he'd been followed—and caught Jake in his trap. Such were the hazards of conducting one-on-one surveillance against a highly trained adversary.

The two men made eye contact.

Walker threw his coffee at Jake's face. Jake ducked the scalding liquid and lunged forward, body-checking Walker backward into the metal doorframe.

Walker bounced back instantly. He launched an elbow strike to Jake's face, knocking out his radio earpiece and nearly breaking his jaw. Jake drove his knee up into Walker's groin so hard that it lifted the traitor six inches off the ground.

Walker doubled over, but he wasn't out of the fight. He reached behind his hip for the pistol he'd holstered there. Jake launched three quick punches into Walker's face and shoved him back into the doorframe a second time. The two men were twelve inches apart when Walker pulled the weapon.

Few people inside the coffee shop had any idea there was a fight going on, much less a lethal battle between two trained killers, and Jake knew that Walker didn't care about collateral damage. If he started firing a gun inside the crowded coffee shop, innocent people were going to die.

Jake grabbed Walker's pistol the instant it cleared the holster and wrenched the barrel up toward the ceiling, trying to break Walker's grip and keep the muzzle pointed in a safe direction, but Walker was just as strong as Jake and just as well trained. He knew one way to get his adversary to release the weapon.

He pulled the trigger.

But nothing happened, and both men knew why. Jake had pushed the pistol's slide back a quarter of an inch—enough to throw the weapon out of battery and prevent it from firing. The two men wrestled for control of the pistol—Walker with his right hand and Jake with his left—but these were no ordinary thugs. These were two elite warriors at the top of their games.

Walker headbutted Jake, but he absorbed the blow and grabbed the gun with both hands, leaving his sides dangerously exposed. Walker didn't disappoint. With one hand still holding the pistol over his head, he rotated his body and used his other hand to fire a brutal punch into Jake's kidney.

Jake staggered, but with his left hand wrapped over the pistol's slide and his right hand around its grip, he used his right thumb to push the weapon's magazine release. Rage spread across Walker's face as watched nearly all of his ammunition drop to the floor. There was only one bullet left in the gun.

Jake released the slide and mashed the trigger with his thumb, firing the last bullet into the ceiling of the one-story building. Heads turned as the gunshot shattered the steady din of the small café. The coffee shop's customers had finally noticed the deadly contest unfolding in their midst, but no one aside from Jake and Walker knew the pistol was now empty. People screamed and ran for cover. The man in the flannel shirt was long gone and the dark-haired woman with the diaper bag was sprinting for the back door.

Walker was furious. He raised his right foot and launched his heel forward into Jake's chest. The kick knocked Jake back through the frosted-glass partition. The glass shattered, enveloping Jake in a cloud of razor-sharp shards as he tumbled backward onto a table, then fell to the floor, twisted up among the metal table and chairs.

Walker leapt through the smashed partition and used a second vicious kick to hammer Jake's head to the floor. The traitor dove on top of Jake, driving his knee into Jake's solar plexus and knocking the wind out of him.

Walker moved in for the kill.

He locked his muscular hands around Jake's throat and drove his thumbs into Jake's Adams apple, using his raw strength and his body weight to cut off Jake's supply of air. Already stunned and gasping for breath, Jake thrashed and struggled to break the hold, but Walker had clamped on tight.

Jake's world started to go dark.

He had one chance left.

Jake reached around Walker with his right hand, raised his left leg, and drew the knife from the scabbard on his ankle. Jake plunged the three-inch blade into Walker's neck and raked it down the side of his throat, severing his jugular vein, his vagus nerve, and his carotid artery.

Walker's strength left him in an instant. He tumbled face-first onto the floor.

Dead.

The entire fight had lasted less than a minute.

Jeff burst through the front door with his weapon up. He scanned the room, searching for threats, but finding only Walker dead, a few frightened patrons, and Jake lying on his back in a growing pool of blood.

"Shots fired, shots fired. I'm inside. Keller is down," Jeff said over the radio.

He shoved the bathroom door open and cleared the men's room, then the women's.

"You," he shouted at one of the people in the shop. "Find the first aid kit!"

The man nodded. He'd been too stunned to leave, but he could follow a direct order.

Jeff holstered his weapon and kneeled next to Jake in the puddle of blood.

"You hit? I heard a gunshot."

Jake shook his head and wiped the blood from his face. "Most of this was Walker's."

"Keller is OK. Repeat: Keller is OK," Jeff said over the radio. *"Walker is KIA."*

"Entering rear," said Clap. He surged through the back door with his weapon up and advanced to the front of the coffee shop, scanning for targets, but finding only a few frightened customers. Clap lowered the pistol when he saw Jeff with Jake on the floor. Clements was right behind him along with the dark-haired woman with the diaper bag.

"Where did you find her?" Jake said as he rose to his elbows.

"Unlocking her car," said Clements as he pulled off her wig.

It was Kirby.

"Fuck all of you," she said. "I want a lawyer."

Clements looked to Jake. "This is your show. What do you want to do with her?"

Jake staggered to his feet, wiped his bloody hands on his jeans, and reached into his pocket. He pulled out Detective Rooney's card.

"Call this guy."

IN LESS THAN ten minutes, half a dozen police cars and three ambulances were parked in front of the coffee shop. Two more cop cars had sealed off the back. Detective Rooney looked none too happy as he walked over to the group clustered around the blood-soaked Jake.

"Are any of you with him?"

"You bet," said Clap.

"Yes, sir" was Jeff's reply.

"Till the end," answered Clements. The associate director of intelligence handed one of his CIA business cards to the police officer. "There are going to be some federal agents here in a few minutes to take this woman into custody."

Rooney grimaced. He'd be lucky to be home for breakfast by the time he finished the paperwork on the case. He waved the paramedics away so he could speak privately with Jake.

"Consultant, huh?"

"As you said, it's a pretty rough job."

"You going to be all right?"

"Never better, Detective."

"You don't look so good."

"I'm just a little banged up right now."

"You know what you need? A nice hot cup of coffee."

SIXTY-EIGHT

JAKE AND GENEVIÈVE strolled arm in arm under the moonlight. After several days of heavy snow, the skies had finally cleared. The air was still and silent. Each step crunched underfoot; every breath vanished in a swirl of vapor. Somewhere in the distance, a pine bough sagging under the weight of the snow shed its burden and sprang back into position.

"What will happen to Ted Graves?" asked Geneviève.

"He admitted introducing Walker to Kozlov," said Jake. "Ted wanted to recruit him as a source because of his relationships with GRU and the Russian president, but after a couple of meetings, Walker said Kozlov wasn't interested."

"But Kozlov was interested—in Walker."

"Kozlov flipped him and brought him on as a hired gun."

"Did Ted know?"

Jake shook his head. "Christine figured it out, but instead of telling Ted, she decided to blackmail Walker."

"Why was she so angry?"

"Ted pushes his men hard. He wants us to be aggressive and

sometimes it gets heated. He challenges, he argues, he presses; but when it comes down to making a decision, if the man in the field can defend his position, ninety percent of the time Ted defers to him."

"Christine didn't like that?"

"She called him a pussy."

Geneviève smirked.

"Christine came up through the army," Jake continued. "She thought that anyone who challenged orders should be relieved on the spot."

"So she had the Russians kill them?"

Jake nodded. "It gets worse. She'd committed treason and the Russians knew it. They owned her. They extracted information from her on our most sensitive paramilitary operations around the world. It's going to take years to assess the full scope of the damage."

"No one else saw it," said Geneviève.

Jake smiled at her. "It was Christine's paranoia that did her in. She knew I was going to Courchevel and assumed I was onto them. I never would have started digging if they hadn't put a bomb on my plane."

Geneviève took a deep, calming breath as she looked out over the valley. Far off in the distance, a snowcat moved soundlessly across the mountain, its spotlights bathing the ski slope in soft white light.

"We should go someplace warm," she said, "someplace with sand, palm trees, and a warm ocean breeze where we don't have to think about espionage for a while."

"What about tonight?" Jake said. "I still have two more weeks of leave."

Geneviève smiled and pulled him in for a kiss.

"Oi," said a voice. "Are the lovebirds just about finished with their holiday plans? I'm freezing my arse off up here."

It was Hunter. He was lying prone in the snow, wearing winter camouflage and looking down the mountain through a high-powered spotting scope.

"What's the latest?" said Jake.

"Oh, are we in a hurry now?" Hunter sneered at his new friend and put his eye back to the glass. "Call it five minutes. There's a thermos in my pack with hot cider if you're thirsty."

"I'll pass," said Jake.

"Bloody ingrate," muttered Hunter.

Geneviève laughed. "Whatever happened to the girl from your gym?"

"The FBI lifted a fingerprint off her job application," said Jake. "They picked her up in Oregon a few days ago and now she's looking at federal charges for attempted murder."

Hunter rose to his knees and handed the scope to Jake. He peered a thousand feet down the mountain at two faint lights moving slowly across the snow.

"It's time," said Jake.

He looked up at the massive cornice of snow in front of them. At least fifty feet high, the wind-driven formation hung precariously over the slope below.

"We should probably back up," Jake said.

"Not your worst idea," said Hunter.

They walked back a hundred feet. Hunter reached into his pack and pulled out a 40mm grenade launcher with a six-round rotating magazine. The weapon looked like an assault rifle with a weight problem.

Hunter offered it to Geneviève.

"I think Jake earned this one," she said.

Jake took the launcher and pointed it at the back of the cornice— an area known as the root. Like the roots of a plant, the section of frozen snow anchored the cornice to the ground.

"I wish Celia and James could see me," he said with a grin.

Jake pulled the trigger.

A 40mm grenade shot from the launcher and buried itself deep inside the cornice. There was a dim flash and a muted thud.

And nothing else.

"Projectile dysfunction is nothing to be embarrassed about," said Hunter. "It happens to a lot of men."

Jake rapid-fired the remaining five rounds into the base of the cornice. Each was followed by a muffled explosion. There was another noise a moment later, but it wasn't an explosion. It was a deep, resonant "whumpf" that reverberated through their chests as the heavy wet snow shifted over the layer of light powder below it.

They each took a few steps back.

The whumpf quickly developed into a deep, rumbling roar as the root fractured, the cornice collapsed, and four million pounds of snow slid down the side of the mountain.

"*Do svidaniya, comrade,*" said Hunter.

A THOUSAND FEET below, Kozlov and his new bodyguard heard the strange noise and looked up the mountain. Even in the dim predawn light, the oligarch swiftly grasped the enormity of the snow mass cascading toward him at eighty miles per hour. Yet, despite Kozlov's innate intelligence, it took his brain a few more seconds to process exactly what was happening, for he knew indisputably that avalanches rarely occurred in the early morning without some sort of external force.

That left five additional seconds for Kozlov to realize that the force had a name, and it was Jake Keller.

COLLEGE FOR THEIR CHILDREN

A portion of my royalties from each copy of *Shadow Target* sold goes directly to Children of Fallen Patriots Foundation, a 501(c)(3) charity whose mission is to provide college scholarships and educational counseling to military children who have lost a parent in the line of duty. The organization is dedicated to serving the families of service members who have died as a result of combat casualties, military training accidents, and other duty-related deaths.

If you have lost a parent in the line of duty, or would like to help those who have, please visit FallenPatriots.org.